One Night at the Lake

 Ballantine Books | New York

One Night at the Lake

A Novel

BETHANY CHASE

Published in the United States by Ballantine Books, an imprint of Random House, a division of Penguin Random House LLC, New York.

BALLANTINE and the HOUSE colophon are registered trademarks of Penguin Random House LLC.

Title page art from an original photograph by Freeimages.com/Blyth McManus

LIBRARY OF CONGRESS CATALOGING-IN-PUBLICATION DATA

Names: Chase, Bethany, author.
Title: One night at the lake : a novel / Bethany Chase.
Description: New York : Ballantine Books, 2019.
Identifiers: LCCN 2018059387 | ISBN 9781524796341
(hardcover : acid-free paper) | ISBN 9781524796358 (ebook)
Subjects: | BISAC: FICTION / Contemporary Women. |
FICTION / Suspense. | FICTION / Romance / Suspense.
Classification: LCC PS3603.H37923 O54 2019 |
DDC 813/.6—dc23
LC record available at https://lccn.loc.gov/2018059387

Printed in the United States of America on acid-free paper

randomhousebooks.com

2 4 6 8 9 7 5 3 1

First Edition

Book design by Virginia Norey

For my son, Dominic.

May your sweet heart always guide you toward kindness.

One Night at the Lake

PROLOGUE

I DREAM ABOUT HER ALL THE TIME, YOU KNOW.

It's always the same dream. I'm standing on the roof of the old apartment building, staring at the stars. As I stand there, face turned up to the sky, I'm wondering if maybe, when the earth eventually gets swallowed up by the ravenous, dying sun and everything goes supernova, she and I will find each other again. It's a thought she would have liked. "My carbon will bond onto your carbon," she would tell me, slipping her arm through mine to illustrate the link.

I smile, and try to believe that it's enough.

1

Leah

Seven years ago

I PROBABLY SHOULD HAVE PRETENDED TO BE AT LEAST A *LITTLE* bit sad about my best friend's breakup, but it was a tough ask considering I knew all along the guy was a mallet-faced shitweasel. And besides, it's not like I've ever been shy about speaking my mind. June knew what she was in for when she called me.

"Babe," I say, "Rick Bergstrom has the personal charisma of a boiled carrot. Are you seriously telling me that you're upset to be done with him?"

"Noooo, I guess not. But if I got dumped by a boiled carrot, then what does that say about me?"

I pinch my phone against my shoulder as I load my laptop into my bag and close the door to the neurobiology lab behind me. "It doesn't say a damn thing about *you*. What it says is that he thought he was just dating a hot artsy Asian girl, and he was shocked to find you in possession of both a spine and a mouth."

"But getting dumped suuuuuuucks," she groans.

"I know it does."

"No, you don't," she fires back, and the zinger makes me smile. June says I'm cocky about relationships because I've never been on the receiving end of a breakup; I prefer to think I've just been lucky.

"Listen to me. You are way too good to be moping over this little turd. He is so not worth your time that I'm insulted I even have to remind you."

She snorts. "Thanks, I guess?"

"I mean it. But if you *are* going to mope, do you want to do movie night? *Clueless* and ice cream?"

"Aren't you meeting up with Ollie?"

"Yeah, but I can cancel. I'd rather hang out with you if you're bummed."

"Ah, you're the best. I've actually got dinner plans with Pooja, but thanks for volunteering for breakup therapy."

"Always, my cherub. *Hasta mañana.* Say hi to Pooja for me."

The warm summer evening hugs me when I step outside, along with the rush of the city. I remember hearing that a lot of people didn't like Columbia's new science building when it first went up, and it's true that the glass-and-steel tower looks like a futuristic Tetris block slammed down amidst the old brick grandes dames that surround it. But I love it. The whole *point* of science is to push forward, even if it offends some sensibilities along the way. To me, this building is about discovery and innovation. And that's the way it should be.

My stomach is grumbling by the time I reach the bar where I'm meeting Ollie. This place is nothing fancy, but it has the most delicious burgers in Ollie's neighborhood, possibly even the whole city—and we'd know, because we've spent the last four years surveying. Noise lunges at me as soon as I open the door: the roar of a hundred conversations, all competing with the squealing guitars of whatever classic rock song is blasting from the speakers. The song sounds vaguely familiar, which means it's got to be one of Ollie's favorite bands; I couldn't begin to guess at which. Ollie has four thousand favorite bands. They *all* sound vaguely familiar.

I push up on my tiptoes to scan the room for him. Crowds activate my barely latent short person's rage, especially because I detest high heels, the universal short girl's coping mechanism. I had a guy tell me once that I ought to consider wearing heels if I was going to bitch so much about being short. I told him he ought to consider dating other people.

Swaying like a car dealership tube man on the tips of my Chucks, I finally spot Ollie at the far end of the room, leaning on his elbows against the dark wood bar. And I'm sorry, I don't care what anyone says; my boyfriend is the dreamiest thing I've ever seen. Now, to be clear, it's not like I'm facing opposition on this front; it's just that any time I mention in passing how hot he is, June rolls her eyes. Which—okay. June rolling her eyes probably has more to do with fatigue with me talking about Ollie than it does with her opinion about Ollie himself. She does put up with an awful lot of it.

But look at him, for god's sake. Although the overall effect falls under "boyishly handsome," his face has this amazing contradiction to it: fair Germanic skin, scruffy brown hair and friendly chin, paired with high cheekbones, sharply hooked eyebrows, a long, narrow nose, and thin lips that can look severe when they're not curved into his usual devilish smile. And he's got the most amazing eyes—the gray-blue of chambray cloth, with a ring of dark slate at the edges. Tonight, he's wearing his usual getup for his job as an advertising account manager—dark jeans and a vintage T-shirt that his shoulders fill out to perfection. He is, quite frankly, delicious. And because he's so absorbed in his phone, that means I can sneak up behind him and give him a righteous slap on the ass.

The phone drops to the bar with a clatter, and then he spins around and I shriek because all of a sudden my feet are off the ground.

"Put me down!" I squeal, but he just grins up at me and keeps his arms clamped around my hips while I attempt to pry myself free.

"That's what you get," he says, then turns to smile at the girls next to us, who are giving us the stink eye. "Excuse us. Just need to punish my girlfriend a little bit here." Once they get a load of him, they giggle as if they'd rather like him to punish them, too.

"Bad idea to keep a hungry woman away from food, Oliver," I say, pushing at his chest until he lets me slide down.

"Good point. Come on, I staked out a table in the back." He gives me a quick kiss and takes my hand to lead me to the open two-top. Which turns out to be a bar-height table. With barstools. At which I cannot reach the footrest.

Ollie makes innocent eyes at me when he catches my glare. "What? You can totally make it this time. I think you might have grown," he says, hovering his palm over my head as if he's measuring me. I smack his hand away and flounce into the seat.

Over burgers and beer, we catch each other up on the past few days. The conversation turns, inevitably, to the plans for our upcoming trip to his family's house on Seneca Lake in western New York. We're leaving next Friday afternoon, and I'm so excited to ditch the city for a week of boating and bonfires and laying out and grilling that I can barely function.

"Oh hey," I say to Ollie, "I wanted to ask you something. Is it okay if June comes with us? She was supposed to go with Rick the Dick to his Hamptons share, but that mosquito of a relationship just met its speeding windshield, so now she's gonna be stuck in the city over the holiday."

"June in a Hamptons share?" He cranes an eyebrow. Ollie can make an entire point with a single eyebrow. When I attempt it, I look like I have a tic.

"Your skepticism correlates with the windshield splat," I say, pointing a French fry at him. "And thus ends June's I-banker experiment."

He shakes his head, bemused. I will admit that, because we have been together for four years, Ollie and I can be a little smug. But honestly, the guys June has been dating in the three years since we left college seem to befuddle her as much as they do us. It's like she says yes to anyone who asks her out without caring whether she's actually interested.

"So, is that cool with you if she comes with? It would be super fun to have her along."

Ollie glances down at his plate, lip pinched in his teeth. "Um, I guess so. Let me check with my mom, though."

"You *guess* so? Babe, you know she's not going to mind. There's nobody else staying with us besides Caleb, right? So June can have the guest room."

"Mm. Unfortunately, June would be sharing the guest room with you. We're going to have to do the late-night tiptoe routine again."

"Still?" I screech. "For god's sake, we practically live together!"

"I don't like it either, but it's my parents' house, so . . ."

"Oh good lord, Ollie," I say, slumping back in my chair. "You are a twenty-six-year-old man without a religious hair on your body. Your mother seriously expects us all to participate in the delusion that you're a virgin?"

This time he puts both eyebrows into it. "Well, I don't exactly want to argue the case. I'm not sure she's ever recovered from walking in on Cal and his high school girlfriend."

I sigh, knowing I'm defeated. I've always loved how close Ollie is with his mom, so if the flip side of that means he humors her bizarre insistence on separate bedrooms, then it's a small price to pay. And despite Ollie's hesitation about June coming up for the week, I know Rachel won't mind.

Now all I've got to do is convince June to join us.

2

June

Present day, seven years later

PERHAPS I'M WRONG ABOUT THIS, BUT I DO NOT BELIEVE THAT any good news has ever followed the words *I need to talk to you about something.*

It's true. I know it's true. No one has ever said those words and then followed them up with "I won the Powerball earlier today, and after I split the pot with the rest of the accounting department, we are coming into six point two million dollars. What do you think we should do with it?" Nobody's *something* has ever been that a mysterious benefactor has paid off the credit card debt. *Something* is never that the doctor interpreted the test results wrong.

So when my fiancé says those words to me over dinner in our Brooklyn apartment one innocent evening in the middle of May, my mind stumbles. It's not a sensation I'm used to, feeling anxious with Ollie.

I set my glass of Chardonnay down on my faded linen place mat and study the person across from me. He appears serious, and not in the way that makes him look like the insides of his cheeks are itching, which is what his face does when he's failing at deadpan. The gray checked dress shirt he wore to work today is in order, cuffs rolled up his forearms like usual, and his hair is minimally tousled on top, which means he hasn't been running his hands through it in agitation. There's a crease between his smoky blue eyes, and his long fingers are spinning his wine glass on his place mat. But I would not go so far as to say he's upset. So far, so good.

"Okay, love—what's up? Is everything okay?"

He smiles and reaches for my hand across our tiny dining table. As soon as his thumb finds its rhythm over my knuckles, the anxiety eases. "Everything's fine. But it's my mom's birthday in a few weeks—her sixty-fifth. And she wants us to come up and visit the week of the party."

"Of course," I say. "Why would that be something to talk to me about in particular?"

"Well . . . it wouldn't be in Rochester. It's a couple of days after July Fourth, so we'd spend the week at the Seneca house."

I jerk my hand away from his so fast that I smack my wrist bone against the edge of the table. Eyes watering from the pain, I pin my hands together between my thighs. I am completely unprepared for this. Seneca, again. After all this time.

Ollie leans toward me and rests his forearms on the table. "I know, baby. You see why I wanted to talk to you. I want you to be honest with me—if you're not up for it, I totally understand."

I take a deep breath, then another, while I try to claw my way back to solid footing. "The whole week?"

"Yeah. The Fourth is a Monday, and Mom's party is Thursday the seventh. Mom and Dad will be there the whole week, and Caleb and Leslie and Eli too."

The thought flickers through my mind that I could send Ollie without me, but I discard it as quickly as it came. I wouldn't do that to him, even if he would let me. We're going to be a family, so that means we stick together. No matter what. And disappointing his parents is not an option.

"Yes," I say, making the word sound strong despite the frantic kicking of my heart. "Let's go. I want to be there for your mom."

He narrows his eyes at me, then turns one hand palm up on the table. "Come on, you're breaking the rule. Cough it up."

I grit my teeth, extract my right hand from its safe space and place it in his. After the first time we got screaming pissed at each other and then forgot whatever we'd been arguing about as soon as he tackled me onto the bed, we agreed never to have a serious discussion or a fight without touching each other. When it comes to fights, it's a good rule. Reminds you that you do in fact love the hell out of the person who's torturing you at that moment. The I-need-to-talk-to-you-about-somethings, though, I'm not as sure about. Sometimes I'm not certain I want him to read me as clearly as he can when his fingers are twined between mine.

"Are you sure about this?" he says softly. "I almost told Mom straight up that we couldn't make it, but I didn't want to speak for you. But seriously—if you're not comfortable, we can skip it. Mom and Dad will understand."

"They would understand, but they'd be disappointed, and I don't want to let them down." My conviction swells as I speak, pushing words out of my mouth. "And honestly, I think it will be for the best. We can't avoid the place for the rest of our lives. Your parents love it there, and I don't want it to be a point of tension. We can go. I will be fine."

Slowly, Ollie sits back in his chair and lets my hand go. "Okay. If you're positive. But just so you know, you don't *have* to be fine. I'm not always—"

"I will be."

"But I'm trying to say that it's okay if you're not. I've been going back there for years, and it still hurts every single time." He pauses, lets his gaze drop to the table before he raises it to meet mine again. "I loved her too, June."

It's like a sudden gust of wind slams open a door inside me that

I'd thought was safely closed; the impact shudders down my spine. Slowly, I push my chair away from the table and stand looking down at my fiancé. "That is something I am unlikely to ever forget."

Seneca Lake, like each of the long, parallel lakes that score the landscape of western New York like the scratch marks of an angry bear, was made over millions of years, as ice gouged a chasm in the softer earth. And like every glacial lake, it is deep.

It's a beautiful area, bracketed by cute towns at the northern and southern points of the lake, with thirty-eight miles of pristine water in between. Houses line its banks on both sides, some of them squatting right against the water's edge while others perch on high bluffs, hidden in the shade of the dense woods behind them. It's the kind of place where American flags flap in the breeze on every lawn, and neighbors stand on each other's docks to chat at sunset.

I hate it like I have never hated anything else on earth. And now I have to go back.

My cells haven't fully put themselves back together since Ollie told me. That was three days ago now, and I still keep catching myself staring out the window of my workshop, watching airplanes glide low over Brooklyn instead of making my clients' jewelry. Anxiety burns in the pit of my stomach, replacing any desire I used to have for food. And a silence has fallen between Ollie and me, which he doesn't know how to start speaking into and I don't want to.

For most of these years, there was no reason to think about going back. Anytime the Finger Lakes came up in passing conversation, I would feel the fist of fear clutch inside my belly, and I'd give a silent shudder, and the discussion would shuffle along to other things before anyone noticed how silent I'd gone.

And then Ollie happened. Ollie, who was at the very center of it all.

I try to remember why we never talked about the lake house last summer, and then it comes to me: This time last year, we were newly together, newly in love, and so addicted to each other that we were spending every single night together and every free hour in bed. He flew upstate the morning of the Fourth, while I passed the holiday at my parents' house outside the city; he was back before I woke up the next day. When he took me home for Passover, not long after we started dating, his parents hosted the gathering at their Rochester house, and that's been the case for every holiday since. I knew, of course, that they still had the place on Seneca, but I assumed the family understood I preferred to avoid it. I guess I assumed Ollie preferred to avoid it, too. Either I was wrong on both counts, or my grace period has run out.

Head bowed, I dig my thumbs into my eye sockets, then drop my hands back to my work table. A client's half-finished engagement ring sits, abandoned, near my right hand, but my eyes drift to the one I wear on my left. A few weeks after Ollie and I started dating, I got a call from a sweet-sounding guy in Minnesota who said his girlfriend was a tremendous fan of my work. Instead of one of the styles showcased on my website, he wanted something unusual for her: a tension setting. I was excited because I'd been wanting to work on a tension set design, but a lot of people are afraid of them because they think the setting isn't secure.

I found a 1.2-carat rose-cut gray diamond, its subtle pewter-gold inner fire like a candle shining through mercury glass, and clasped it between two delicate, diagonally arching arms of brushed 18-karat yellow gold, with tiny white brilliants scattered over the arms for extra shimmer. It was stunning, unique, everything I'd hoped it would be, and I was more in love with it than anything I'd made in years. When the ring was finished, I photographed it, packed it lovingly, and shipped it off to Minnesota.

And then it appeared two months later in the palm of Ollie's hand, while we sat wrapped in a blanket on the beach at Montauk, splitting a bottle of rosé and watching the sun set over the ocean.

Sighing, I get to my feet and lock up the studio. I pause by the large window at the end of the hallway, as I often do, and gaze out toward the harbor. Open sky always reminds me of Leah.

"God, I wish you were here," I whisper, throat burning. The wish, the ache, are familiar; they are with me every day. But it surprises me, sometimes, how raw the sudden surge of pain still can be.

The last time it happened was when I went to try on wedding dresses. The lady dropped the first gown over my head—I don't even remember what it looked like—and pinched back the extra fabric and sent me out to be *oohed* and *aahed* over by my crew. I looked from my mom's skeptical face to my cousin Jang-mi's kind smile to my recently-ex-roommate Pooja's eagerly clapping hands, and I got as far as saying "Where's L—" before I remembered. And then my throat closed on an ugly wail. I stood there in that froth of lace and sequins that should have filled me with delight, and I sobbed.

And, of course, there is the other thing here. The terrible thing, the unjust thing, the thing that can, at the most random moments, throw acid on my very joy. The thing that kicked me in the stomach as I walked home, love-drunk and dizzy from my first weekend with Ollie, and practically shaking with how badly I wanted to share it all with Leah. I could see her, twirling the ends of her ponytail like she always did when she was listening, her brown eyes gleaming with excitement. That's when I discovered the new dimension that my longing for her had just taken on. It wasn't as simple as *God, I wish you were here.* Not anymore. It was also this: *But we wouldn't be having this conversation, if you were. After all, he was supposed to be yours.*

3

Leah

MY PHONE RINGS AT A PREPOSTEROUS HOUR THE MORNING after my burger dinner. There is no reasonable explanation, so I bury my head under the pillow and ignore it. The silence is a thing of beauty. And then it all goes to hell again.

Ollie groans and nudges my calf with his foot. "Make it stop."

I climb over him and reach for the phone, abandoned on the night table and nearly out of juice.

"Goooood mawnin'," says June in an exaggerated drawl. "I assume you forgot about our Bikram date, so I'm taking your mat and some workout clothes with me to the place. Any particular top you want me to bring?"

Shit. This idea of mine, I'd thought it was such a stroke of genius at New Year's. When I was drunk and full of gusto for adventure. And oblivious to possible consequences like early morning wake-ups.

Because of *my genius idea,* June and I have been on a Groupon initiative since January, finding one new thing to try or visit somewhere in the city each week. Our activities have ranged from fun to tedious to bizarre, but this week's selection is 100 percent June-oriented: yoga, which she is way better at than I am, and scheduled to occur at a frankly offensive hour on a Saturday morning.

June is one of those bloody-minded "morning people" who like to spring out of bed early on weekends and "get things done." I like to sleep. It's what God intended.

"Ugh." I flop onto my back and stare at the ceiling, trying to decide exactly how bad it would be to skip.

"You know the rule," says June. "No bailsies."

"Unless we don't feel well. And I kind of—"

"You are not sick," she says, still with that maddening calm. "You just don't want to get out of bed."

"Don't be mean. I legitimately feel like my burger last night might have been undercooked. Something does not feel right in my tummy area. I think I have a burger hangover. June . . . I have a burgover."

Next to me, Ollie snorts.

"Okay," she sighs, "you can skip this one if you promise not to miss any more."

"Done!" I say, pouncing on the plea bargain. "Have fun!"

As I put the phone down, Ollie shakes his head at me, *tsk*ing mockingly like a disappointed auntie. But the guilt has barely begun to warm up when Ollie's phone rings. I lunge upward with a quickness, but he grabs it before I can intercept him.

"Why hello, June," the devil says, grinning at me. "No, actually, she seems quite hardy. In fact, I'd have to say if there's anything ailing her, it's nothing a little—wait, what were you guys doing today? Right. Nothing a little sweaty yoga couldn't cure."

"Traitor," I whisper.

"She thinks so, too. Yep. She's sitting up and pulling her clothes together . . . and now she's putting her hair in a ponytail. . . . I think she'll be rolling out of here in less than ten minutes."

From my prone position next to Ollie in his bed, I glare at him for his betrayal. He's displaying quite a lot of warm bare skin right now, with his sheets having fallen down to his waist when he answered the phone, and this is of far greater interest to me than yoga. I slide a hopeful hand over the plane of his lower belly, but he stops it in place and presses the phone mouthpiece against his shoulder.

"She's already on her way to meet you, Leeb. Don't blow her off."

Oliver Bierman, voice of my conscience. I heave a sigh and withdraw my hand.

"Okay, yes," he says into the phone, "she is technically still in bed. I was giving you a glimpse into the future. The future of the next five minutes," he says, shoving me gently but inexorably toward the edge of the bed. "She'll meet you there. Have fun."

"See? That was actually pretty fun, wasn't it?" June takes a sip from her latte mug, roughly the size of a soup tureen, and bats her long eyelashes at me. We are brunching at a coveted sidewalk table at Friend of a Farmer, which I sense is my roommate's compensation for the undignified rousting and even more undignified perspiring that she just subjected me to. My crotch smells like roadkill and my body is encased in a thick coulis of dried sweat. But, unsurprisingly, I'm the only one of us who looks worse for wear.

June is tall and slim as a ballerina, one lovely shape flowing into another: long neck, elegant collarbones, willowy legs and arms. She's a jewelry designer who wears her craft all over her body: Gold ear cuffs glint amongst her choppy, bobbed black hair, and she always wears a long pendant necklace or stack of delicate bangles to polish off her otherwise plain outfits. Yoga clothes purr when she puts them on.

If June has the kind of looks that make guys ask her if she's a dancer, then I have the kind of looks that pit me in a never-ending battle against the word *cute*. Short and curvy, with big brown eyes, freckles, and dimples—I'm doomed. And I absolutely hate it. Especially since my PhD research is in a STEM field where my male colleagues treat me either like a kid sister or a target. Right after we started dating, Ollie made me a screenshot from the "What?" scene in *Pulp Fiction*, where Samuel L. Jackson is waving his gun in the other guy's face and threateningly daring him to say "what" again, except Ollie's caption read "Say 'cute' ONE MORE GOD DAMN TIME." I showed it to June, and when she finished laughing she gave me the phone back and said, "Does he have any brothers?"

Now, as it happens, he does. I heartily wish he had a different one. If June comes to Seneca, I will guard her like a dragon to keep Caleb away from her. Coming off a breakup like she is, she might get taken in by his suave routine.

"Hmph," I say to her now, nipping a bite of omelet off my fork and chewing contemplatively. "I question your definition of fun."

"Please, you did great," June says.

I glare at her. She knows as well as I do that I sucked. I was a soccer player in high school, and a very effective one: fast, compact, and powerful, just like a cannonball. My teammates co-opted my last name, Tessaro, into "the Tessile." Cannonballs do not graceful yogis make.

"Well," I say, spearing another bite of omelet, "if I forgive you for this morning—which I may not, I haven't decided yet—then you should come with us to Seneca. We're leaving the Friday before the holiday, and spending the whole week up there. It's really fun; Ollie's parents are super chill, they let us mind our own business, so we just tool around on the boat and swim and have cookouts and bonfires."

"You think I'd prefer that to watching the fireworks on TV and making s'mores over the stove burner?"

I snorfle into my mimosa. June's deadpan humor gets me every time. "Well, I know it's no Hamptons share, but . . ."

She tosses back a wing of black hair. "Touché. It sounds fun, but I feel like I'd be a third wheel."

"No way. Ollie's brother will be there, and a few friends who live nearby; there's always people milling around."

"What did Ollie say when you asked him?" she says, staring at her coffee as she absently stirs it.

"He was fine with it," I say. "He has to check with his mom to make sure, but I know she'll be down. She's making me sleep in the guest room again, anyway. So you can join me in the Chamber of Maidenhood."

I expect an outcry over the injustice of the guest room, but instead June frowns. "Well, that doesn't sound like he was fine with it, if he was using his mom as a potential out."

"She's not an out; he's just being considerate."

"What if he wanted you all to himself? Isn't it your anniversary that week?"

My mouth freezes, half-open. I hadn't thought of that. Hadn't even occurred to me. The all-to-himself part, not the anniversary part. The anniversary is actually the week after. But still, that completely explains Ollie's slight, but unusual, hesitation on the matter of June's attendance. The two of them are buddies; they go to see live music together, getting stomped on by drunken strangers while I study at home in peace. There's no reason he wouldn't want to have her around. Suddenly, exhilaration gushes through my chest, almost uprooting me from my seat. "Oh my god, Junie. What if he's going to propose?"

"Oh, wow!" she says, eyes going huge.

I stare at her, hands pressed over my mouth as if that will push back the elation. Not that I'd really want to, anyway. You have to understand, I've been ready for Ollie to propose to me since our first date. Our first date, which lasted seventeen hours. The night we met, I'd been telling him how, since I was spending my last summer of college in the city to work on thesis research, I missed the lazy afternoon cookouts in my parents' Westchester County backyard. So when I came over for the date, he took me up to the roof of his Murray Hill high-rise and proceeded to cook us burgers on a rickety charcoal grill of suspect legality. When the sun rose over the railing of the roof deck the next morning, we were lying on our sides in Ollie's tiny camping tent: still dressed, still awake, and still talking.

Unable to process my excitement, I start flapping my hands in the air like Kermit. "Holy crap, this could totally be it. This could *totally* be it."

Across the table, June's face lights up. "You're gonna get engaged, Leebee!"

I squeal incoherently.

"But the thing is, though," June says, her smile faltering, "that means I really shouldn't go. You guys should have this to yourselves. You're not going to want a sidekick."

I catapult out of my chair and tackle her with a hug so tight that her breath coughs out in a little "puh" sound. "Shut up, you maniac. You're my sister from another mister. Of course I want you there. Hell, having you there is the one thing that could make it even better. Ollie will figure something out. You are coming. Are we clear?" I pull back and give her my best threatening look.

Her straight dark eyebrows drift upward at my vehemence, but the smile that curves her lips is indulgent. "Yes, madam. We are clear."

"And no weirdness about third wheels or any of that crap. I *want* you there."

"No weirdness," she promises, squeezing my trembling, sweaty hands in her cool ones. Her eyes are warm with affection. "Babe, whether he proposes on this trip or not, whenever it happens, I am going to be so damn happy for you."

4

June

I DON'T RECALL THE EXACT DAY OF SIXTH GRADE THAT I NO-ticed Leah, but I do remember the silent adoration that swallowed me. She was everything that let her fit in in the way I didn't— confident, popular, outgoing, white (there were only a few more Asians living in my corner of Westchester County, New York, when I was growing up than there were mermaids)—but those things weren't why I liked her. She was just so goddamned good. Not in a Pollyanna way—she could be tart to people who deserved it; but she was *principled*. She approached the world with an assertive kindness that I don't think is all that often found in twelve-year-old girls. She had this ability to recalibrate herself to other people's tender spots, so that no one ever felt lesser when she spoke to them; and god help the fool who picked on the kid who might be gay, or the disabled kid, in front of Leah. Those were the only times she got in trouble: when she took flight as a red-faced, razor-tongued angel of justice. I could tell she felt everything that I so deeply felt about what was right and what was wrong—but unlike me, she was bold enough to yell it out loud.

With single-minded obsession, I had spent most of my early childhood begging my parents to get a dog. Their obvious reluctance did not deter me, nor did their outright refusals. It's always amused me that people assume only children are spoiled; that guideline must not apply to parents who'd wanted more children as badly as mine had.

But at long last, that fall of my sixth grade year, my persistence was rewarded, possibly because I'd been at my fancy new middle school—the middle school for which my parents had uprooted our family and my dad's camera store, from the much larger upriver town of Poughkeepsie to a cramped townhouse in the NYC commuter village of Briarcliff Manor—for two months without making a single friend. As I walked toward the grocery store with my unsuspecting mother one afternoon, I spotted a table set up near the entrance with a hand-lettered sign spelling the magic words: FREE PUPPIES. My skinny legs were propelling me across the parking lot before my mother even saw what sparked me. By the time she caught up to me, I'd already reached into the squirming, yipping box atop the table, and a puppy had melted into my hands.

"Please, *Umma*, can I keep him?" I breathed, holding the warm, wriggling little creature against my neck, which he industriously set about licking. "Please please please please please?"

"All right, Ji-Eunah," she sighed. "But you are responsible for him. His food, his walks, his poop—everything. He's yours to take care of."

My new puppy beeped with alarm as I squished him into the hug I gave my mom.

Winfield was a dog of indeterminate origin, although he had the expressive eyebrow markings of a Rottweiler and the size and tenacity of a large Jack Russell. I was determined to prove to my parents that I was worthy of their trust, so not only did I scrupulously look after him each and every day, but I undertook to train him in his manners all by myself. Winfield and I drilled for hours: sit, stay, come, heel. I can still remember the flush of pride I felt each time he began to obey one of my commands, shiny black eyes alert and tail swishing for his treat.

And then there was the day, a late gray-skied afternoon in the middle of December, when Winfield and I went out for a walk just as the first snow of winter began to fall. Winfield was enraptured, his doggy nose twitching at the air, and as the flakes began to mass on the ground, he spun and leapt, barking, wild with excitement over this strange thing befalling his landscape. By the time we reached the park where I liked to walk him, he was jerking at his leash, tangling his legs in it, so I made him sit while I unclipped it. I wasn't supposed to let him off leash, but he'd learned his commands so well. Every time he ranged too far away, I called him to come to me and he did, prancing around me with his tongue lolling. I was just about to clip him back up for the walk back to our house when he saw the squirrel.

"Winfield! Come!" I shouted, but he shot off like a bullet, hot in pursuit of that audacious rodent, through the damp brown leaves that littered the ground. I chased Winfield and squirrel up a small rise, which I crested just in time to see Winfield launch himself off a steep bank of earth, directly into the path of a gray Range Rover driving too fast up the opposite side of the hill.

"Winfield!" I screamed again, but by the time I reached the street I could just make out his small black form, motionless on the snow-glazed asphalt in front of the Rover. More flakes drifted through the headlights to land on his body. "Winfield," I sobbed, reaching to stroke his head but too scared to touch him.

"Oh my god, I'm so sorry, I didn't even see him," a woman's voice behind me said. Then there was a rush of motion and somebody was kneeling by my side.

"It's okay; he's breathing," a girl's voice said, calm and strong. "Mom, he's still breathing, we can save him. Help me pick him up; we can take him to that vet down near the train station. Remember we took Rory there when he swallowed that ball?"

Dazed, I watched as the girl and her mother gently lifted Winfield and set him on the back seat of their car. Only then did I notice who they were. As if the situation had really needed to get worse.

"Well, are you coming?" Leah said, voice sharp with impatience. "He'll feel better if he knows you're there."

I wiped my nose on the back of my wrist and climbed into the car next to my dog. He looked even more terrible up close—his two hind legs were horribly bent, and there was an odd hitch to his shallow breathing that clawed me with fear. Winfield was going to die, and it was all my fault. My stupid fault, for letting him off his leash when I knew better, *I knew better*. A fresh wave of sobs overcame me.

"You're June, right?" The sound of my name snapped me out of my hysteria, and I looked up to find Leah peering at me around the passenger seat. "June Kang, from school?"

I felt a flicker of surprise that she knew my name. Pronounced it right, even. Silently, I nodded.

She tucked a hunk of her curly brown hair behind her ear. "Right. Well, I'm Leah if you don't remember, and this is my mom, Cheryl. We'll call your parents as soon as we get to the clinic, to let them know what happened."

I shuddered at the thought of my parents' reaction. Winfield hurt, because of my stupidity, and now these strangers having to know about it and spend their own time to rescue me.

"I'm so sorry we hit your dog," said Leah, her businesslike manner dropping for the first time. "But he really is going to be okay. Look, he's trying to wag his tail."

I knew she was just saying it to make me feel better, but as the car glided smoothly down the hill toward the Hudson, I tried to believe it. I tried to be as strong as she was.

My dad arrived a few minutes after a very worried-looking vet tech swept Winfield off to surgery. Leah and her mother both got to their feet when he entered the waiting room, melting snow clinging to his plain canvas jacket.

"Are you Mr. Kang?" Cheryl Tessaro said. "I'm so terribly sorry to have hurt your dog. He darted right into the street before I even saw him."

"Why was the dog off his leash?" my father said, ignoring her and speaking to me. I withered all over again under the force of his disappointment.

"He slipped out of his collar," said Leah boldly. I cut her a warning look—it hadn't gone well for me the one and only time I'd ever tried to lie to my father—but she raised her chin and continued. "His fur was wet from the snow and it made him slippery. June is extremely upset," she said, putting an arm around my shoulders.

My dad flicked his assessing gaze from me to Leah and back again, and I guess he could tell the one thing she was telling the truth about. He nodded briefly. "Thank you for helping my daughter. You can go now."

I flinched. My Korean-born father had been mocked enough to be self-conscious about his English, so he tended to speak tersely in front of Americans he didn't know well; his short sentences often sounded curt. But Leah just shook her head.

"No, I'll stay. If you wouldn't mind dropping me off home once they tell us Winfield will be okay. My mom needs to get home to my brother."

"Leah, honey, June has her dad here now, so she won't be alone. Don't make him go to extra trouble to drop you off later."

"Mom, how far can they live from us? Briarcliff is tiny."

"It's no trouble," said my dad. "I will take her."

Leah's mother shrugged in defeat. Defeat, I would come to learn, was a position everyone in Leah's life had to come to terms with.

And so Leah stayed. As the last dim light drained out of the sky, we sat side by side in that waiting room that smelled of antiseptic and bandages, and she kept up a ceaselessly scrolling chain of chatter, one thing after another, whatever it took to keep my mind off my little dog who was dying on the surgical table because of my unforgivable carelessness. I heard how Leah's favorite class was science, but it made her mad that Mr. Paulson always called on the boys even though she usually knew the answer. I heard about her younger brother, Sam, who had been injured falling out of a tree a couple of years ago, and how no one could make him be able to use his legs again, but even though he got frustrated sometimes, he never felt sorry for himself or said how things were unfair. I learned that Leah wanted to become a research scientist who studied the nerves so that she could figure out how to reverse paralysis. It was no wonder she wanted so fiercely for Winfield to heal.

Finally, well after seven o'clock, a tired-looking woman in scrubs walked out from the back of the clinic. "Miss Kang?" she said, and I gulped down a breath as I made myself sit upright to receive the awful news. I felt Leah's hand clutching mine.

"The good news is, Winfield pulled through his surgery, and he's going to be all right," the veterinarian said. I sagged back against the seat as the air whooshed out of me, so relieved I almost missed her next words. "The bad news is, it's going to be a long recovery. He had several broken ribs, some internal injuries, and two broken legs. Unfortunately, his back right leg was too shattered to save."

"What does that mean?" My voice was a reedy croak in the quiet room.

"It means we had to amputate his leg just below his hip. Once his other leg heals, he's going to have to learn to walk on three legs. I promise you he can do it," she said kindly. "It won't be easy, but he will learn. Because he's a smart, strong little dog, and he'll have you there to help him, right?"

My eyes blurred with tears as I nodded, thinking of where my training and "helping" of Winfield had gotten him this time.

"I'll help too," said Leah. "My little brother can't walk so well either, so I know what that's like."

"See? There you go. It's great that you and Winfield have a friend," the veterinarian said to me.

I could almost physically feel the warmth of Leah's smile as she squeezed my hand. It lit up that dark, dreary room and beamed through my shame and grief, making me believe that I could teach Winfield to be okay. From that day onward, she was my beacon. There is only one person on earth I have ever loved more.

When I open the door to my apartment, the silence I step into is as suffocating as the air. I cross to the living room windows and heave open the heavy sashes, a swell of summer sound rushing in on the breeze: the groaning compressor of the A/C unit upstairs, a car passing on the street below, a man calling out a greeting to a neighbor on her stoop. Ollie is mystified by my disinterest in air-conditioning, but I love an open window more than a chilly draft. I like the sounds of the world around me, just like I like to watch the sights of it from the window. The faces of the buildings across the street offer a checkerboard of light and dark. Each bright room has a story. Someone is home safe.

I walk to the turntable and drop on a Van Morrison record. I used to think listening to music on vinyl was a hipster affectation, but after the first weekend I spent ensconced in Ollie's old apartment, watching the late winter snow fall and making love while we worked our way through the highlights of his encyclopedic music collection, my tune—pun regretfully permitted—changed swiftly. As Van's soulful voice fills the room, I pour myself a glass of wine and sink into our silky leather Eames lounge chair. The chair, a real '60s vintage one, was one of Ollie's dad's prized possessions until he gave it to us in honor of our buying this apartment in Carroll Gardens a few months back.

The thought of Ollie's father reminds me, like nearly everything in the last three days has somehow reminded me, of Seneca. God, that place. My mind is stuffed with memories, which I both hate and can't bear the thought of being without. It's odd to think that, if things hadn't happened as they did, I'd have forgotten most of them by now. But instead, there they all are—gleaming sharp and hard as a set of heirloom sterling I can't stop polishing. The mist that clung to the treetops of the Catskills valley we drove through on our way there, after an early evening rain; firelight flickering on Ollie's face as he played Fleetwood Mac's "Landslide," my favorite song, flawlessly on his guitar; the rich, heady air, full of the scents of summer grass and blooming flowers and the clear, cold lake water. The vertigo of falling in love.

And of course, Leah. The sharpest, hardest gleam of all.

I can't pretend to Ollie that I am happy about this trip, but I meant it when I said that I was willing. And yet he didn't seem convinced that I'd be strong enough. I will be, because I have to be. It's as simple as that.

One of the reasons I love him is the way he gives everything he has to his people, every single time—that's the way I've lived my own life as a daughter, a lover, a friend. So I will always do the same for him. He is an elemental requirement for me: food, water, sleep, Ollie. And when you love somebody that much, you give them what they need. I just have to forgive him for needing this.

I wake in the darkness when Ollie brushes my hair off my face and kisses my forehead. When I open my eyes, he's lying close, head propped on his hand, studying me in the dim light seeping into our bedroom. Heart surging with love, I reach up to cup his cheek, relishing the familiar texture of his beard against my palm. The first time we slept together, he asked me if its roughness bothered my sensitive skin.

"I love it," I said. "It makes you *my* Ollie."

I regretted it immediately, of course, because the last thing I wanted was to remind him of Before. But it's never become less true than it was that very first day.

"Baby," he says now, and kisses my lips. "We have to stop this. I can't take the silent treatment."

"I wasn't trying to punish you," I say, as he skims his hand under my nightshirt—an ancient, threadbare Allman Brothers T-shirt I co-opted from him ages ago. "I was being quiet because I was upset." I can feel every fretting callus on his fingertips; my nerves respond to his touch like grass does to the wind.

"I know," he says, "but when you want to be quiet, that's exactly when you have to talk to me. That's how this works." He shoves the shirt up to my collarbones and trails his tongue down the center of my body.

Lightning shoots along the path he takes. "Ollie, this isn't— *whoa*—we shouldn't talk about this right now. Why do you always—oh. Mmmmm."

"Why do I always use sex to get you over being upset with me? Because it fucking works."

He is right. It does. I'm aware that it's a bad idea to let my partner distract me from a disagreement with sex, but my body doesn't care. Orgasms unlock me, and Ollie knows it.

"I think I can talk to you now," I say when I can form sentences again.

"I noticed that," he whispers against my lips as he sinks inside me with a slow roll of his hips.

I wind my arms around his shoulders and bury one hand in his hair. "I felt like you didn't believe me when I said I could handle going to Seneca. Like you thought I was too weak."

He stops moving and pins me with his gaze. "No, absolutely not. I would never think of you that way. It's not that I didn't believe you; I know you want to do this for my family, and that means the world to me. I was just worried about you. Not because you're weak; because I want to protect you. There's no way this won't be hard on you."

Dread drags at me like undertow. Am I kidding myself to think that I can manage this? Being in that house again, standing on that dock, looking at that water?

I stare up at Ollie's precious face, and everything he feels is right there for me to see: the love, the worry, the hope. And I understand then that there was only ever one answer I could have given; and so I give it again. "It will be okay. I will be okay. I'm not who I was seven years ago, and I really want to do this. Have faith in me."

He nods slowly. "I do. And I'll be with you the whole time. I remember what it was like, my first time after." He looks away for an instant, and it makes me hate that we weren't together then, that I wasn't there to help him. When the shadow passes, he meets my eyes steadily again. "You're the most important thing in the world to me. I promise I'll take good care of you."

My eyes drift closed as I kiss him to promise him back. But in the darkness there is Leah. I can see her, twirling by the water's edge, face turned up to the sky with a sparkler in each hand and the silhouette of her long hair and her skirt billowing against the starry night. Leah, spinning.

Leah, sinking.

5

Leah

WHEN YOU LIVE IN MANHATTAN, HEADING OUT FOR A ROAD trip on a spit-shined summer afternoon always sounds so much more epic than it turns out. First you have to wrangle all your people to show up at the appointed place and hour, then find room for everyone's shit and snacks and water bottles and phone cords and Jesus Christ already. And then, on a holiday weekend like the Fourth of July, you're guaranteed an absolute minimum of one hour spent gnashing your teeth at the Hudson River crossing of your choice, followed by enough New Jersey to make you truly believe you will die there.

None of us can relax until we're out of the Garden State, mainly because Ollie is in commander mode. For a guy with such a mellow personality, he's a nightmare about anything related to driving directions and traffic: It's like he beams all the neuroses that the rest of us spread over various topics onto this single, completely uncontrollable element. He will not engage with any of my attempts to converse, just shifts his eyes with obsessive focus between the road and the GPS screen, occasionally barking responses to relevant queries but mainly being a total grump.

But at last, once the snarl of exits and overpasses in eastern Jersey finally coughs us out onto the interstate, Ollie deems it safe to shut off the GPS lady and turns on the radio. It's in the middle of a Billy Joel song, because of course it is, and Ollie lands fearlessly on the high harmony of "He works at Mr. Cacciatore's down on Sullivan Street." It isn't really a road trip until Ollie starts singing along to the radio. I smile at myself in the side-view mirror, kick my Havaianas off, and plant my feet on the dash so I can admire my juicy pedicure.

"Are we there yet?" says June, popping her head into the empty space between the front seats.

"No, but Ollie's butt cheeks have finally unclenched from the traffic, so maybe now we can have a civilized conversation."

"Oh, was that the wheezing noise I heard a minute ago?" she says, swatting the middle finger he waves in her face. "Okay. Civilized conversation: Go."

"I would like to discuss the fallout from the Rick the Dick breakup," I say. "I can't believe he tried to booty-call you after he dumped you."

"I can't believe you slept with somebody who thinks Blink-182 is one of the best bands of the last twenty years," Ollie says.

"Oh, like you never made a bad call before you hit the jackpot," snaps June. "Leah told me about the selfie girl from college. Didn't she almost fall in some mountain stream because she was so busy trying to get the perfect face angle?"

"That got personal quickly," Ollie says.

"Excuse me, you guys started it! It's not cool to make fun of me for being single. I'm not your entertainment."

"Vacation rule number one," I say in a loud voice, staring meaningfully at Ollie. "Ollie and Leah will not tease June about her love life."

"Thank you," June huffs, flopping back against her seat.

"Life rule number four hundred and three: June will not date anyone who admires the music of Blink-182, Sugar Ray, Aerosmith, Fall Out Boy, Nickelback, Creed . . ."

"Ollie!" I yell, but June is laughing.

"Okay, okay, fair," she says. "You can formally disown me if I ever date a Nickelback fan."

"Case rested," says Ollie complacently.

"Speaking of bad music," I say, picking up my phone to scroll through Facebook, "can we flip this station? Billy Joel is grandpa music."

Ollie and June erupt in identical shouts of indignation.

"Oh god, here we go," I groan. Tangling with either one of them about music is like a game of fetch with a single-minded Labrador; both of them at once is like getting tackled by a pair of Labradors in the grips of a face-licking, leg-humping frenzy.

"Billy Joel is one of the best songwriters of all time," says June, while Ollie leads with the far more direct "Only people without souls could hate Billy Joel. Or ears, people without ears."

"My ears are present and accounted for," I say. "This music is so cheesy, I don't know how you guys can like it. 'Uptown Girl' and 'River of Dreams' and the one that's just a big long list of stuff and—"

"Okay, so your problem is with bad Billy Joel songs, not Billy Joel per se," Ollie says. "It all went to hell in the eighties, but the early stuff—"

"*Nylon Curtain* was early eighties; that's a great album," says June, who only ever acts like a know-it-all about music—but boy, does she get intense about it. And she really, really loves to get the drop on Ollie.

"Sure. But Leah's talking about the stuff he wrote after he was a sellout. What about the early stuff, like 'Big Shot'? 'Miami 2017'? 'Honesty'? 'You May Be Right'? 'Summer, Highland Falls'?"

I am so bored with this conversation. "I have no idea what you're talking about."

"'Only the Good Die Young'?" June says, then breaks into song in the back seat, shimmying her shoulders and snapping her fingers to the rhythm. Although her speaking voice is low and smoky, her singing sounds as bright as the sun glancing off the windshield.

"Okay, yeah. I do like that song."

"Aha!" Ollie is grinning proudly at me. "I knew you weren't a cyborg." He reaches over and wiggles my knee, and my skin sparks at his touch. "Besides, that song could have been written for you. Sweet, proper Catholic girl gets coaxed into sin by a guy from the wrong side of the tracks . . ."

"Don't flatter yourself," I tell him, and he squeezes my leg again.

"Love you too, Leebee."

As we make our way northwest through a pretty valley somewhere in the southern Catskills, we stop for a late lunch at a country diner that Ollie saw recommended online (he detests rest stop food and will happily stop for a longer meal if he can find a place with soul). My brother, Sam, calls just as we're finishing up the meal, and I have to unstick my thighs from the vinyl banquette one by one before I can focus on the conversation.

"Where are you guys?" says Sam.

"Little less than halfway there. What about you?"

"Just got here. MJ and Karly went to pick up groceries, so Rob and I are chilling here for a second."

It never fails to amaze me that my brother's girlfriend is so literally his dream girl, right down to her name—although the red hair is far from a natural coincidence.

The bell on the door of the diner jingles as I push it open. "How's the place, is it nice?"

He snorts. "It's a park-in-front motel on the Jersey Shore. We're college students. How nice do you think it is?"

"Got me there."

"So, is Ollie's mom really making you sleep in separate rooms?"

I can't hold back a smile. Sam likes to act like he's an old pro at everything related to sex, even though he only started doing it a few months ago. This question of his is an entrée to teasing me with the fact that, though he may be spending his holiday week-end in a roadside dump that's costing him a week's earnings at his programming internship, he will also be spending his holiday weekend in the same bed as his girlfriend. "She really is," I say, as I take a seat on the bench in front of the diner and stretch luxuri-antly in the sunshine.

"Ooooohhhh," he groans. The sound is equal parts sympathy and delight. "That suuuuucks."

"It sure does. We'll just have to get creative," I say, and he makes a dramatic retching noise as if he hadn't been the one to bring the topic up. "Right, babe?" I call in a louder voice to Ollie, who has just emerged from the diner, June behind him.

"'Right babe' what?" he says, walking closer.

"I was just telling Sam—"

"No, you were not telling Sam," Sam says in my other ear. "Sam doesn't want to know. Sam wants you to get your groove on in your own particular way, but he doesn't need to know *any* of the details."

Ollie smiles as he watches my shoulders shaking with laughter, and holds out his hand for the phone. "What's up, bud? How's the beach?"

I should probably tell him that Sam might be too old for Ollie to call him by the nickname he used when Sam was sixteen—but then again, I'm pretty sure Sam secretly likes it. He banned me from calling him "Sammo" in front of Mary Jane, but Ollie can get away with pretty much anything as far as Sam's concerned. Al-though it's not like I'm any better. From the minute he smiled at me in that dive bar on MacDougal Street, I was toast.

Once we leave the Catskills behind, the land gradually flattens out, like a shaken blanket settling down on a bed. We leave the interstate and travel over two-lane local roads, while pastures dotted with silos and barns and farmhouses roll past around us. The roadsides are lined with wild orange daylilies, and the land is so green you could almost get high off it, bursting with lushness at the peak of summer. I crack my window a few inches and suck in a chestful of the rich, intoxicating air. And then before I know it, we're entering the town of Watkins Glen, which hugs the southern point of Seneca Lake.

"Junie, we're here!" I yell, and she snaps to life in the back seat.

"We are? Where's the lake?"

"Watch out your window," Ollie says, and within a few minutes we've passed through the town and begun to climb the rise along the western edge of the lake.

"There!" I say as we pass a clump of trees, and the lake comes into view below us, glittering in the early evening light. Beyond the boats bobbing in the Watkins marina, hills rise on the other shore, a mile away.

"It's pretty," June says.

"This is just the beginning," Ollie says, clearly feeling she is insufficiently impressed. "It's thirty-eight miles long."

"Holy crap!" says June. "That's gigantic."

"That's what she said," Ollie says, before one of us can beat him to it. After we do the expected groaning and snickering, he continues. "But yeah, it's the biggest of the Finger Lakes. And the deepest. Goes down to almost seven hundred feet in some spots. That's a seventy-story building."

"Yikes," says June.

"There's a naval station in the middle of the lake, not too far from the house. The navy built it so they could test sonar equipment."

"And there's all kinds of wineries along the shores," I say, taking over the tour guide routine. "We can do a winery crawl one day, it's really fun."

Now that we're in the homestretch, I can't sit still. I start tapping my fingers on my armrest, eating up the familiar landscape
with my eyes. There's the farm stand that has the sweetest corn for
miles, and the soft-serve ice cream place, and the brewery that
just opened up last year, which is an awesome spot to park yourself at a picnic table in the sun with a beer. The car slows as Ollie
prepares to turn, and I cheer. The lake briefly dips out of view as
we descend toward it, past a neighbor's cornfield with its huge red
barn that lists slightly sideways off its stone foundation. We pass
from the meadow into some woods and then, finally, surrounded
by a group of tall trees that cover it in shade, the house appears.

This house is just so perfect. It tells the story of the people who
live here. You can still see the small shape of the original structure, a bare-bones lake cottage that Ollie's father bought as a real
estate investment when he was single, which was added to repeatedly as Howard acquired a wife, a stepson, and a new baby, each
of whom came with visiting family and friends of their own. A
narrow pathway, grass sprouting between its uneven flagstones,
leads from the driveway to the front door, which is flanked on
both sides by hydrangea bushes popping with blue flowers.

At the *thump-thump-thump* of our car doors, the front door
opens and Ollie's dad appears in the doorway. "They're here!" he
bellows back into the house, then strides forward to welcome us.
He swallows Ollie into a hug, then turns to me. I've always thought
Ollie's father was a ringer for Sam Elliott, with his shaggy gray
hair, grizzled beard, and dashing swagger. I wouldn't go so far as
to say I think my boyfriend's dad is hot, because that is disgusting,
so I will simply state that Howard Bierman is a lady-killer. A lady-
killer, I should add, who is completely devoted to his wife; Ollie's
parents are notoriously, and sickeningly, in love.

Ollie's mom, Rachel, appears a moment later, shielding her eyes
against the slanting sun. I toss my bags on the driveway and gal-

lop over to her, arms raised, and she squeezes me tightly around the waist. Rachel is my favorite.

With everyone talking at once, we bustle inside, bags bumping the walls the whole way. I inhale the familiar scent: a mix of fresh air, wood smoke, and dampness that belongs to this place alone. As always, it's bordering on too warm inside, because Rachel is a tree hugger who deplores the energy wasted by air-conditioning. Everybody teases her about it, but they all also go along with it.

Spencer, the Biermans' golden retriever, dives excitedly into the scrum, tail swishing as he prances from person to person, licking and barking. I rub his head as he passes, and June drops to her knees to ruffle his ears.

"Hi, buddy! Hi, hi, hi! Oh, aren't you handsome!"

As June fusses over the dog, a pungent odor like boiled broccoli fills the room.

"Pardon Spencer," laughs Rachel. "He farts when he gets excited."

I wave my hand in front of my face. "Whew! That was a strong one. Think my nose hairs are curling."

"Hey, we all have to strive for a personal best," says Ollie.

"Hashtag goals," says June.

"Hashtag hustle," Ollie fires back.

"Hashtag believe in yourself."

"Both of you knock it off before I smack you," I say. I hate when Ollie and June go off on one of these banter tangents, because I can never think of jokes fast enough. I know I'm plenty funny, but I don't like feeling slow.

"Your house is so cozy, I love it," June says to Rachel, head swiveling as she takes in the rag rug spread across the worn floorboards and the LIFE IS BETTER AT THE LAKE sign hanging against the bare pine wall paneling over the couch.

Rachel smiles. "Thank you. I'm so thrilled you were able to join us; any friend of Leah's is someone we need to add to our wacky crew."

"C'mon, Junie; this isn't even the best part," I say, tugging her toward the sliding door. She follows me out onto the deck and there, spreading out to the distant horizon beneath the bluff the house is perched on, blazing with the sinking sun, is the lake.

"Woooow," she says. "This is incredible."

Around us, the air chimes with cricket song, and the wind rustles in the leaves overhead. While we stand there, a solitary kayaker slips across the water, silhouetted against its bright surface. I raise my hand, and the unknown person waves back in reply. The sliding door screeches in its tracks behind us, and then Ollie steps close and wraps his arms around my waist.

"Happy vacation, babe." He kisses the top of my head.

I close my eyes and smile.

6

June

EVERY MILE WE TRAVEL, CURVE AFTER CURVE, HILL AFTER VAL-
ley, stacks another pound of iron onto my shoulders. Cold, hard
iron, pressing me down with relentless force. It was easy enough
to agree to this trip when it was safely in the future; actually being
in a car headed to Seneca Lake is something else entirely.

Ollie has been driving with his left hand since we hit the middle
of the George Washington Bridge; his right one is wrapped around
mine. Every so often he adjusts it, gathering my listless fingers
together, trying to tangle them tighter with his, as if that will make
me feel better. Maybe it makes him feel better; I don't know.

I'd rather have left late enough that we'd be traveling mostly in
darkness, but Ollie quietly said he'd like to be there for dinner and
the bonfire. And so, as we swirl through the lush summer-green of
western New York, I am reading. "Reading." Staring at the tablet
in my lap, trying to concentrate on the young adult book I started
last week. I used to love suspense novels, with their mysteries and
twisty tension. Now I read stories about young people alight with
possibility.

By the time we approach the southern tip of the lake, it's too
dark to see much. I remember my first sight of it, how insubstan-
tial it seemed. How indifferent I was. My body blazes with yearn-

ing for that feeling, for there to have never been a reason for me
to hate this place. As we turn off the main road onto his parents'
lane, Ollie slides his whole forearm under mine. I close my eyes.
The car rolls forward for a few minutes and then draws to a stop.
I don't move.

"We're here, baby," Ollie says.

I swallow against the burst of saliva that floods my mouth. My
eyelids flutter open, and a quick impression of the house—
windows glowing with yellow light, trees overhead silhouetted
against the sky still faintly lit with sunset color—burns into my
eyes before I slam them shut again, shuddering. I hear myself
make a low, unwilling moan.

Ollie unbuckles his seatbelt and leans over, arm along my back
and fingers against my neck, underneath my sweaty hair. "Are you
okay?" he says, voice gentle.

I nod and silently accept the water bottle he presses into my
hand. The water restores a little calm as it slides cool and steady
down my throat. I can't believe I thought it was a good idea to arrive at night. It was not a good idea at all.

"Better?" Ollie says, and when I nod again, he pulls me into his
arms, lips against my hair as he talks to me. "Listen, if you don't
think you can do this, we can go home tomorrow."

I shake my head. "I'll be fine."

"Fuck it, we can turn around and leave right now. Just say the
word." His voice sounds weird, and I can't tell whether leaving
would make him feel disappointed or relieved. This place is hard
for him, too, he'd said. It must be. He loved her every bit as much
as I did. And then, of course, there was the lake.

It's tempting, the thought of sparing both of us from this. But I
don't want to let fear make any decisions for me. A few years ago,
I would have. Since then, I've learned how strong I can be when
there's somebody else who needs me to. "No. I'll be okay. Just need
a minute."

"Okay. But the offer to leave is always on the table. I know how hard this is. And I can't thank you enough for doing this for me. I love you."

"I love you too," I mumble. "All right, let's go."

The house looks different. There's a small porch over the front door now, empty and pointless. I think there used to be some flowering bushes here, which must have gotten uprooted to make room for the porch. I don't know why anyone would do that. Who would pull up beautiful plants to make room for a dinky little porch? It looks like they repainted, too; rather than the weathered gray I remember, the wooden siding gleams chilly white against the surrounding darkness. As we approach the porch, the door nudges open and my future mother-in-law heads straight for me.

"June, honey," she says, awkwardly fitting her arms around me between the bags hanging from my shoulders. "It's so good to see you."

"Happy birthday, Rachel," I say automatically, hugging her back.

She cups my cheek, evaluating me with her steady blue eyes. "Thank you," she says. "And thank you for coming." Then she drops her hand and turns to her son.

As I watch Ollie embrace her, I remind myself that this is why I'm doing this. My fiancé has a wonderful mother whom he adores, and that is a good thing. I am showing him that I value that; showing her that I value her.

Another wave of nausea crashes over me the moment I step inside and breathe in. That smell. Woodsy air and long-gone smoke; the sugary exhalations of the shrubs and clover-filled grass around the house; that faint dampness that blows up from the water. They're in my camp about air-conditioning here; it's open windows and ceiling fans, even when it rains. It's all far, far too familiar from memories embedded like shrapnel in my mind.

Except it seems smaller somehow, claustrophobic, in spite of the freshening that has gone on inside, too. Flat white paint on the wall paneling that used to be bare; scuffed and humble wood floors refinished to a stylish, mirror-polished chocolate. The comfortably worn furniture has been entirely replaced, with the effect as if Rachel just scrolled down the landing page of the Pottery Barn website: *One of these, and one of these, and a sand dollar in a hurricane glass because why not.* It looks sterile. As sterile as if they were trying to wipe something away.

"Glad you decided to join us for dinner," says a deep voice, and I turn to find Ollie's half brother, Caleb, strolling out of the hallway to the bedrooms. "At the extremely convenient hour of nine twenty-six at night."

"Couldn't get out of work any earlier," says Ollie, clapping his brother on the back. "I'm pretty sure you didn't starve."

"June," says Caleb, arms wide for a hug. "You look beautiful even after a long car ride."

While Ollie heads into the bathroom, I kick off my shoes to buy a couple of seconds before letting myself be engulfed. "Hey, Caleb. Nice to see you. Where's Leslie?"

"She's just getting Eli down. He's a little wound up from all the excitement of coming to the lake."

"Ah," I say, with a vague all-purpose smile. But that's all I've got to offer. I'm never great at conversation with Caleb one-on-one. "Do you need help with anything, Rachel?" I say, turning to her.

"No thanks, honey. Howard put the steaks on the grill a few minutes ago, and everything else is ready. Oh! Unless you'd like to set the table? We're going to eat inside because of the bugs—place mats and napkins are in the console over there."

Gratefully, I focus on my task, setting six neat places at the gleaming wood dining table. When the linens are done, I duck into the kitchen for plates and silver. Just like elsewhere, this space looks new; pristine white cabinets reach to the floor and ceiling, bisected by a tasteful granite countertop and subway tile backsplash. Instead of the homey golden glow I remember, the overhead lighting is blue-white and scorchingly bright; must be some energy-efficient bulbs Rachel adopted instead of incandescent. I survey the lay of the land and correctly guess that the plates are in the cabinet to the right of the sink, but after that I get stymied. "Um, where is the silver?"

"To the right of the dishwasher," Rachel says, and when I tug open the drawer, my heart hiccups.

"It's the same silver."

I don't realize I've said it out loud until I sense Rachel standing next to me, staring down at the drawer full of silverware, each piece with a ceramic handle in the shape of a vaguely cross-eyed fish. "Yeah, we love these silly things," she says, lifting a knife so the light glints off the smooth steel. I have a sudden visual of it in Leah's hand, the fish part turned toward Ollie as she menaced him with it, Ollie tilting backward in his chair to escape her, laughing.

Rachel cuts her eyes to me and opens her lips to say something, but just as she's about to speak, Ollie's dad barrels into the room, accompanied by their dog, Spencer.

"June bug!" Howard wraps me in a steak-scented hug. "So good to have you. Where the hell is that boy of mine? We're ready to go here."

I bend down to pet Spencer, who wags and gazes at me with his sweet brown eyes. The fur on his face is white with age now, but he's as loving as ever. "I think he went to the bathroom."

"Pops!" Ollie bellows from the open screen door behind us, from which issues a waft of meaty smoke. "I came out to check the steaks. Only way you'd think they're done is if you're a coyote who brought this cow down in the field."

"Boy thinks he knows how to grill better than his old man," Howard mutters, shaking his head in mock disgust.

"Remember the pork chops from last year?" Rachel says sweetly, and Howard grunts.

"No respect," he says to me. "I get no respect from my son, no respect from my wife. I suppose you'll be colluding against me, too, huh?"

"Never," I say solemnly, but the effect of it is ruined as Howard sidles sideways and swats Rachel on the butt. She yips and giggles.

A few minutes later, we are seated around the table, including Caleb's wife, Leslie. She is a former Syracuse cheer captain, the perfect petite blond counterpart to Caleb's Don Draper masculinity. They got married a couple of years before Ollie and I got together—in the photos, she looks like a Swedish princess—and conceived Eli at a prompt but appropriate interval after their wedding. I suspect they will shortly get to work on baby number two; Leslie is a goal-setter.

"So, how was the drive up?" says Rachel. "Not too bad, I hope?"

"Well, getting out of the city on a summer Friday is always like the traffic scene after they announce the apocalypse in a disaster movie," says Ollie, "but once we got onto 80 it wasn't bad."

Rachel glances briefly at Howard before speaking. "I really appreciate—*we* really appreciate—you coming up here for my birthday. Especially you, June. I know being here can't be easy for you. Please let me know if there's anything we can do, anything at all, to make you more comfortable."

A half-hearted "um" is all I can manage. In my family, we don't discuss our feelings over the dinner table. We don't discuss our feelings at all. I've been forced to get better at it since I've been with Ollie, working out that muscle more and more, but Rachel's just asked me to do a deadlift. There's a long, dreadful moment where the only sound is the *tick-tick-tick* of the ceiling fan spinning over our heads. "Thanks, Rachel," I say finally. "That's kind of you to say."

"We take care of our family," Howard says gruffly. Caleb's shoulders twitch in a silent snort, and Howard sets down his knife and fork with a clatter. Ollie rests a hand on his father's wrist before he can speak. After a deliberate beat, Howard slowly resumes eating, and I exhale.

"Thank you," I say again, and I squeeze Ollie's knee so he knows I'm including him in that. "I'm glad to be spending time with you. So, what sort of stuff do you have planned for the Fourth of July party?"

Rachel follows my blinking conversational detour sign, and we move on. By the end of the meal, the day's strain has tightened an invisible band around my head, but it isn't over yet; we still have the bonfire. It's one of the Bierman family traditions: The first night of the July Fourth weekend, they build a big blaze in the fire pit down near the water, and their friends come over for beer and s'mores. It's so nice and neighborly and warm.

I am so goddamn tired.

Once we've cleared away the dishes, Howard slings an arm around Ollie's shoulders. "Come on, boy, let's go set some shit on fire."

Ollie looks back at me. "You coming, baby?"

"I'll be right there," I say. "Just gotta make a pit stop first." Rachel and Caleb follow the other two outside; I can hear their voices drifting up from the lawn as they walk toward the dock. When they're gone, I stand alone in the living room for a few minutes, quietly breathing in and out. I've been here over an hour, and I'm still alive. I'm not even curled up in a fetal position on the floor. I'm going to survive tonight, and from here I think it can only get better. There's just one other thing I need to do. I suck in a chest full of air, open the sliding door screen, and step out onto the deck.

The lake is alive. Glimmering with moonlight, it spreads to the north and south of the house, as far as I can see. Tiny waves lick the shore below the house, but the lapping, trickling sound that fills the air isn't just from the water—it's the fish. Out of sight in the darkness, countless tiny fish are feeding and playing in the shallow water near shore, leaping into the air for bugs and splashing down again. I didn't believe it the first time I came here: It had been a still night, and Leah and I couldn't understand how the waves were making so much noise when the wind was down. Grinning like a guide getting to his favorite part of the tour, Ollie jumped down to the shoreline and shone his phone flashlight over the water, and there they were, swirling.

Down by the shore, an orange glow sparks in the darkness, growing brighter while I watch, illuminating the people standing nearby as the fire devours more and more of the wood. I walk down from the deck to the terrace, my mind echoing with the eager slap of Leah's flip-flops against the plank steps. When it came to anything fun or adventurous, she had one speed setting: zoom.

From the terrace to the lawn, then down the stairs that descend from the steep bluff the house sits on to the shoreline. Ollie sees me coming and meets me at the stairs.

"I missed you." He curls his arms around my waist and kisses me.

I set my hands on his warm, solid shoulders. "After five minutes?"

"Five lonely minutes." He tugs me closer, arms sliding downward from my waist to my hips, and kisses me again. I feel the dull ache swell low in my abdomen and, as if we share a single nervous system, he makes a satisfied little noise and kisses me harder.

"Ol," I say breathlessly, forcing myself to pull away. "We can't make out in front of your parents."

"Nobody's looking," he murmurs against my lips.

"They will be."

"Come down to the dock with me."

I give a half laugh, half pant, and glance over my shoulder at the raised structure at the end of the Biermans' dock—the roof that shelters their two boats is built out into a seating platform that no doubt still houses a group of chaise longues and a table. "Ol . . ."

"I don't like it out here after dark." His words are so quiet I almost could have imagined them. "Distract me."

I rub my thumbs along his collarbone, frowning. "You don't—"

"Ollie!" One of the shadowy figures near the fire separates itself and moves toward us, and when the firelight catches the man's handsome face, guilt, sticky as syrup, drips down my spine. Ollie didn't tell me Terrance was going to be here.

"What's up, man?" Ollie walks to Terrance and embraces him warmly.

"Good to see you," says Terrance as they pull apart, and then he turns to me, still smiling. "Hey, June. It's nice to see you again."

Same voice, low and soft. Same infinitesimal pauses between the sentences that let you know he's thought about what he'll say before he lets it out. "Hey, Terrance."

He steps forward and folds me in a light hug. He even smells the same: subtle, piney aftershave cut with sunscreen. "You guys up here for the week?"

"Yep," says Ollie. "Couldn't miss Mom's birthday. You gonna be able to come to the dinner?"

"No," says Terrance. "Wish I could, but I booked a couple of gigs in Rochester during the week so I could take these weekends. It should be a nice week, though. Weather's supposed to be good."

I side-eye him. "You didn't used to be a guy who'd make conversation about the weather. Boy, how about this heat wave, huh? Hot as tarnation, all the way up here. I do declare."

His laughter is low and pleased. "Still snarky, I see."

"You see that?" I say, pointing at the ground. "That's the broken ice."

"Well done," he says, holding up his hand for a high five. "And now that you have, let me ask you a groundbreaking question that nobody's ever asked you before. How's the wedding planning going?"

Ollie answers. "It's good, man. We're mostly done with the big stuff at this point, just have to send out the invitations, pick the food—"

"Micromanage the playlist," I add, and Terrance laughs.

"Oh, I believe it. It's in Montauk, right?"

"Yeah, little beach shack–type of place. Right on the water."

"Did you think about having it up here at all?"

"No, we—" Ollie looks at me and pauses uncertainly for a second. "We're pretty New York focused these days."

Terrance rubs the side of his face. "Damn, I can't believe I asked you that," he says in a low voice. "What a stupid question."

Ollie waves it off. We both tend to freeze up in response to direct allusions.

"Well, at any rate, I'm looking forward."

"You gonna have anybody to bring with you?"

Terrance wrinkles his nose. "Nah. I'm traveling so much for work, it's hard to get anything going."

"The devil named 'music' has stolen your life?" Ollie says.

"I'm not gonna complain about it," Terrance says. In his rueful smile, there is pride that he's making a living as a musician; it makes me happy to see it. "But hey, come on back to the fire. My folks want to say hello to June."

There are twelve, maybe fifteen people gathered around the bonfire, talking—Ollie's family, Terrance's, the neighbors on the other side, and a few assorted friends of Ollie's dad's. Ollie's arm is firm around my waist as we make the rounds: "This is my fiancée, June." In response to the inevitable "How did you meet?" he smoothly gives the answer, the one that's true but only tells a fraction of the story: "Through a mutual friend." Normally, it's safe as can be: What more unremarkable story is there? No one ever asks for more.

But up here at Seneca, I wonder. I'm not especially memorable on my own, but there's no question I stick out up here; somebody might remember having seen a tall Asian girl with haunted eyes hanging around the house the day they came to try to help. I was in a photo in the local paper, hugging Rachel, my face twisted with tears. I should never have even seen that article, but I found it a few weeks afterward, in one of my late, burning nights in front of my computer screen. More often than not, those nights occurred on days when Ollie had tried to call me.

Ollie, always my cause and effect.

When the bonfire is headed for embers and the guests have gone home, we make our way back to the house and say our good nights. Finally, this endless day is over. Limp with relief, I sag onto the living room rug to cuddle Spencer. Ollie lifts our bags to take them to his room.

"Can Spencer sleep with—wait, where are you going?" My hand stills on the dog's soft head.

Ollie peers up at me from halfway down the stairs. "We sleep in the downstairs bedroom now. Eli has my old room so he can be close to Cal and Leslie."

It makes sense. But I hadn't expected it. I flit after him and grip the stair banister in sweating hands. "Um, what about . . . is the couch in the family room still a pull-out?"

Ollie sets the bags down gently. "It is, but we wouldn't have any privacy there."

"Well, it's not like sex is a priority when we're at your parents' place."

"I meant a place to sleep with walls that block the noise from upstairs. And a door that keeps out dogs and toddlers."

He has a point. And I did say I would be okay with this. I *will* be okay with this.

Ollie holds out his hand to me. "Mom redid the room to be really comfy. Why don't you come down with me and check it out?"

Before I can stall again, I lift my handbag off the floor and follow him down.

The fact that the furniture in the family room has changed doesn't make a bit of difference. There's only one way to lay out this room, so they've just put new things directly in the places of the old: two slipcovered couches angled toward the woodstove and the windows, a wide coffee table in the middle. I blink, and for an instant Leah is there, her bare feet with their coral-red nail polish propped on the table. She was so obsessed with that color. I blink again, and she's gone.

She is always, always gone.

I release my breath and follow Ollie to the bedroom. A king bed dressed in crisp white linens fills the center of the room. With the stiff sisal rug and the dense curtains covering the screen door to the terrace behind regimented pleats, the room looks polished. Trying too hard.

"Those are blackouts," Ollie says, nodding his chin at the curtains. "She'd be so relieved we finally took mercy and decided to let people sleep."

Whenever one of us says the pronoun *she* or *her* without a name attached, it's always Leah. Of course he's thinking about her, too. But in a calm, almost casual way. I don't know how he does it.

All I can think about, being in this room, is her ratty old duffel bag, a leftover from her high school soccer team that she refused to throw out in favor of something less disreputable. She was attached to the memories. And now the sight of it sitting open at the foot of her bed is permanently etched into my brain.

I sit down on the side of the bed and put my face in my hands. Ollie scoots until he's behind me and wraps himself around me.

Arms around my waist, spine arched to echo mine: Every inch of him that can bend is curved toward me.

"God, it hurts, Ol," I whisper. "It hurts so bad."

"I know, sweetheart."

"I keep remembering. Just little things here and there . . . but I feel like the big things are waiting underneath. They can't not be."

He hugs me tighter and kisses the back of my head. "Yeah, they might be. But don't be scared."

"'Don't be scared'?" I twist free of his grasp till I can face him. "How the hell am I not supposed to be afraid of this?"

For a moment he doesn't answer, just traces a circle on my knee with his fingertips. "Sometimes being afraid of something hurts you worse than actually facing it," he says. "I'm here. And I've got you. It's going to get easier every day. A little bit at a time."

I know he believes it; he wouldn't say it if he didn't. It would be so easy to let him comfort me. An hour ago, I was telling myself the same thing he's telling me now. But walking into this room obliterated my foolish optimism.

It isn't going to get better the longer I'm here. It's going to get worse.

7

Leah

REMEMBER HOW I SAID I WASN'T A MORNING PERSON? MORN-
ings are the only thing I hate about Seneca Lake. Ollie's parents'
house faces due east, so as soon as that big old ball of burning
hydrogen pops over the tree line across the lake, *blammo.* So long,
sleep.

When the rising light has pried itself all the way under my eyelids, I thrash around with a groan and sit up. The room presents
the usual microcosm of June's and my habits: her side tidy, bed
made impeccably, and clothes folded inside her open suitcase; my
side strewn with my belongings, my duffel bag barfing out T-shirts
and running shorts like the guts of Luke Skywalker's tauntaun. I
rope my hair in a topknot and harness myself into a bra; the last
thing I need is to run into Caleb while I'm au naturel.

I draw back the curtains covering the sliding door and step out
onto the terrace. Mind you, the only time I like an early morning
is when I see it 'cause I've been up all night talking. A morning like
that, it feels like a victory. But this morning is so gorgeous it's
obnoxious—*Look at me, I'm a perfect summer morning; don't you
feel like a scumbag for all the times you've slept through this?* Everything's all sparkling lake and trilling crickets and golden light

bouncing off dewy grass. June, seated on the love seat next to the door with one knee drawn up under her chin, puts down her creepy-looking paperback and smiles at me.

"This is pretty stinkin' fantastic," she sighs happily, releasing a deep breath of Seneca air and stretching her arms out to her sides. "Thank you again for inviting me."

I pluck her hand out of the way and sit down next to her so I can rest my head on her shoulder. "Yeah, it is. And you don't have to thank me. I'm so happy you came. Kinda seems weird now that you *haven't* been here before, actually."

"So what's our agenda for today?" she says, when I yawn and raise my head. People tell me *I'm* cute, but right now June has the air of an eager squirrel—dark eyes inquisitive, nose sniffing at the air.

"Breakfast on the deck, change into bathing suits, hit the boat," I say. "Drink on the boat, snack on the boat, pull each other along the water using ropes attached to the boat. Swim, lunch, lie out on the dock, sunset cruise, dinner, bed . . . and repeat."

"Oh my god, I'm never leaving," says June, getting to her feet with a decisiveness I cannot summon. "Should we get started on the breakfast part?"

Hmm, except that I am deeply enjoying this whole sitting on my ass in the sun thing at the moment. I look up at her, contemplate, and quietly burp.

She rolls her eyes and kicks lightly at my outstretched foot. "Come on, lazy-ass. I'll make you coffee."

Those are the magic words, and she knows it. I trot obediently behind her into the house and up the stairs.

Ollie's dad has perfected the art of cooking breakfast for a lot of people: throw a dozen eggs in a pan along with some diced-up ham or sausage and a mountain of peppers, onions, and mushrooms, stir until delicious, and serve. Once June has unearthed her coffee supplies from the colony of Wegmans bags and produce that litters the counter, we are pretty much ready to go; only Ollie is missing. And unfortunately for him, I am starving.

"Wake up wake up wake up!" I yell, leaping onto Ollie's bed and bouncing on my knees so the mattress jostles wildly. He groans and tries to duck under the covers, but I will grant no mercy. "Don't scowl at me—your face looks like a butthole when you do that. It's time for breakfast."

He stares at me in horror for a second, then tips his head back and stares at the ceiling as if in prayer. "Dear God, thank you for this woman. Her grace, her sweetness. You really outdid yourself." I try to shove his face, and he traps my hand. "I always hoped that one day my girlfriend would tell me my face looks like an anus."

By this point, I'm flopped down on top of him, giggling into his chest. "I didn't mean it in a bad way . . ."

"My face looks like a butthole in a positive sense?"

"I just meant . . . kind of pinched and frowning and angry," I say, voice squeaky with laughter. "You've got to admit, that does pretty much sound like a butthole."

Ollie drills his finger into my ear. "You know what? Maybe you should just stop talking. Get off me, you mini hell spawn."

One of the unique properties of Ollie is that not only does he get away with teasing me about my height, but I actually like it. I slide onto my feet and ogle him while he pulls on jeans and a T-shirt. As soon as he's ready, I reach for the door.

"Oh hey, Hell Spawn?"

"*Whaaaaat?*" I spin around on my toes, teeth bared. Holy pumpkins, why won't he let me eat? He *knows* what happens when I don't eat.

A shit-eating grin creeps across his face. "You just answered to the name *Hell Spawn.*"

I snarl incoherently and snatch the door open.

Caleb looks up from pouring a mug of coffee when we trail into the kitchen. "Morning there, baby brother," he says to Ollie. "It was well worth waiting an hour for you to grace us with your presence so we could eat."

"What time zone are you living in, Caleb?" I snap. "June and I only came upstairs twenty minutes ago."

"Relax, Leeb," Ollie mutters.

Caleb gives a lazy smile as he runs a hand through his longish dark hair. "That would be Ollie Time, Leah. I'm sure you're familiar with it. We all live on Ollie Time."

"Yesterday Ollie Time included a seven-hour drive to bring our guests to us, an hour-and-a-half trip to Wegmans, another half hour at the wine store, and twenty minutes trying to fix the speaker connection on the boat," says Howard. "What have you done with Caleb Time lately?"

Ollie squints his eyes shut and pinches the bridge of his nose. "Let's just eat, please."

After the meal, June and I leap to help wash up, then head back to our room to get ready for the boat. Ever careful of her surroundings, June retreats to the bathroom to apply her sunscreen lest some stray droplet land on the carpet.

"What's the deal with Caleb?" comes her disembodied voice. "Is he always that crabby?"

"No—he can be cool when he forgets to try to impress everybody. But he's awful around Howard. The two of them can't stand each other."

"That's weird to me. Howard clearly loves Rachel like crazy; you'd think he would love her son, too."

"I think he used to," I say, before I remember that I really shouldn't be spilling Ollie's private family business—even to June.

She waits for me to go on, then lets the topic stay dropped. "But Caleb's here for the whole week?"

"I guess a free lake house to stay at is worth it to him. He usually goes off with his own friends a fair bit. I'm sure his girlfriend will be down at some point today, too. Which won't stop him from staring at my boobs like my nipples are glowing."

"Seriously?" says June. "Gross. Doesn't Ollie notice?"

"Of course not. He's oblivious. And it's not worth making a big stink over. Besides, to be quite honest, Ollie is often staring at them too."

"Oh, speak of the devil. Good morning, girls," June says to my bare chest as she breezes out of the bathroom. "Haven't seen you in almost twelve whole hours."

Okay, so I'm a bit of a nudist. Around June, and other women generally. It's not that I *want* to be looked at; I just never really got the point of all of the turned-back, folded-arm, pointed-elbow contortions that some girls go through to preserve their modesty from each other. Tits are tits are tits. And right now my goal is to make sure mine are completely submerged in sunscreen before I go outside. Anyone who believes that can be accomplished with a bikini top on is kidding themselves.

While I grease myself, I stare enviously at June's lean body as she slips a tank and board shorts over her sporty black bikini. This has been our dynamic ever since we stumbled into puberty (well, I'd sprouted boobs by the end of sixth grade, so admittedly I started lurching first): I lovingly envy her clean lines and absence of visible body fat; she lovingly envies my D cups and my soccer booty. We both know it's ridiculous to be such *girls* about it, but what are you gonna do?

After much milling about, collecting of sunglasses, filling of water bottles, and loading of beer and snacks and towels, we are finally ready to hit the boat. Last year, Ollie's dad replaced their old, basic speedboat with this ridiculous double-decker pontoon. The thing is basically a giant floating couch with a motor: a wide, flat base ringed with cushy upholstered seating, a built-in cooler, and an attachment for a grill that hangs over the side of the boat.

(Because nothing says safety like open flame at sea.) There's a smaller platform overhead from which you can access a slide that will shoot you, squealing, into the lake. This boat is really obvious bait to get us to come up here—and boy, is it effective.

The glare of sunlight and glittering water almost blinds me when we step outside, but when my poor pupils recover, I can see that Ollie's friend and next-door neighbor Terrance is already down at the dock, futzing with something on the boat's console panel. I grin to myself, because I love me some Terrance. He's one of those people who always make you feel at ease, no matter who you are. Further, he is an eyeful. The fitted T-shirt he's wearing clings to his ever-so-manly frame and dark brown skin, and he's wearing his hair in short, spiky twists that look stylish and playful at the same time. While I watch him, a Taylor Swift song blasts unexpectedly from the speakers, and he recoils as if he'd been attacked by a rat. Great—I'm outnumbered among music nerds.

"Ahoy!" I shout.

Terrance waves and boosts himself back onto the dock. "Yo, Ol!"

"Hey!" Ollie calls back. "Nice T-shirt. Do they sell it in adult sizes?"

"Nice haircut," says Terrance as Ollie walks up. "Did your hairdresser give you back your Ellen DeGeneres inspo pic?"

They do a back-slapping bro hug, then Terrance grabs me around the waist and spins me. Another casualty of being a short girl: bodily dignity. Men cannot resist (do not attempt to resist) the urge to lift me up and toss me around. I guess it makes them feel strong. Never mind that June, eight inches taller than I am, weighs only six pounds more. Nobody tosses June.

Terrance keeps it quick, though, and sets me down after one revolution. "How are ya, Leah? Been a while."

"Last summer, I think. How's school?"

He rolls his eyes and blows air through his teeth. Terrance is in the second year of a master's of music degree for violin performance, after which he's going to work in a classical symphony orchestra—which is about the coolest job I've ever heard of.

"Eh, I'm just happy to have a break for now," he says, and then his eyes track behind me. "Well, well, look at this. After all these years, a fellow *Mayflower* descendant arrives at Seneca Lake."

I turn just in time to watch a slow grin spread across June's face. I know that grin.

"You sure you don't need to see my DAR card?" she says.

"Shoot, girl, I know you're in," he says. "You must be June."

"Don't believe I've had the pleasure," she says, practically purring. For a Korean girl from Westchester, June does an uncanny Southern belle. But the slightly unhinged Vivien Leigh version, where she's a predator underneath the sweet-tea charm.

"I'm Terrance," he says, meeting her for a handshake that lasts a couple of seconds longer than necessary. "My parents live next door." He angles his head toward the small gray-blue house a hundred feet away, perched close to the water with a couple of kayaks tugged onto the gravel beach in front. "I'm psyched to finally meet you; I've been hearing stories for years."

June holds up a graceful forefinger. "I want you to know that there were extenuating circumstances regarding the chinchilla incident."

Terrance laughs. "Is that a fact?"

I raise my eyebrows at Ollie, because this is an intriguing development. He gives me a slight frown of confusion. Damn, guys can be dense sometimes. I feel faintly slighted that June and Terrance managed to notice each other before the idea occurred to me, but it's just as well; she hates it when I throw guys at her. I'll just have to be vigilant for opportunities to unobtrusively nudge it along.

While Ollie checks around the boat and lowers the hoist, the rest of us claim seats on the wraparound banquette, then Ollie jumps in and starts the motor. The *chug, chug, chug* of the propellers slowly churning as the boat reverses away from the dock is such a happy summer sound that I break into a grin.

As we pick up speed, bumping gently over the waves, and move further out into the lake, June and I turn our faces to the wind. The sky is the kind of blue you almost don't believe is real, empty except for a few stray cotton puffs drifting slowly along. The lake is thickly lined with trees on both sides, with houses along the water's edge. Most of them are small and modest, many with decks and additions clearly assembled after the fact, like the Biermans' house. Ollie has told me that unlike the other Finger Lakes, like Canandaigua and Keuka, whose smaller, shallower dimensions keep them warmer and therefore tend to be more socially oriented, people who live on Seneca come for peace and quiet and fishing. In ten minutes of cruising, we pass only two other boats and a Jet Ski.

Once we get beyond the spit of land that pushes out into the lake on the middle of the western shore, the wind drops off and the water smooths out. Ollie slows the boat and cuts the motor.

"All right, who wants first turn on the skis? Leeb, you ready?"

"I was born ready!" I say, springing to my feet. And this is true. Waterskiing isn't easy: The combination of balance, strength, and intuition for the water that it requires is definitely a challenge. A challenge for most people, that is. But not for me. Because I am an effing waterskiing *goddess*. Ollie proclaims that my remarkable prowess at skiing is because of my low center of gravity; I prefer to credit my natural athleticism.

When the towrope is in place and everything is ready, I take a deep breath and plunge off the back of the boat into the lake. Despite knowing exactly what I was in for, I still do a closed-mouth shriek as the water swallows me. Seneca Lake in early July is cold. You can call it refreshing, you can call it bracing; and you can also call it straight-up *cold*. Aided by my life vest, I pop back to the surface and shake my head like a wet puppy to clear the water off my face. Ollie hands me the skis, and I quickly attach them and get into position. "Punch it!" I yell, and Ollie retreats, grinning, to the driver's seat and starts the engine. And then we're off.

As the skis catch the water and pull me up to my feet, I scream with sheer joy. Ollie has cranked up my favorite summer anthem, "Party in the USA," and I'm ripping across the lake at twenty-five miles an hour, my strong legs absorbing the undulations of the water, guiding me effortlessly back and forth over the curling wave of wake on either side of the boat.

"Yeah, Leah!" shouts Terrance, while June waves and cups her hands to her mouth to yell "Woo!" I wave back at them and they cheer. As we rocket down the lake, I begin to play, cutting my edges against the wake to try to get a spray, and lifting one foot a little bit to test my balance. I've been wanting to try the single slalom ski—Caleb bought it a couple of years back in a fit of ambition, but it hasn't gone well for him—and I think I'm definitely ready.

After a nice, long run, I signal that it's somebody else's turn, and Ollie slows the boat so we can trade out skiers. As I swim up, I see Caleb waiting at the back, and he leans down, smiling, to offer me a hand up into the boat. "Great run, Leah!"

"I'm good," I say, ignoring his outstretched hand, but that doesn't stop him from staring at me as I climb up the ladder. His gaze slides over my bare skin like oil. I snatch the towel June is holding out and wrap it around me even though I don't really want it. June throws Caleb a nasty scowl, which regrettably is wasted on him.

"Hey, Caleb, when is Tamra coming down?" I say, stuffing the end of the towel under my armpit.

"'Coming down'? To the lake? She's not. *Going* down, on whoever she's sleeping with these days?" He does an ostentatious check of his watch as he stands up to take his turn on the skis. "That I cannot tell you."

"Wait, you didn't tell me you guys broke up," says Ollie.

I stare at Caleb and tip my head to one side. "Geez, the way you talk about her, it's hard to imagine why she'd ever look elsewhere."

"Leebee," says Ollie in a warning voice. He hates it when I give Caleb a hard time for his crap. But I'm sorry, I'm not going to not say something just because it makes Ollie uncomfortable. Ollie telling me to slow my roll is a tale as old as time. "What happened, Cal?"

Caleb shrugs. "Doesn't matter. But it happened right after I got laid off and lost my paycheck. You can draw your own conclusions."

"That sucks, man, I'm sorry," says Ollie.

I catch eyes with June, who flares her nostrils eloquently. One of my favorite things about June is her sneakiness. The first thing I noticed about her when she started as a new kid at our middle school was how observant she was—those dark eyes didn't miss anything, especially because she was usually the one listening while somebody else (like me) was busy getting high off the sound of their own yap. But the second thing was the sneakiness. She doesn't have quite the poker face she thinks she does, and watching for her subtle tells delights me. A faintly arched brow, a half smile, a perfectly timed side-eye: Those are her tools. If you speak June, you can learn exactly what she's thinking just by watching her face.

"Great job on the skis, babe," says Ollie, walking over and hugging my wrapped-burrito form against him. "You're the queen of the lake."

"I want to try the slalom next," I tell him.

"Okay, but we should get you practicing first. We'll do some more runs later where you can start with two skis and then drop one."

"I am the queen of the lake. The queen of the lake doesn't need training wheels."

"The queen of the lake doesn't want to get injured, either. We can—"

"Oliver!" yells Caleb from the water. "A little less talk, a little more boat driving?"

Ollie goes back to the driver's seat. I shamelessly stare at him sitting there with that faint golden tan on his skin, the tops of his eyebrows just visible over his aviators, a look of relaxed concentration on his face as he scans the lake for traffic and keeps an eye on Caleb in the rearview. Looking at Ollie is just such a rewarding experience. His only physical imperfection, if you can even call it that, is his breastbone, which instead of sitting flat on his chest, is concave and somewhat sunken. But the thing about this is that, since he's always been self-conscious about it—largely thanks to Caleb, who teased him about it as a kid—he obsessively works out his upper body to minimize the impact of it. So what you notice, if you're a person who likes dudes and who happens to be ogling Ollie, is a whole lot of fine, followed—*maybe*—by "Oh huh, I guess there's something funky about the middle of his chest." Caleb is crazy jacked and I guess it's cool if that's what you're into, but I will take lean and ripped over Hulk Smash every time.

As the morning turns into afternoon, we break open the cooler and start handing around the beers. Ollie's parents are big believers in local pride, so all the beer is from upstate New York—Saranac, Ommegang, Ithaca. We snack and talk and bake in the sun, and everyone takes a couple of turns on the skis except for June, who cannot be persuaded to try it.

"I'm a spectator, not a participant," she says, shaking her head. "I know my lane."

"It's easier than it looks," says Caleb. "I bet you'd be good at it if you gave it a shot." He's giving her a big, warm smile—the smile that always reminds me that he really is Ollie's brother. And just like that, my antennae are quivering. He had better not be getting any notions about June.

"Totally," says Terrance. "All of us had to learn how to do it before we got good; nobody's going to make fun of you."

"I wouldn't go that far," Ollie says, reaching into the cooler for another beer. "I will certainly make fun of you."

"Ignore that fool," says Terrance. "He lacks basic manners."

"For real, though," says Ollie, "it's not as hard as it looks. If you're good at yoga, then you're strong and you've got good balance. All you need besides that is practice."

For a second June wavers, looking tempted, and Ollie bounces his eyebrows encouragingly. Then she scrunches her nose and it's over. "It was a good effort, guys, but I'm gonna pass. I will take another one of those beers, though."

"Come on, Junie, let's float." I get to my feet and hold my hand out to Ollie for a life vest. "Diaper, please." While June watches with amusement, I turn the open life vest upside down, step through the armholes, wrestle it up my thighs, and yank the zipper closed. "Voilà!" I say, turning in place. "The Finger Lakes diaper." I cannonball off the back of the boat, and when I bob back to the surface, my lower half is comfortably supported by the life vest. "Beer me."

Ollie passes me my beer, then splashes in after me, followed by Caleb. June walks to the back platform of the boat, gets her diaper on, and immediately bursts out laughing. "I feel ridiculous!"

"Don't knock it till you've tried it," says Ollie, and digs a handful of water at her.

"Ahh, that's cold!" she gasps. "*Not* the way to get me in there!"

"Terrance, you want to do the honors?" Ollie says.

Terrance gives a solemn nod, then quickly steps behind June, wraps his arms around her waist, leans back so she's off her feet, swings her sideways for torque, and launches her. Guess I was wrong—it looks like somebody does toss June, after all. She has a brief, glorious flight, accompanied by an angry squawk, before she lands ass-first in Seneca Lake. And then she comes up fighting.

"You *asshole!*" she shrieks, splashing frantically at Ollie.

"Why are you attacking me? He's the one who threw you!" he laughs, grabbing her wrist.

"Because you told him to," she says between gritted teeth.

"Hey, Terrance has free will," Ollie says. "And anyway, you're in now. Chill out and float."

From the back of the boat, Terrance wiggles her beer back and forth in his hand like bait. June releases a huffy breath and swims over.

"Sorry, but it had to be done," Terrance says, grinning. "Otherwise you were just gonna sit here on the boat and swish your feet around."

"Because it's *freezing* in here," she mutters, and takes a reluctant sip of her beer.

"Yeah, I can see your goosebumps," says Terrance, brushing his thumb along her shoulder. I give a subdued squeak of excitement; that guy has got *moves*. "But now you're stuck. If you get out again then you're admitting defeat."

June nods in concession, but I notice that her right hand has disappeared underneath the water. Terrance, lovestruck fool that he is, is too busy smiling at her to notice what her hand is doing until she swoops it up toward him, nailing him right in the face with a handful of Seneca. He rocks backward, laughing and sputtering, and then he sets down his beer and dives right over her head. She looks around, alarmed, then yelps as he grabs her from underneath.

I roll onto my back and paddle toward Ollie, who wraps his arm around my shoulders. "Ah, young love," I say as we watch June and Terrance splashing.

"You think?" says Ollie.

"Are you kidding me?" I crane back to peer at him upside down. "You didn't see him looking at her like she was a human ice cream sundae?"

"Terrance flirts with everyone."

"Yeah, and look how much she hates it."

He frowns as he watches them. "I better say something to him. She just got out of a relationship."

I lean up and kiss his jaw. "You're sweet to be protective. But she's fine. Rick the Dick was hardly a blip on her radar. The only person you need to keep away from her is Caleb. And look at them, they're having fun."

June has now attached herself to Terrance's back like a turtle shell, and he's trying unsuccessfully to dislodge her while remaining afloat. Their laughter bounces over the water, sparkling above the music—this one I can ID, it's the Gov't Mule version of "Soulshine," one of Ollie's favorites—and I sigh and rest my cheek on Ollie's chest. I lazily stretch my arm out, and my fingertips brush a delicate stalk of seaweed that's drifting by, its bright green vivid in the shaft of sunlight that filters through the water. A funny trick of the lake is the way cooler currents from below mix with warmer ones at the surface; so even if you're holding perfectly still, you will feel a pocket of warmth slip over you, followed by a swirl of cold and then another momentary break just as you start to shiver.

Ollie told me about this phenomenon called lake turnover, which happens in a deep lake like Seneca where only the upper layer of water gets heated by the sun throughout the summer. As the days shorten and the surface water gets colder, its molecules contract and grow denser, which makes the cooling water sink below the water that used to be beneath it. The water underneath then rises to the surface, bringing with it everything that was at the bottom—dead fish, decaying plant matter—which remarkably echoes the way humans exhale carbon dioxide when we're done with our air. The mixing of the layers cleanses the lake of the junk at the bottom and replenishes the oxygen levels in the water.

The whole goddamn lake is *breathing*.

8

June

THE SERENE, ROSY LIGHT THAT RISES OVER SENECA LAKE ON the morning after our arrival promises me that things are going to be better now. Determined to fake-it-till-you-make-it my way to a sense of ease, after breakfast I park myself in the hammock underneath the weeping willow at the corner of the lawn, accompanied by my cellphone, a big iced coffee, my tablet, and Spencer. Ollie lounges alongside me, but I notice his head tipping up from his book every time he hears the buzz of a Jet Ski motor from the direction of the lake.

"Go," I say, patting his foot that's resting near my shoulder. "I don't want you to sit around in the hammock just for my sake."

"But I like sitting in the hammock with you." He takes hold of one ankle and shifts my leg until it's resting on his chest, then begins stroking the back of my calf with two fingertips. Ever since he discovered the particular sensitivity of my skin, Ollie loves to touch me in ways that look completely innocent, yet will quietly drive me nuts until I cry uncle and drag him somewhere private: a restaurant bathroom, a dark bedroom at a friend's party. We like sex with a hearty side of mind games. I don't know what that says about us.

I close my eyes and absorb the sensations: the drone of a lawn-mower in a neighbor's yard; the scent of the cut grass it leaves behind; the warm breeze on my face; Ollie's fingers on my skin. If I can just wrap myself inside these things and stay there, I'll be fine.

After another few minutes, Ollie's hand has crept up until he is stroking the inside back of my knee with his two first knuckles. On me, that represents an explicit statement of intent.

"Baby," I manage. My voice is thick and dark as high-summer honey, even to my own ears, and he chuckles softly when he hears it.

"What is it, sweetheart?"

My eyes flutter open. His eyes are half-closed, sleepy, and he's watching me melt from inside out with one side of his lips lifted in a faint, smug little smile. God, but he makes me want to screw his brains out when he looks at me like that.

Maybe that's exactly what that haunted bedroom needs.

I have one foot on the grass when Caleb's shout rings across the yard. "Hey, lovebirds!" He's striding toward us in a bathing suit and T-shirt, a beach towel wadded in one hand. "Mom took Eli and Leslie into Geneva to go to the playground," he says when he gets closer, "so I'm off kid duty for a bit. You guys feel like hitting the Jet Skis?"

Ollie clears his throat. "Ah, actually June and I were going to—"

"It's okay," I say quickly. There is no verb he could use to finish that sentence that Caleb wouldn't intuit to mean "do it," and I do not need him commenting on that. "You guys go ahead. I think I'll stay right here and read until I fall asleep."

"You sure?" says Ollie. And he means it. But I saw his whiskers quiver when Caleb said those magic words.

"Of course. Go have fun. I'll see you when you get back."

"Okay. Don't worry, we'll be careful." He plants a smacking kiss on the side of my head and hustles back to the house to change into his suit.

"Whatcha reading?" says Caleb, nodding his chin at my tablet. I shudder inside at the pointlessness of answering the question. The title won't mean anything to him; neither will the designation *young adult book.*

"Just a novel," I say.

"Well, I hope it's more interesting than that," he says, nodding toward the hardcover memoir Ollie abandoned in the hammock. "Is that another one of his NPR fire-sale specials?"

My tablet bounces on my belly as I laugh. Generally, Ollie lives on a steady diet of music biographies and *American Songwriter,* but he's periodically seized by a spasm of guilt that he isn't doing enough "serious" reading. Whereupon he buys the most ponderous literary novel or depressing memoir that our local bookstore can recommend, lugs it home, and proudly displays it on his night table, reading one-third of one page per day until he buckles under my teasing and puts it out on our stoop for takers. "Yes," I say, "it is definitely more interesting than *that.*"

Caleb shakes out the towel in his hand and smooths it over one forearm. "You know, we were thinking of coming down early for the wedding—maybe spend a day or two in the city before we head out east. I'm sure you guys will be busy getting ready, but if you had a couple hours to meet us for lunch or something, that would be nice."

This is an unusual request. In the year and a half I've been with Ollie, I've never known Caleb to propose spending time together outside of larger family gatherings; usually it's Ollie bouncing out invitations, which get ignored or brushed aside. "Oh! Um, I'll have to talk to Ollie, but I'm sure we can figure something out."

Caleb nods and, evidently satisfied that he's done his conversational duty, turns to look out over the lake. But just as I am edging my tablet upward in my lap, he speaks again. "It must be weird for you to be here."

For a second, I just stare at him. This is so far from a topic I ever would have expected him to raise. "Um . . . yeah. It is."

He nods again. "Me too. For different reasons, but still. I hadn't even been here in a few years, but Leslie insisted. She's got this cute idea that Howard and I will learn to love each other if we just spend enough time in the same room together. And she doesn't listen when I tell her it's the opposite. I lived with the son of a bitch for eleven years before I left for college. *That* was the chance for the happy family thing. Not now."

I could ask him why he decided to share this with me, but I already know. All my life, people I don't know well have told me their secrets. Whether I wanted to hear them or not—and I usually haven't—I've been the recipient of confessions, observations, and gossip. I think it's partly because, to white people who can't be bothered to pay attention, my social read is "quiet Asian girl." If that's what you're expecting me to be, my outward demeanor can arguably fit into that slot. Especially in contrast to the ebullient loudmouth I used to have for a best friend, I look like the human version of a dark well you could throw your shiny copper penny into, never to be seen again. Still waters run deep, or something. When I told Leah that a guy I'd started dating had said that about me, she made one of the jerk-off gestures in her varied repertoire. "Your quiet act is such a load of horseshit. If this dude is only now realizing that, just cut the poor boy loose."

I repeated the still waters comment to Ollie once, as a test. He slid his hand up my throat until his thumb fit under my jaw, and then he looked into my eyes and shook his head. "Baby," he said softly, "you are a waterfall."

* * *

Once Ollie and Caleb have headed off to the lake, I feel unexpectedly lonely. On the grass nearby, Spencer sighs and shifts position in his sleep; even if he were spry enough to make it into the hammock, I don't think he'd be comfortable. One of the many things I miss about Winfield is his affinity for lap cuddling.

I pick my phone up to check for messages, but there are none. I'm not a heavy texter myself, but friendship with Leah got me in the habit of frequently checking my phone; anytime I wasn't physically with her, and she wasn't studying or in class, my phone would fill with messages from her, bubble after bubble popping up on my screen. Mostly it was a one-sided conversation, but while I did not have to respond to every volley, I was nonetheless expected to read and absorb. Woe betide me if she ever had to utter the words, "But I texted you about that." Seven years later, I'm still checking my phone more often than I need to. Seven years later, something still yanks inside me every time I see that dark, empty stretch of glass.

I read an article recently by a neurologist whose research challenged the disease model of addiction. I like reading about brain and nerve science, because it makes me feel a little closer to Leah for a moment; I always wonder what her opinion on the topic would be. Addiction, this scientist said, was not an illness but rather a destructive offshoot of the healthy processes of memory. The changes that happen in an addict's brain, that building and strengthening of neural pathways around one particular source of reward, are essentially just the brain revisiting a route it's taught itself to enjoy. The mind seeks out that pathway again and again, in a relentless cycle of craving, satisfaction, and loss, because it favors the repetition of the experience; and the more it repeats, the more deeply ingrained it becomes. There's a reason the word *habit* can mean both a routine and an addiction.

As I stare, a text blinks onto my phone. *How is it?* The message is from Sam, Leah's little brother, all grown up now and writing algorithms for Google. He's playing it close to the vest, as usual. I'm pretty sure Sam lives his entire life close to the vest; but when it comes to Ollie and me, those cards don't even leave his pocket.

It's weird, I write back. *Mostly awful. They've changed the whole house around, but I see her everywhere.*

How's Ollie?

Better than me. He's been coming back here for years.

It isn't different, having you there this time?

I don't know. We haven't talked about it too much. I pause, then fire off another message. With Sam, I am in the unenviable position of having nothing to lose. *Your mom mentioned that you're staying for a couple of extra days next week. Would really love to see you once we're back from Seneca. Both of us would really love to see you.*

He doesn't respond. I sigh, then remind myself that he didn't say no. He didn't say no, and he could have. That has to count for something.

Apparently, the blessing I'd given for the Jet Ski excursion covered an entire day's worth of activities. Ollie and Caleb reappear after an hour, stay long enough to grill some burgers on the deck, then evaporate amidst some muttering about taking the new boat out for a spin to see what it can do. I catch eyes with Leslie, who lifts an eyebrow in a silent expression of sisterhood, but I'm afraid that being left alone with her and Rachel will result in some well-intentioned probing, so I retreat downstairs for a nap.

My "nap" lasts for almost four hours. Ollie texts me photos of himself, Caleb, and Terrance enjoying the new boat, which is a low-riding craft specially designed for wake sports.

Looks fun, I write.

It's awesome. Would be way more fun if you were here, though.

Sorry, lover. I'm spending the week on dry land.

A little while later, he writes again: *I think it would be good for you to come out.*

I pull a Sam and decline to answer.

Half an hour later, he's back, blue eyes supercharged against a fresh bloom of sunburn on his nose and forehead. He pours me a glass of white wine, takes my hand, and leads me to a shady corner of the deck.

"Listen, baby," he says. Belatedly, I notice that his fingers are preemptively wrapped between mine. Uh-oh; here we go again. "I honestly do think it might help you to come out on the boat. I was talking to my therapist about the situation, and—"

"You have a therapist?" I say. Surprise floods the words before I can stop it.

"I saw someone for the first year or so after everything happened," he says, his thumb stilling on the back of my hand. "And I've been talking to someone a bit recently. Is that such a shock?"

I guess he's right; it shouldn't be. My friend Pooja hounded me for months to "get some help." But the thought of spending a metric ton of money—as if I could've gotten my hands on it, which was not likely, considering my parents think psychiatrists are only for people too weak to cope with life on their own—to spill my personal business to some stranger was not an appealing one. It feels odd that I'd never known that Ollie needed that. Let alone that he apparently needs it now. Why wouldn't he just talk to *me*?

I brush aside the faint sense of betrayal. "I'm sorry. So you were talking to the therapist?"

"And she said that, if a person is afraid of something and they actually confront what they're afraid of instead of avoiding it, they can overcome the fear once they realize they're not truly in danger."

I stare at the deck railing, where his and Caleb's damp towels are draped to dry, flapping fitfully in the breeze. Even the towels are different now; the ragtag assortment I remember has been replaced by blandly matching gray-and-white stripes. "The thing is, though, that I don't believe I am in danger. I know I'm not in danger. I know *you're* not. So I don't see why this applies."

"You're afraid of reliving it," he says quietly. "You're not afraid of your surroundings; you're afraid of your memories."

"And *you* are out of your depth." I try to tug my fingers free, but he holds them tight.

He knows he's pushed me too far when my voice drops that low, but as usual with us, my burst of stubbornness seems to trigger one of his own. "Maybe so. And if you really can't stand it, then you shouldn't. But I'm so proud of you for coming here . . . it was the right choice. I don't want you to be afraid of the lake for the rest of your life. And I don't want you to be afraid of our bedroom, or my parents' house, or my parents' boat, or anything in the whole damn Finger Lakes area. I don't want you to be afraid at all. Because I love you."

I turn and rest my palms on the railing so I can look out at the water. The lake is so broad and open that its surface has its own specific pattern, a subtle shift of sheen and shade as the wind brushes across it and the current eddies underneath. It's early evening now, starting to slip toward sunset; this was my favorite time of day when I was here before. I guess I had figured that being here would be my big statement of how okay I am; I hadn't thought through the specifics of everything I might need to ask of myself. But there's truth in what Ollie's saying. Am I seriously going to give up sunset boat rides forever?

"Okay," I say. "But let's bring Cal and Leslie and Eli."

9

Leah

THE FIRST TIME OLLIE AND I HAD SEX, I WAS SO ASTONISHED BY how good it was that I blurted out in the middle of it, "Jesus Christ, did they send you to school for this?" After he recovered from the shock of me yelling a complete, grammatically correct sentence not containing the words "oh god" and realized that I was complimenting him, he couldn't stop laughing. And once I started, I couldn't stop either. I don't know if you've ever tried to have sex with someone while you are both laughing uncontrollably, but it is ridiculous. And bumpy. But after that, Ollie's school—which in our minds resembled a sort of dirty Hogwarts—gave us bottomless amusement.

Ollie, when he climbed back up my body after going down on me till I woke up his roommates: "Learned *that* in McGillicuddy's cunnilingus class." (Me, panting: "There must have been one hell of a wait list.") Me, when he got me off from behind for the first time in my life: "Remarkable technique there. Was that AP reacharound?" He put his face between my shoulder blades and laughed against my skin, and that, right there, that was the minute I loved him. Like I said, I knew by the end of our first date that I *would* love him; the only question was how long it would take me. And the answer was a week and a half. I made it till the minute he had to stop screwing me because he was laughing so hard at my reach-around joke.

What can I say? I have a weird idea of romance.

That was just the rush, though. The funny thing about love is that as mystical as it feels, it's really just a bunch of chemicals. Of course, that's all there is to any of us—chemicals, minerals, water, and goo. But humans always talk about love as being a thing of the heart, even after we learned that it's all in the brain: oxytocin and dopamine, neurological firecrackers exploding into joy and craving and affection and connection. And because that crazy, head-spinning high of falling for somebody is pure dopamine, which is whoa-nelly strong stuff, it's pretty much a crapshoot whether the person who's causing it to blast off inside your brain is actually worth it or not.

I knew that Ollie was. You won't like it if I tell you I *just knew*, but it's the truth. And the ways he proved it to me, that's when the real love began. From the beginning he saw exactly who I was, and he enjoyed me and respected me without feeling any itch to try to make me into more of a lady. Or to make me more like him. (I was never going to be more like him.) It was the opposite; he got out of his comfort zone to *know* me: reading articles about neurology so he could discuss my field with me; tracking down a snowflake-patterned adult onesie after I told him about the one I had as a kid; learning the barometer of my moods so well that he could take one look at me as I sat down for dinner and know I'd just had another fight with my parents. But it was the topic of those fights that really taught me to love him.

When Ollie and I first started dating, Sam was heading into his junior year of high school, and my family was split down the middle over what the plan for college should be. Sam and I on one side, lobbying for him to apply wherever the hell he wanted because he was damn well smart enough to get in; our parents on the other, convinced that he'd do better living at home and attending our local SUNY. My folks and I had spent sixteen years looking out for him, cushioning him as best we could against the hurts and frustrations that a kid who used a wheelchair would face, so it was hard to break the habit and adapt to the fact that he was becoming an adult.

But, in an episode of unprecedented emotional clarity for which I have humbly and repeatedly thanked God, I had done it. One night after my freshman year of college, I was telling Sam the story of how June and I spontaneously decided to drive to Nashville over our spring break, and I spotted the hunger in his face. To have what I had. Not my undamaged spinal cord—my unquestioned right to independence. And that's when I realized the way to help the young man was different from the way I'd helped the child. More than he needed protection, he needed trust, freedom, and respect. Right then and there, I resolved to stop shielding Sam and start listening to him.

Ollie resolved to corrupt him. Even before he fully understood the issue, or the currents swirling behind Sam's bouts of stubborn silence at family meals, he treated Sam like a kid brother whose only difference was how tightly he'd been smothered. A few months after we got together, the three of us were watching *Saturday Night Live* in the family room one night after my parents were asleep, when out of nowhere Ollie said, "Oh, I almost forgot— I brought you something," and dove into his satchel. He emerged holding a copy of *Playboy,* which he presented to Sam with a flourish. "I was actually telling the truth when I told the bodega guy it was for my friend."

Sam inspected it skeptically, then glanced back at Ollie. "Thank you for this . . . very weird and probably inappropriate gift. You do realize I've been mainlining Internet porn since I was fourteen?"

Ollie and I both gaped at him in horror.

"I mean, this is cool in, like, an ironic way," Sam said, gesturing at the taut-assed blonde on the cover. "It's . . . vintage."

"Don't hang out on those websites too much, man," said Ollie when he had recovered. "That shit will give you a lot of wrong ideas."

Sam darted his eyes at me, clearly wanting to hear more about the wrong ideas but unsure how much I would tolerate.

"No girls actually like jackhammer sex," I said, "and rough bareback anal is not the pinnacle of our dreams."

"Jesus," Ollie snorted. "I was going to say, don't expect to go forty-five minutes your first time out of the gate. But . . . yeah, no girls actually like jackhammer sex."

"Suddenly feeling *super* awkward about getting sex advice from you," muttered Sam.

"Oh, I've never had sex with your sister," said Ollie. "I've never even seen her naked."

"We just kiss a little bit," I said.

"No tongue," said Ollie.

Sam shook his head, disgusted. But he didn't give Ollie back the *Playboy*.

Ollie was also responsible for Sam's first joint (they smoked it together on the roof deck of Ollie's building the night after Sam's high school graduation, giggling like schoolgirls whenever a neighbor walked past and commented on the smell) and his first hangover (Ollie decided that, prior to entering the Wild West of his freshman year of college, Sam needed to learn to pace himself at drinking; it turns out that pacing themselves at drinking is not something eighteen-year-old guys can do, at all). Teenage Sam worshipped Ollie so much he even forgot to try to conceal it. And nothing on earth has made me love my boyfriend quite as much as the fact that my brother does.

Our second day at Seneca, the wind picks up enough throughout the morning that the lake is crested with whitecaps. A spin on the boat would risk somebody's breakfast winding up on their flip-flops, so we decide to do a winery crawl instead. Because there's zero chance of anybody vomiting as a result of that.

"I'll be designated driver," says June, as we walk toward the car.

"That's lame for you, though," says Caleb. "We should take turns."

"Don't fucking use that word," I snarl, and his head kicks backward in surprise.

"Uh . . . okay," he says, with a *wow, crazy lady* laugh.

"It's not a joke. I wasn't kidding. It's disparaging to people with disabilities. *Do not* use it."

"That's obviously not how I meant it," says Caleb, as Ollie puts his hand on my shoulder to settle me. "Jesus. Oliver, calm your woman."

"Leeb, he didn't know," Ollie says quietly.

"Trust me, I'm fine driving," says June, jumping into the awkwardness. "I don't really want to drink wine all day."

"We're going on a *winery crawl*," says Caleb. "Who doesn't want to drink wine all day?"

"Asian people who have a hard time metabolizing it," says Ollie.

Caleb glances back at June, then gives a short laugh. "Huh. What else can I come up with to endear myself to the group right now?"

"Just get in the car," Ollie sighs.

Terrance, the opportunist, slides into shotgun like a fox into a henhouse, which leaves me pinched in the back between Ollie and Caleb. Stick the short person in the hump seat. Happens every freaking time. Ugh, and Caleb is taking up a seat and a half. He's a big dude, but he's not *that* big. You just know he's one of those guys who ride the subway with their thighs spread, like the contents of their crotches are a gift they're offering the world. He is doing it right now, in fact. His left thigh rests against my right, and it absolutely doesn't have to.

The minute June parks the car at the first stop on our tour, I almost castrate Ollie trying to climb over him to escape the back seat. I dart over to Terrance and poke him in the chest. "Dibs on shotgun from now on," I inform him.

"Try me, punk," he mutters, twitching his hand in what I think he thinks looks like a gang sign. I'm not sure I've seen anything more ridiculous in recent memory than a classical musician trying to make a gang sign.

I pat him on the arm. "Yeah, don't do that again. Definitely not in front of *her*."

Fox Run Vineyards, just up the road from Ollie's parents' place, is a well-known winery with a great site—a large, restored barn overlooking the lake, with acres of grape vines marching up the low hill behind the building in tidy lines. In the tasting room, we learn about the Finger Lakes wine region: how the minerality of the soil, along with the late springs and lingering fall warmth generated by the enormous water mass, combine to create an ideal viticulture environment. But I'm not so busy listening that I miss Terrance passing tiny sips of his tasting wines to June. Nor do I miss the way he brushes her fingertips with his as he does it. And then there's the way she raises her eyebrows and smiles as she lifts each glass up to her lips. This is *so good*. I'm twitching with impatience for an opportunity to talk to her about him. But I have to be subtle about it, or she will get her hackles up.

After the tasting, we buy a couple of bottles we liked, and sit down with a robust cheese plate on the sunny terrace facing the lake. I decide I better pee before we head back to the car—Ollie says my bladder is scaled in proportion to my overall size—and when I exit the bathroom, Caleb is waiting outside the door, arms and ankles lazily crossed as he leans against the wall. I feel a twitchy impulse to step back into the ladies' till he's gone.

"Is the men's one full?" I ask, confused.

He shakes his head as he uncoils from the wall and looms

toward me. With his shaggy hair and watchful eyes, he sometimes reminds me of a lion. "No. I wanted to apologize for what I said before. I forgot your brother was handicapped. I didn't mean to be insulting; I didn't know that was a bad word to use." His voice is quiet and sincere, and the tightness between my shoulders relaxes.

"It's okay," I say, feeling a familiar rush of regret at having lost my temper. Caleb pisses me off sometimes, but he's Ollie's brother. *My future brother-in-law*, I think, with a tingle. "A lot of people don't realize. I'm sorry I bit your head off."

Caleb gives me that Ollie smile again. "Thanks, Leah. That's nice of you. How's he doing these days, by the way? Your brother?"

"He's great. He and some friends are spending the weekend on the Jersey Shore. He has this all-terrain chair—the thing looks like it's made out of Legos but it gets him on and off the sand."

"Oh, wow. I guess regular wheelchairs can't make it on the beach, huh? I never thought of that."

"There's a whole world of stuff that the abled never think of."

He nods. "I believe that."

Well, color me intrigued. Never would have expected to be having a conversation about able-bodied privilege with Caleb Burwitz.

"By the way, do you think I should say something to June, too?" he says.

I frown, then remember his comment from earlier. "Nah. You had no way to know about her alcohol thing. She knows you weren't being malicious."

He sighs and drags a hand through his hair. "Sometimes I think everything I say gets taken the wrong way. At least around here. I know I have a big mouth, but I swear I'm not really an asshole."

The wry, beleaguered expression on his face makes me laugh. "I know the feeling," I say. "Brain to mouth, no filter in between."

"You really get me," he says in a deliberately corny voice, hands clasped over his heart; then when I laugh again, he grins and pulls me in for a one-armed hug. As we turn to walk back toward the others, he rests his hand at the small of my back the way guys sometimes do, like *Please, after you.* It's supposed to be genteel but it's so not my thing. I'm not a *lady;* don't gentleman me. But I don't want Caleb to think I'm rude for shaking off his little outburst of brotherly affection. There's no creature on earth so easily wounded as a man who just wants to show you a little affection.

Although I like wine, and enjoy ridiculously pretending to be fancy about it, I'm really more of a beer person. And of course, tequila is where the magic happens. But wine just makes me sleepy. So by the time we straggle back to the house after the fourth stop on our wine tour, that unmade twin bed in the Chastity Room is looking mighty fine indeed.

"I'm going to nap," I announce, flinging myself facedown on the bed and crawling under the sheet. It's midafternoon, so the air inside the house is still too warm to warrant a blanket, but through the open screen door I can hear the *wush-wush* of the waves the wind's beating against the shore, and that will put me right out, no question about it.

"Yeah, I think I might join you," June says, sitting down on the edge of her bed to check her phone. Her face is a little pink from the accumulation of Terrance's wine samples, and she looks unguarded, so I decide to test the waters.

"I'm so glad Terrance is here this week. We haven't seen him much since he started his master's. He almost got into Juilliard, you know."

"No, I didn't know. Why would I know that?" Her lips are curved into a smile that she is failing to repress. She is *so* into him.

"Well, I just told you, so now you know. Ollie said the competition among violinists is especially tight because it's such a popular instrument. But I mean, he doesn't only play classical; he can do anything. I've heard him play; he's incredible."

"I'm sure he is. Is Terrance also a dog lover, by chance?"

Well, that sailed out of left field. "I have no idea. Why?"

"You're trying so hard to sell him to me."

"What?" I sputter. "No, I just think he's a cool guy."

"You are a terrible liar and a worse matchmaker."

"I'm not matchmaking!"

"I'm nah mahmahmah!" says June, wagging her head from side to side as she mimics my indignant tone.

"I'm not!"

"You are, but I forgive you. So you can stop arguing."

"I was trying to be subtle," I say, crestfallen.

"Leeb, you're about as subtle as a bulldozer. You are . . . as subtle as a rhinoceros. As a Mack truck with naked ladies on the mud flaps, screaming down a hill at eighty miles an hour. As—"

"Okay!" I yell, then launch myself onto her bed and squirm around so I wreck her tidy bedding. "Look at me being subtle all up in your blankets!"

June rocks forward, laughing, then watches, cheek sucked between her teeth, until I've exhausted myself. "So, after all that, aren't you going to ask me?"

I glare at her with one eye from the depths of her pillow. "Ask you what? For another metaphor for my subtlety?"

"What I think of him."

"Oh!" I shoot upright and give her an intense stare. "What do you think of him?"

She does a Scarlett O'Hara smile. "Hottest dog-loving, Juilliard-adjacent violinist I've ever met in my life."

"Yessss!" I do a couple of wild fist pumps since, you know, I'm so subtle and all. "Terrance is such a great guy. I mean, on all levels. There's not a lot of guys who are hot and funny and smart *and* actually good-hearted on top of everything else."

"Is this going to turn into an Ollie monologue? Because it sounds like it's about to turn into an Ollie monologue."

There's a sharpness to her voice that takes me by surprise. That's the thing about June: Unlike with me, where I blat everything out as soon as I feel it, June's flashes of pissiness are as mysterious as they are rare. "No," I say, stung. "I was talking about Terrance. I don't make everything about Ollie."

"Yes you do. But it's okay," she adds when she sees me filling up my lungs to argue. "And hey, speaking of, have you picked up any clues about you-know-what?" She flattens out on the narrow bed, and I lie down next to her.

"Not yet," I say. Although, come to think of it, that was a very pointed question from her. Kind of out of nowhere, really. I wonder if she knows anything she hasn't hinted at. Because in fact, there is one very specific item she might know a great deal about. "Hey, Junie?"

"Yeah?"

I rotate onto my side until I'm facing her. "Did Ollie ask you to make an engagement ring for me?"

Staring at the ceiling, she shakes her head. "No," she says. "He hasn't."

"How do I know he didn't make you swear a blood oath of secrecy?"

She turns to me with her face screwed up into one big *duh*. "Because I wouldn't have sworn it. I would have laughed in his face at the idea that I could keep that a secret from you."

I feel a little swoop of disappointment, because she's right. As much as I would love for my best friend to design my engagement ring, it wouldn't be fair of Ollie to force her to sit on it for months while she made it and then he waited for the right moment to ask me. He wouldn't risk her accidentally letting something slip.

"Have you talked with him about what you want?" she says.

"No, but he knows my taste. Something simple but classic. Platinum or white gold. Square stone."

"Princess cut," she says, and I make a face.

"Ugh. Really? That's what it's called?"

"Yup. For sweet little Princess Leah," she says, in a saccharine voice.

"Stop, you're gonna make me barf. Okay, so you're not going to work on the engagement ring. But will you make our wedding bands, then? I know my taste is kind of different from what you usually do, but I would still love to have something you made for me. Actually I can't imagine *not* having what I wear on my hand for the rest of my life be something you made for me."

"Of *course*," she says, snuggling closer. "I'd never forgive you if you didn't ask." She picks up my left hand with her right and holds it in the air above our faces. "Maybe some micropavé," she says, touching my ring finger with her index. "Super delicate."

"*Princess* and *delicate* are two words nobody has ever used in reference to me before today," I say. "And all this after you wouldn't even let me have *subtle*."

She snickers. "I know. You have the impact of a Mack truck, but your hands are little. You'll need a little ring."

"What even is that word you just used, by the way?"

"Micropavé. It's lots of teeny stones, set in a row. You can build up a couple of rows to form a surface. Sparkles like you wouldn't believe."

"That sounds pretty," I say. We both stare in silence for a moment at my bare knuckle, then she turns her hand, threads her fingers between mine, and gently squeezes. We look so funny together—my tiny critter paw with its bare, stubby nails and the scar on my index finger; her beautiful hand with its smooth olive skin and elegant nails, three hammered-gold knuckle rings scattered across her tapering fingers.

"You know I love you like my sister, right?" June's voice is unexpectedly thick. She sounds like she's trying not to cry.

"Of course," I say, turning to face her. "Same for me. Always. What brought that on?"

She sniffs and shakes her head, then nudges moisture away from the corner of one eye with her free thumb. "Just . . . thinking. I didn't know if I'd said it in a while, and I just wanted to be sure you knew."

I look at our hands as I squeeze hers tight in mine again. "I know, Junie. I always will."

10

June

WHEN WE REACH THE LAKE FOR THE SUNSET CRUISE, THE dock brings a fresh onslaught of memories. The worn but sturdy wood of the planks, slightly bowed in spots from age and dampness. The slurp of the water against the pilings; the school of minnows that darts and dances in the shallows like an underwater sparkle. The impossibly rich, clean fragrance of the water. I remember Leah sucking it down, breath after breath, like she was trying to huff it, saying, "Damn, if you could just bottle this stuff, you could sell it in bars in Manhattan, make a killing. Lake country air, imported from upstate New York. Twenty bucks a pop."

There's the platform over the boats where we lay out in the sun, Leah periodically lifting the strap on my bikini to inspect me for signs of tanning. My skin soaks up UV rays like a sponge made of melanin, and no matter how many summers we spent together, it drove her bonkers that I didn't like it. "I would *kill* for this," she would say, poking my arm with her small finger. "This perfect color, no freckles, no burns . . ." She couldn't understand that it wasn't worth the earful from my mother ("Ji-Eunah, you're so dark! You have to be more careful!"). But for the most part, for someone who'd been raised by parents who regarded her as their very own personal miracle, Leah got it. She used to tell me to stop my mom's disapproval from getting to me by holding an imaginary umbrella over my head. "Let her rain around you while you stay dry," she would say. I've gotten stronger as I've gotten older; but even after all this time, sometimes I open up that damn umbrella.

When I step from the Biermans' dock onto the boat, my stomach wobbles right along with the floor I'm standing on.

"I've got you," says Ollie, hand firm under mine as he helps me in.

From the banquette, Terrance gives me a thumbs-up and an encouraging smile.

"Oh, are you in on Project Healing, too?" I mutter to him as I sit down, and he has the grace to look abashed.

"I don't know what that is, but I can guess," he mutters back. "And if it is what I think it is, then yes. I'm in favor."

"Cal, do you wanna drive?" says Ollie. "I'm going to sit in the back with my lady." He sits down next to me and wraps his arm around my shoulders, tugging me close.

While we get ready to pull out, I study Leslie, perfectly outfitted for a summer evening boat ride: Her thick blond braid nestles lovingly against her throat, and a chic navy-and-cream-striped sweater drapes her slim arms. Her diamond-studded bridal set sparkles blue-white against her tan fingers as she fastens two-year-old Eli's life vest around his small body. He doesn't like it one bit, and fights her with cries and stomps and flailing arms.

"You said you wanted to come with Daddy on the boat, buddy," she says. "And if you're on the boat, then you wear the puffy jacket. That's the rule."

I expect him to parry by pointing out the indisputable injustice that he is the only one in a puffy jacket, but by the time we begin sliding backward away from the dock, he's resigned himself to his fate and settled down on his mother's lap.

"You got him, hon?" says Caleb.

"Sure do," Leslie says, smiling back at Caleb as she tightens her arms around their son. Her face is soft with contentment. Whenever I spend time with them, I'm always a little surprised that it's *Caleb* who has managed to inspire such devotion from this woman, but still it's nice to see. Ollie made a passing comment once that Leslie had a pretty rocky start growing up, so I can understand the satisfaction of creating her own stable family life. I bet that's why she's been after her husband to get along better with Howard; maybe she was even the impetus behind Caleb's suggestion of spending time with us in New York before the wedding. I should try to spend some time with her this week, and get to know her better.

Carefully, Caleb backs the boat around and points us north. I grit my teeth and sit back to "enjoy" the ride.

And yet, breath by breath, I relax. The wind from our motion rushes through my hair and raises goosebumps on my bare calves, but I'm toasty inside my sweatshirt, and Ollie's arm makes a warm ring around my body. The lake is every bit as beautiful as I remember. The water is calm and smooth, reflecting the peachy sky like dark glass, and we are almost the only people out on the lake. Small houses in shades of blue, gray, white, and red sit in a tidy line along the western shore, many with pale green weeping willows at the water's edge that trail their graceful fingers toward it. Inner tubes and floats of all descriptions sprinkle the ground as if beached there by a high tide. We sail past people sitting in brightly colored Adirondack chairs on their docks, and kids splashing in thigh-deep water with Labradors romping nearby. Every time we pass someone, Caleb waves, and Eli follows suit. Everyone waves back.

"Why are the seagulls so particular about what roofs they sit on?" I say to Ollie. "Look at them."

He follows my pointing finger to a row of boathouses ahead on our left, where a large cluster of gulls inhabits one—and only one—of the roofs. "I have no idea," he laughs. "They must have their reasons."

As we approach, the birds take flight in consternation and spin, honking, over the water.

"You guys, you guys," Ollie narrates for the birds, in a sort of Forrest Gump–ish voice, "you gotta see this spot right over here, it's simply the best spot, I think I might have seen a fish, come on, quick—"

"That arsehole and 'is bleedin' magical spot," says Terrance, as the gulls land again, flapping vigorously, on the exact same rooftop they deserted en masse just moments before. "Always mouthing off, saying 'e's seen a fish when 'e 'asn't, chasing us off the roof for no bloody reason—"

"Wait, why is your seagull a cockney?" I say, laughing.

"I've always thought gulls would sound like cockneys if they could talk." He makes some squawking sounds that, now that I think about it, actually do sound a fair bit like an East London voice.

After a while, Caleb turns away from the shore and moves out toward the center of the lake. To the west, the sunset floods the feathery clouds with luscious coral pink—it looks like a heavenly phoenix wing, blazing against the darkening sky. The water mirrors it back, with the crest of each tiny ripple glossy and rose.

"Okay, that's pretty beautiful," I murmur to Ollie, and he kisses my nose. We soak it up in silence, staring over the left side of the boat, until Eli's small voice breaks the trance.

"Daddy, what's that?"

I look at where he's pointing, directly ahead of us, and my gut clenches with dread.

"That's the testing station, buddy," says Caleb. "The government made it so they could research technology. Did you know that when we make noise, it actually wiggles in the air?"

As Caleb begins attempting to explain sonar to a two-and-a-half-year-old, I stare at the approaching complex. Therapy or not, the thing is creepy. The base of it is a large platform that supports various hunks of machinery and equipment, including two tall structures that loom like smokestacks. Railings and cables crawl all over it: up, down, across. Several large concrete-topped buoys float in the water surrounding it, with more cables extending from their tops back to the mother ship. And it's deserted. There's no sign of life there but birds. Not gulls; these are larger, black animals, and they're everywhere—grouped on the buoys and perched on the cables, silhouetted against the sunset.

I glance at Ollie to see if he's remembering what I am, but he's smiling as he watches Eli mimic the sound-wave motion Caleb's making with his hand. We draw closer and closer to the station until Caleb cuts the motor and motions Eli up to sit on his lap. I stare up at the sky, trying to ignore the unease simmering inside me and get back to my simple enjoyment of the evening.

Ollie gets to his feet and strips his shirt decisively. "Might as well jump in while we're stopped. Last dip of the day." Moving fast, he steps onto the back platform of the boat and dives into the water, graceful as an arrow.

My breathing shudders to a halt. The boat rocks gently from the disruption of his movement, but in an instant I'm up on my knees on the seat, looking for him. Facing this direction, away from the sunset, the light is so much dimmer; the water is deep blue-gray, licked with black, and an early rising planet gleams just above the horizon. There are absolutely no other boats in sight. Panic strains inside me like a racehorse at the gate.

Ollie surfaces ten feet away, shaking the water off his face.

"Anybody joining me?" he says. "It's gorgeous in here."

"Ollie," I say in a low voice, as my hands tighten on the side of the boat. *"Ollie."* But it's like one of those dreams where you're being chased by a killer, and though you know crying out might save you, your throat can't make a sound. Ollie flips like a duck and dives downward. I can see the ghostly whiteness of his skin, blurry and diffuse under the dark water—shoulders, back, legs, feet—until suddenly it's gone. He's gone. The water near the naval station is five hundred feet deep, and Ollie is gone.

"Ollie!" I scream. "Ollie, Ollie, Ollie!" I'm screaming so loud my throat lights up with pain, but I can't stop, because he's gone. I lean over the edge of the boat to try to find him and there are arms around me, pulling me down onto the seat, and I'm fighting and screaming because I still can't see Ollie, and then I'm drenched and shivering because Ollie is holding me and he's covered with water but he's here. He's here.

"Don't ever do that again," I sob, clinging to him with my face jammed against his wet neck. "Don't you *ever* fucking do that again."

He crushes me in his arms, under the damp towel he's pulled around us. "I'm so sorry, baby," he whispers, voice thick with tears. "I'm a complete moron. I'm so sorry. I'm *so* sorry."

I nod, but I can't speak; somehow all I can do is wail. I hear Eli whimper, and I know I should pull myself together because I'm scaring him, but I can't.

"Get us home," I hear Ollie say to someone, and then the motor starts and the boat is moving again, skimming across the lake much faster than we drove out. I burrow closer to Ollie's warmth, keeping the towel across my face even though it smells like dampness and old sunscreen, because I just cannot stop crying. I'm crying like I've never cried at all.

I feel another hand clasp my shoulder for comfort—Terrance. And then his voice, calm but certain, speaking to Ollie: "I think you need to be a little more careful with your healing therapy."

Ollie rocks me back and forth as he gathers me closer, and kisses the side of my forehead once, then again. "I'm so fucking sorry, June. I wasn't thinking. Will you try to forgive me?"

But all I can do is cry.

* * *

The next morning, I wake up with a sickening emotional hangover from shame at having caused a scene. All I remember after Ollie got back in the boat is a blur of watchful faces, concerned voices, low-spoken explanations. I think Caleb offered me one of his Ambien, and Leslie, a nurse, waved it off. Ollie was permitted to give me a Benadryl, and he stayed in the dark beside me until I fell asleep.

But this morning the birds are squeaking and trilling outside the screen door, their voices rising over a string chorus of crickets, and when I pull the drapes aside, I can see it's barely after dawn. The sky across the lake is warming from deep rose to pale gold, and the light has that fragile, gossamer quality to it that makes early morning so uniquely beautiful.

"How are you feeling, sweetheart?" Behind me, Ollie's voice is rusty with sleep.

I turn to him and smile. He's pushed up on one elbow in bed, trying to look alert but still blinking at the sunlight like a mole. Tenderness rushes in a warm river through my veins.

"I'm better," I say, sitting down beside him. I rest my head on his shoulder and inhale the earthy scent of his skin. "Much better. I'm sorry I lost my head like that."

He shakes his head as he tucks a skein of hair behind my ear. "Don't apologize. I was thoughtless. I'm so sorry I frightened you."

"You were only swimming," I say. "There was no reason to have a meltdown over seeing you get in the water. It was just . . . so dark. And then when you dove under, I couldn't see you anymore, and . . ." My throat compresses like someone stepped on it.

"I know," Ollie says, pressing a kiss to my cheekbone. "I shouldn't have talked you into going on the boat. I'm sorry. I honestly thought it would help you. It helped me."

"I thought it would help me, too."

He rests his forehead against mine and stares at me, his eyes moving as they try to focus on mine from so close. "June, do you want to go home?"

I close my eyes, and for a moment I hover over it. I imagine kissing Rachel on the cheek and climbing back into the car, firing up my John Prine playlist, and letting Seneca Lake slip into the distance behind me. The relief makes me so weightless I almost drift to the ceiling.

But Ollie needs me. He needs this.

My eyes pop open, and he smiles because he knows what I decided. "No. I want to stay. You were right yesterday. I can't be afraid of everything forever."

"Okay. But we'll take it one day at a time. And maybe I'll stick to swimming during daylight hours, huh?"

"Yeah. That would be good."

That smile of his, it's like the sun coming out from behind the clouds. "Okay. Let's go upstairs. Mom and Dad were worried about you; they'll be glad to see you're feeling better. Oh, and Terrance and his parents invited us over for dinner tonight, just the two of us . . . you up for that?"

"I would love that." Getting away from the concerned stares of Ollie's family sounds like exactly what I need right now.

The route to Terrance's family's house takes us along a path that descends from the steep hill of the Biermans' property to the water-level lot where the Holleys' Craftsman bungalow sits. As I remember the last time I walked this path, my skin flushes hot and I'm glad that Ollie, walking behind me, can't see my face. But this house, unlike Ollie's, looks exactly like I remember it: shingle siding painted a mellow shade of blue-gray, with sturdy white pillars across the broad porch supporting the second story above. Large planters at the foot of the porch stairs are exploding with geraniums, while cheerful white-and-yellow daisies along the foundation wave in the evening breeze.

Terrance is reading in a rocking chair on the porch, and when he sees us coming he does a double take at his watch. "Holy shit, I didn't even have to lie to you," he calls to Ollie, putting down his book and standing up. "Mom said seven-thirty, so I told you seven-fifteen. And here you are at six minutes after the hour."

"June's a good influence," says Ollie.

"How you feeling today?" Terrance says to me. His voice is light and undemanding, letting me decide how to answer the question.

"Much better," I say with a smile. "Thank you."

"Glad to hear it. Well, I just checked on Mom and she's in good shape for now, so why don't we go down to the dock?"

The Holleys have a broad area at the end of their dock that's just large enough to accommodate a dining table, which is already laid with five place settings and a steel bucket chilling two bottles of wine. Near my feet, the water laps at the pilings, evening-smooth except for when a boat passes out in the lake. Mellow amber sunlight glimmers amongst the ripples, illuminating the small, algae-covered rocks on the lake floor a few feet beneath us.

After a little while, Terrance's parents appear on the front porch, each bearing a large tray of food. I jump to my feet and hurry toward them, but his mother, Michelle, waves me off.

"We've got it, honey. Lots of practice."

"But check this bad boy out," says Terrance's father, Wilson, as he approaches me. "Caught him this morning, and here he is for supper."

I peer at the outstretched tray, which holds a trout that must be nearly two feet long, its silver scales seared with grill marks and dripping with lemon and herbs. My stomach rumbles audibly, and Wilson laughs.

"You and me both. Come on, let's eat."

The trout is every bit as delicious as it looked, and so is everything else: tender grilled asparagus, a Greek salad made with tomatoes so juicy they burst with sweetness in my mouth, and for dessert a bowl of grilled peaches glazed in butter and brown sugar. I'm guessing it's all from the Mennonite farm stand on Route 14 that we visited last time. I remember Leah stuffing bag after bag with fruit and veggies, even things like radishes that she didn't like, just because it was all so beautiful and so fresh, with little crumbs of the earth it was grown in still clinging here and there. And I remember staring at those radishes a week later, wilted on the counter while fruit flies swirled.

"So, June," says Michelle, scraping her spoon along her bowl to catch the last of the peach juice, "Terrance mentioned you're a jewelry designer. I'm so curious how you got into that field."

"Well, I went to school for it at FIT, in New York. And after I graduated I had a couple of different jobs to learn the retail and distribution aspect of the business, while I worked on my own designs and started taking on some freelance clients. I launched my line about three years ago."

"So I guess you decided against the MFA in metal?" Terrance says, grinning. "More useful than mine, and *so* much more badass."

I laugh. I'd forgotten about that conversation. "No, no badass MFA. That was just a bid for credibility with my parents. I was scared, but I got over it. I decided to pursue my own stuff instead, and it's taken off pretty well."

"Because you worked like a demon to build it," Ollie says, then turns to the others. "Don't let her act like it's an accident that her line is sold in twenty-one boutiques. That's a huge achievement in three years."

"That is incredible," says Michelle. "Does the line have a name, or is it just your name as the designer?"

"It's called Elements," I say. "Like the periodic table. My best friend was a scientist, and she used to say that the chemical elements were the thing that linked our work. Her biology research and my metalsmithing. Even diamonds are just a specific form of carbon." I pause, thinking of the photo on the "about" page of my website: Leah in her safety glasses from the lab, me in my magnifier headset, both of us grinning like dopes. "And because my work is a little raw compared to other jewelers, I guess you could call it elemental. It kind of all goes together."

"I love that," Michelle says. "Is this your work?" she says, tucking her fingers under my left hand to lift it. "May I see?"

"It is, yeah. Although I didn't know I was designing my own ring when I made it."

"Especially since we'd only been together a couple of weeks when she got the commission." Ollie always says this as if he's admitting he's crazy, but the truth is we both love how fast it happened, how quickly we knew. We share a smile. Terrance coughs, and I roll my eyes at him. Of the many things a couple can potentially be gross about, we're allowed to be a little gross about our engagement ring.

As Michelle moves my hand gently from side to side in the slanting evening light, the ring shimmers like a tiny ember made of brushed gold and diamond. Like always, my heart glows as I look at it.

"It's stunning," she says, releasing my hand. "Simply stunning. I love that it's so warm. My daughter Sonya has a platinum and diamond set, and it's beautiful, but to me it looks a little cold."

"Well, people do call it ice, honey," says Wilson, with that endearing awkwardness unique to later-middle-aged dads attempting slang.

"Yes, and Sonya's is very traditional. Platinum band and a square solitaire stone, what's that called—princess cut?"

"I want to hear how you made the ring without knowing it was for you," says Wilson.

But I'm not paying attention anymore. Until just now, I had forgotten: Leah had wanted a princess solitaire. And that is exactly what she would have been given by this man whose fingers are rubbing a warm stripe along my thigh, the man I'm in love with—because he was in love with her first. Once again, I feel like a thief, and my beautiful, heart-glowing ring is a fake.

"Everything okay, baby?" says Ollie softly.

Shake it off, June. I refuse to collapse in histrionics every time something punches a sore spot. Right now I am one giant, walking bruise; the hits are bound to keep on coming. "I'm fine."

Terrance lifts the open wine bottle and holds it over my glass. "Want some more?"

I notice the label: Fox Run Vineyards, the first place we went to on our wine crawl that day. I've drunk this Riesling before, in a tiny splash at the bottom of Terrance's tasting glass, while I buzzed with warmth from his attention.

Yeah. The hits are bound to keep on coming.

As the sky gradually swallows the last of the light, the sweeping curve of shoreline to the south of the Holleys' house begins to erupt with sporadic firecrackers. I forgot that people up here start warming up for their July Fourth a day or two early.

"I'm assuming we'll see you for the party tomorrow?" Ollie says to our hosts.

"Wouldn't miss it," says Terrance, but his parents exchange a look.

"We'll be there, too," says Michelle. "But actually, Ollie, part of the reason we invited you two over by yourselves is . . . well, we're concerned about your mom."

Ollie frowns and leans closer. "How so?"

"Well, with all this silly gossip about Caleb, and that waitress or whatever she was. Of course we know it's ridiculous, but it must be hard on Rachel. Some people will believe anything they hear—"

"Guilty until proven innocent in the court of public opinion," says Wilson.

"Exactly," Michelle says. "And I've tried to talk to your mother, to let her know we support your family, but she freezes up and won't discuss it. I don't want to pry. But I do hope she's managing all right."

Dumbfounded, I stare at Ollie for guidance. And even in the faint light from the citronella candle flickering on the table, I can see that he has no idea what she is talking about. He will not admit it—though his family is far more prone to *internal* discussions than mine, they are every bit as clamlike about external ones—but I can see his eyelashes flickering like crazy. This is what he does when he's digesting a piece of news he doesn't like, but is trying not to show he's upset.

"Thank you for being concerned," he says after a moment, in a steady voice. And I suddenly realize I've never witnessed before how convincingly he can lie. "I really appreciate it, and I know she does too. She's managing okay. We all are." There's a pause while the Holleys wait to see if he will continue, and he waits to see if their next comment will give him any signposts for the swamp he's just stumbled into.

"Of course," says Michelle. "Please don't hesitate to ask us if there's anything we can do to help out. We'd be glad to."

"I will. Thank you. Truly."

I dart a look at Terrance, who clearly has no more idea what the hell is going on than Ollie does—there's a deep furrow of confusion between his eyebrows. But he doesn't want to cop to it, either.

"Well, it's probably time for us to head back up the hill," Ollie says, getting to his feet with his usual limber grace. But the hand that reaches for mine is trembling.

"Thank you so much for having us over," I say, as we all take turns embracing. "We'll see you tomorrow afternoon."

Terrance moves as if to see us off the dock, but Ollie dismisses him with a quick shake of his head. "See you tomorrow."

I look back at Terrance as Ollie tows me away. With his back to his parents, he makes a grimace of dismay and concern. I shake my head to show I don't know what this is all about, either; then immediately regret it. I should have closed ranks.

"Ol, what the *hell* was that about?" I say, as soon as we're out of earshot.

Ollie, charging up the hill like the fiends of hell are behind him, doesn't answer.

"Ollie!" I snap, and he jerks to a halt. "Answer me."

"I have absolutely no fucking idea," he growls. "But I promise you I'm about to find out."

11

Leah

APPARENTLY, CALEB IS MY FRIEND NOW. EVER SINCE OUR TALK outside the bathrooms at Fox Run yesterday, he seems to believe that we have left behind our awkwardness like a butterfly shaking off its crusty old cocoon. He has helped himself to the nickname that June and Ollie call me. He laughs at all of my jokes, and looks at me when he lands the punch line on his own. If he's close enough, he'll bump my elbow in a nudge-wink maneuver that I didn't know anyone actually did in real life. And, because Ollie's father either doesn't laugh, or says something just a little too snide in response, I laugh for Caleb.

It's a weird dynamic he has with Howard. I don't like it. It's always been the one thing that holds me back from loving Howard without reservation: the way he treats his stepson. Granted, Caleb's never been exactly my favorite, either, but he deserves better than this. It's not his fault who his dad is or how the guy treated Rachel.

We've been busy all morning helping to get ready for the Fourth of July party. Rachel's red, white, and blue bunting is hung from the deck railing overlooking the lake; Howard's bonfire and his monster stash of illegal fireworks are waiting for a match. We've set up a dog-and-burger assembly station at the grill, with condiments and mountains of buns, the edges of their plastic bags drifting in the breeze, stacked nearby. Four huge coolers of beer sit on the deck and down by the water.

Once everything is set, Rachel kicks us out of the house to work off our excitement before the guests arrive, like we're little kids. Which I, for one, certainly am. Ever since June caught me poking around for information on Terrance, I've abandoned my subtle approach and have been digging with the abandon of a backhoe.

"Did he kiss you yet?" I say, as we lie baking our hides on the platform over the boats.

"No."

"Did he try to touch your butt?"

"What guy would go for my ass before he kissed me?"

"Do you want him to kiss you?"

"Yeah, I wouldn't be mad about that."

"If he doesn't kiss you soon, will you do it first?"

"Yes, Leah, I'll close my fangs around his jugular and bring him down."

I flick her on the side of the head.

"That might have hurt if you didn't have those tiny koala fingers," she says without inflection.

I grunt and lie back with my baseball cap over my face. Seneca time is prime opportunity for my usual game of chicken with the sun: How long will I go between intervals of sunscreen? Will I get caught out in a burn? Can I avoid tan lines this year or am I screwed? ("Why does someone who knows damn well what UV rays do to human skin enjoy their poison kiss so much?" is a question only answered by "Because Italian.") I unhook the clasp of my halter-neck suit and tuck the straps into the cups. Better.

Beneath us, I can hear Ollie and Caleb playing with Spencer, inciting him with a Frisbee to jump off the end of the dock. The dog's enthusiasm for the game is endless; time and time again, he launches into the air in pursuit of the Frisbee, belly-flops into the water, grabs the Frisbee in his teeth, and paddles back for more. I think the guys are trying to measure the distance of his leaps, like they're training him for a competitive event. The splashing and shouting and laughing, along with the heat beaming down on me, lull me into a drowsy haze.

Until a blast of icy water falls out of the air and drenches my chest.

I scream and jackknife up to sitting, one hand clutching my rudderless bikini cups. Caleb is standing out of my reach, smirking, while an empty bait bucket dangles from his hand.

"Why the hell would you do that?" I gasp, swiping water off my belly with fast, angry jerks of my free hand.

He gives a low, slippery chuckle. "'Cause it was funny."

"It was obnoxious." I start to bend down to retrieve my hat, but pause when I feel my breasts shift against my containing hand. I don't want to bend down in front of Caleb. I don't want Caleb looking at me in a bikini at all. I didn't like it before he decided I was his new favorite person, and I like it even less now that he has. June's spot on the lounge chair next to me is empty; I can hear her voice from below, calling to Spencer.

"What was your goal here?" I say to Caleb. "You ruined my nap, you harshed my buzz, and you annoyed the shit out of me. Was there anything else specific, or was that everything?"

He tilts his head to the side like a little boy trying to ingratiate himself. "Ah, I was just playing. Didn't think you would get mad over it."

"Well, I did," I say. We stare at each other for another moment—him waiting for me to quit being pissed and agree it was an awesome joke, me waiting for him to leave me alone so I can rehook my bathing suit and pick up my stuff without him watching every move. Then he startles me by grabbing one of the lightweight lounge chairs and dragging it, feet scraping across the wood planks of the dock platform, near my chaise.

He sits down in it and leans toward me, resting his elbows on his thighs. "I wish you liked me," he says quietly. I search his face for a clue to the joke, but he is completely serious.

I wiggle my head in confusion. "What do you—I mean, I do. Like you. I just didn't like you dumping ice cold water on me while I was napping."

He shrugs and leans back in the chair, folding his arms over his chest as he looks at me. "Nah, but that's not it. I just feel like I never get it right with you. I wish we were friends. You're a cool girl."

"Thanks," I say. The word sounds like a question, and I'm not sure why. It's just a bland little compliment.

He waits for me to say something else. As the silence grows, I nervously adjust my hand that's holding my bikini in place. Caleb's smirk trickles back onto his face as he watches me. "Need a hand with your situation there?" he says, pointing in the vicinity of my neck.

"Fuck off," I mutter. "Seriously, what are you still doing here?"

He sighs and gets to his feet. "Ollie asked me to get you up so you can get ready for the party. People are going to start showing up soon."

"Okay. I'll be up in a few."

"Cool," he says, as he walks toward the stairs down from the platform. "I'll see if I can find some tequila for you."

Once he's gone, I adjust my suit and blot the last of the water from my body with a faded yellow towel. Like all the Biermans' towels, it smells of sunscreen even though it's freshly washed. I wrap it around me, tuck one corner between my front teeth, and gnaw.

I should be nicer to Caleb. I know he's just trying to be friendly, in his awkward way. But it's like he never outgrew the third-grade approach of communicating with girls by tugging their ponytails.

I just don't like the way he stares at me. I mean, I will certainly acknowledge that I'm the proud owner of some seriously first-rate boobs, but they're not the only boobs in western New York. But you'd never know it where Caleb is concerned. And I don't know how to get him to stop. I've thought about asking Ollie to talk to him, but I don't think he'd really get why it bothers me. And I *know* Caleb wouldn't. There is literally no point in trying. Especially since a proposal might be looming . . . complaining to Ollie about his brother is not the way to maximize his feelings of romance.

Excitement zings down my spine at the thought of the proposal. Who knows—today might even be the day. I'd always kind of figured Ollie for a private proposal type of guy, but I could also see him going for something with his family around. His parents' love story is so special to him; I can see how he would want them to witness the official start of his own.

I can't say I've never thought about it, because that is a lie. I've thought about it often. It won't be a flowery speech; that's not Ollie. Nor will it involve an elaborate setup; no rose petals on my twin bed in the Virgin Room. My parents aren't going to show up with Sam. It'll be something simple, straightforward, but heartfelt. *I want to spend my life with you. . . . Please say you'll be my wife.* And I will yell "Yes!" and throw myself into his waiting arms. Alone on the dock platform, I stamp my feet and squeal.

"Leah!" Ollie shouts from below. "Come on, babe, we gotta go get ready!"

"Okay, I'm coming!" I yell back.

I grab my scattered things and clamber down the stairs, where I find June still on the dock, waiting for Spencer to return from his last Frisbee dive of the day. Proudly clutching his treasure in his mouth, he paddles to the shore, then scrambles onto the dock and runs toward us. He drops the toy at June's feet, looks up at her expectantly, then wriggles his whole body, sending hundreds of water droplets flying into the air, where they sparkle like tiny jewels.

"Blaagh!" laughs June, shrinking away from him; but once he's done shaking she grabs the plastic disc and tosses it toward the shore. "Let's go, Spencer!" As she chases after him, towel fluttering around her calves, Ollie turns to me and smiles. Hand in hand, we walk back to the house together.

The Biermans' July Fourth shindig deserves its fame among the residents of west middle Seneca Lake. By midafternoon, over forty people are here, mostly neighbors and their kids and dogs, all of whom are scattered on the lawn engaged in games of tag and chase. The men wear baseball caps and knee-length shorts, and the women are in tank tops or light cotton dresses that reveal the varied patterns of sunburn on their shoulders.

Classic rock pumps from the outdoor speakers—Ollie gets his music taste directly from his dad—and the grill is going nonstop, filling the air with the scent of roasting meat. I've made it a personal mission to see that grillmaster Howard, face red and sweaty below his Willie Nelson–style bandanna, is never without a fresh cold beer. Every time I hand one to him, he winks.

Terrance has locked on to June like a love-seeking missile. Whether I'm with them or spying on them from across the deck, it's the same story: heads close in conversation, adoring smile on his face, happy smile on hers. I'm on pins and needles waiting for the moment I look around and *don't* see them, because that will mean he's finally pulled her off somewhere to kiss her. Ollie has been made aware of the circumstances and is on alert to encourage the blush of love at every opportunity.

As the sky dims and the air cools down, a kind of summer magic takes hold. Firecrackers start popping off all around the lake, one whistling shriek and sharp snap after another. Gradually, people start moving to the heavy stuff, and the horizon fills with shots of color—green, gold, red, and white—as fireworks burst against the darkness like paparazzi flashbulbs. The night air reverberates as the explosions echo back and forth across the water. I can feel the percussive boom of the nearest fireworks all the way inside my chest.

Not to be outdone, Howard abandons the grill and races toward the grassy stretch above the shoreline, where he has stockpiled his supplies. Ollie and Caleb hover, waiting to assist, and before long, we're off: Hissing, a tail of golden sparks shimmies into the sky, then with a *pow!* it bursts into a shower of light. It's followed by another and another, each more gorgeous than the last.

I seize the box of sparklers resting on a nearby table and pass them around. June, Terrance, Ollie, and I hold ours together to light them, and they fizz into life with a crackle. As I peer at the three faces so close to mine, all lit up by the sparklers, I tingle with sudden certainty: This is the future, right here. The four of us. Together.

Before I do something foolish like blab it out to them, I give a deranged little shriek and grab more sparklers out of the box. With three in each fist like some kind of pyro pixie, I twirl away from the others, spinning in circles as I watch the sparklers blaze against the dark. Their beauty only lasts a scant few seconds, but they burn fast and bright as I spin and spin and spin.

12

June

IT TOOK A GOOD SIX MINUTES OF PLEADING AND REASONING, last night out there in the noisy summer darkness of the path to the Holleys' place, to stop Ollie from bombing into his parents' house and raising unholy hell. Only Rachel's being already asleep spared her a late-night interrogation. I could tell that Ollie's ignorance unsettled him as much as the mysterious rumor. If there was some kind of alarming gossip about his family, why the hell didn't he know?

This morning at breakfast, all the sharp angles in Ollie's face have convened: jagged brows drawn together over his knife-edge nose, lips compressed into a flat line. He's responding to his family in tight monosyllables only. Rachel darts me a look, which I dodge; for the woman who raised him, it's always struck me as odd how alarmed she gets when he appears upset about something. As if she's surprised he has a full complement of emotions beyond loving devotion and wiseass humor. After the meal, I take myself downstairs to shower, and when I come out, Ollie is leaning against the sliding door with his arms folded, staring out at the lake. I move next to him and rub my hand on his back.

"So what's going on?"

Silently, he shakes his head. "I don't know. None of it makes any sense."

"What doesn't?"

"What my mom said."

"Which was *what*?" I say, shaking his arm a little. "Maybe I can help it make sense."

He tucks a piece of hair behind my ear, and for a second I think he's about to tell me. "I don't think so. I don't know the whole picture yet. I need to wait to talk to Caleb."

There is a certain opacity to Ollie when it comes to his brother. It's all the more disorienting because everything else about him is so transparent: his love for me, for his parents, his friends, his career, for music. It's like looking into a pool of clear, sunny water and then something moves in the corner and the water clouds with sand. I cannot see what's back there. I never have.

I wait for him to say more, but he doesn't. That's it. That's all I'm getting. I raise my hand and poke at the air around his shoulder. I try again, closer to his face.

"What are you doing?"

"Locating the force field. It wasn't here an hour ago, but now it is. I can't reach you." I tap my finger above his forehead and make a *dink, dink, dink* noise as if I've hit an invisible barrier.

He gives a wistful smile. "I'm sorry. I just really don't know what's happening here. I want to get all the information first before I talk about it with you."

"But why? I'm supposed to be here to help you. How can I do that if you won't tell me what's going on?"

"I've wondered that before myself," he says.

After the past few days of model summer weather, today is hazy and overcast, the dim sky turning the surface of the lake as flat and gray as hammered tin. It feels hotter than ever, though, and the humid, motionless air clings to my skin. Rachel has conceded to reality and turned the A/C on while we get ready for the Fourth of July party. Which, I can't help noticing, feels considerably more subdued than it did the first time I was here. Last time, there was an infectious excitement in the air; Leah was bouncing off the walls, and the rest of us were on a contact high. But today, Rachel and I work quietly side by side in the kitchen, chopping and rinsing fruit for the massive salad that will be one of the desserts. Since Ollie wouldn't tell me what the issue is with Caleb, I can't bring it up with his mother; and I can't seem to think of anything simple to chat with her about. The silence hangs as heavy as the clouds outside.

The party is less than half the size that I remember. It's mainly the same people who were here the night of the bonfire, including Terrance and his parents. I'm talking with Ollie, Caleb, and Leslie at one point when Howard meanders over, beer in hand. "Small turnout this year," he says to Caleb. "You have any guesses why?"

"Maybe people got tired of your King of the Lake shtick," says Caleb. "It was getting pretty old."

Leslie's fingers tighten on her husband's arm, but Howard just raises his eyebrows as if he's bored. "Is that the story we're telling?"

"Howard, you can tell any tale you want."

"Honey," says Leslie quietly, just as Ollie says, "Enough."

"Think I'll get a refill on my beer," I say, except once I'm away from them, I don't head for the cooler at all. With a glance behind to make sure Ollie isn't watching me, I dart down to the lawn, where I spotted Terrance and his parents talking to a couple of other neighbors.

"Can I talk to you for a second?" I say, touching his wrist, and he excuses himself and follows me. I head for the trail to Terrance's house. There's an old split-log bench with a nice view of the water just past the start of the trail, screened from sight of both houses by the woods and the angle of the land. It's a good spot for a private conversation. Belatedly, I realize that I know this because this bench is where Terrance led me, as afternoon turned to evening on the Fourth of July seven years ago, and kissed me in the deep green shade of the overhanging trees while the leaves rustled in the breeze.

"So what's up?" He sits down next to me, hands knotted loosely together between his thighs. If he's thinking about the last time we sat here together, he's too much of a gentleman to show it.

"What the fuck is going on with Caleb?" I say, too far beyond caring about saving the family's face to keep pretending they've seen fit to inform me.

"You didn't hear yet?" he says. "Damn. I could tell you hadn't heard last night, but—" He trails off at the look on my face. "Sorry. Well, I didn't know anything about it either, but I asked my folks after you left. They said Caleb's been accused of sexual assault by a waitress at some bachelor party he was at in Rochester a few weeks back."

"Sexual *assault*?" I gasp. "Not sexual harassment?"

"That's what they said. I know, I asked the same question." His tone is as grim as his face.

"As in, he hurt someone? Or he raped someone? What does that even mean?"

"I don't know, June. I think you need to—"

"I need to talk to Ollie," I say. "He spoke to his mom this morning but he wouldn't tell me what she said; he said he wants to wait to talk to Caleb. Which I'm sure won't happen till tomorrow, with the house crawling with guests today and everybody three sheets to the wind. So, yeah, I guess I just told you that he didn't know about it, either."

"It's okay. I could tell yesterday."

I think of how smoothly Ollie tried to conceal his ignorance, and feel a stab of alarm. "Did your parents notice?"

He shakes his head. "No. I can just read him. Which . . ." He pauses, then smiles slightly. "Okay, I probably shouldn't say this, but—"

"But wait, though. Why wouldn't they have told him? You said this has been going on for several weeks?"

"It sounded like it, yeah."

"So why not tell Ollie? He hates being caught out like that. Especially about something as big as this."

"Your guess is as good as mine. Maybe they wanted to talk about it in person, and they figured it could wait until this week."

"I guess so. But we've been here for three days, and nothing."

He shrugs. "Who knows? Families are nuts."

I scrape my hand through my hair and sigh. "Ain't that the truth. But so . . . was that all your parents said about Caleb? There must be more to it than that."

"They said it was in the Rochester news a couple of weeks back, and word started spreading. You could probably find the article if you googled Caleb's name."

I flinch. The last time somebody I knew was in the newspaper, it was Leah. And the Biermans, too. They must despise this kind of public attention, having gone through it once before. But, my god . . . Caleb accused of sexual assault, and the whole area talking about it? How on earth is everyone walking around in any sort of facsimile of normal? I remember Leslie, the image of contented wifely devotion on the boat the other night. Even assuming she disbelieves the accusations, it's bizarre to me that she could be so *calm*. I reach inside my skirt pocket for the hard shape of my phone, itching to look up the article Terrance mentioned.

"Well, on a lighter note, it was funny hearing you tell my folks about your ring last night." Terrance reaches for my left hand and angles it forward so he can see the ring. "This really is beautiful. I never actually got to see it."

Distracted from the Caleb issue, I frown. "What do you mean?"

He frowns back. "What do *you* mean?"

"Why would you have seen it before?"

"He never told you?" He shakes his head briefly—*that crazy kid.* "What am I saying, of course he didn't tell you. It was my brother-in-law that Ollie asked to buy the ring from you."

My lips drop open. No, Ollie never told me that. I asked him once who he'd enlisted for help, but he deflected it somehow, and I never remembered to ask him again.

Terrance gently sets my hand back down on my lap. "Yeah, it was my sister Sonya's husband. Derek Adams."

"Yes! I remember his name. I think Ollie just told me it was a friend of a friend. Good grief, why wouldn't he tell me? That was so nice of you to help."

He raises his eyebrows with a faint smile and looks away.

"What? What is that supposed to mean?"

"You can't think of a single reason why, out of his entire depth chart of friends, he asked me for help with the ring?"

I start to speak, then falter. "No. I mean, not because . . ."

"Yeeeeeesss," he says, low voice teasing.

"But that's absurd, it was a million years ago. And he loves you."

"But he hates *that,*" he says.

"That's ridiculous. I never even would have seen you again if I hadn't started dating him. Which, I mean . . . I'm sorry I—" I break off, flustered.

Ever gracious, he lets it slip past. "No, but he knows how much I liked you."

I roll the hem of my skirt between my fingertips. I know how much Terrance had liked me, too. I owe him an apology, but it's so far underwater now that it would be worse to dredge it up than let it lie.

"And anyway, you can't hold Ollie to logic where you're concerned. Ever since you guys reconnected, the dude's been possessed. I think it scared the shit out of him to realize he almost—"

Just then, Ollie shouts my name from the lawn near the start of the trail.

"Well, lookie here," says Terrance, as Ollie approaches. "Speak of the devil and he shall appear."

"What are you doing hiding away down here?" Ollie demands, scowling, as he reaches me. "I thought you went to get a drink but then you didn't come back. I was looking all over."

"Well, gracious me, I just can't think of the slightest reason I'd have left behind that charming conversation," I say sweetly, and Ollie sighs.

"I know. Cal and my dad are worse than usual. I'm sorry." He pauses, sizing us up to see if Terrance has told me what he knows. I almost cop to it, but I know it would make him feel like shit that I had to go to his friend for information. Even though he deserves it.

"Terrance was just telling me that it was his brother-in-law who did the hand-off for the engagement ring," I say. "Which, curiously, is a fact I never knew until today."

"Speaking of awkward conversations," Terrance murmurs, patting his thighs decisively and getting to his feet. "I'll see you back there."

Once he's gone, Ollie gives a soft half laugh and turns to me. "Yeah . . . I'm a jackass. That's all I've got on that one."

I shake my head, bemused. "It's such a silly little thing. Why would you never tell me?"

"It bothers me that you were involved with him," he says quietly.

Wow—Terrance was right. "Ol, that is honestly ridiculous."

He runs his fingers down my arm, his eyes searching mine. "Is it? You guys were a good fit. If everything hadn't happened, you would have kept seeing each other."

"But everything did happen."

"He asked me about you. More than once. In the months after it happened . . . he asked me how you were doing. I hated that I didn't even know. June," he says, nudging my chin up to face him, "why didn't I know?"

"Because," I say, and then my voice falters. Too many reasons, and none of them ones I want to talk about right now.

Ollie watches me, waiting for me to speak. When I don't, he raises his hand to my face. I think he's going to caress me, but at the last second his fingers stop short.

"Dink, dink, dink," he says.

13

Leah

THE NOT-SO-SECRET HISTORY OF HOWARD IS THAT BEFORE HE moved to Rochester and settled down, he spent ten years traveling the country as a lighting and effects designer for bands. Thirty years later, he retains both his passion for rock and roll and his deep love of combustion. The fireworks might be the main event in a nominal way, but the bonfire is the after-party: And it's the after-party that people stay for.

With a showman's panache, Howard lets a moment of stillness fall after the last firework fades into the dark; then, while everyone is peering at the traces of sulfurous smoke still hanging in the air, the bonfire roars to life behind us, as Ollie's match makes contact with a robust application of lighter fluid. This fire is like something out of a Viking legend: huge, chunky logs as tall as a person, stacked on end around a bed of kindling six feet around, all of it covered in ravenous orange flame that writhes into the black sky above. The heat it throws off by the time it really gets going is enough to warm an Icelandic night, let alone a Finger Lakes one, but the contrast of the scorching heat against the front of my body and the chilly air against my back is a sense memory that will always remind me of Seneca.

An hour later, the fire has calmed, and everyone is loitering in

Adirondack chairs ringed around it, talking and laughing. There's one final phase of this party, which takes a little bit of alcoholic lubrication to get to, but I sense that we are almost there. I smile to myself when I see Howard walk over to Terrance, clap a hand on his shoulder, and mutter something in his ear. Terrance gives a quick nod, then, with obvious reluctance, lets go of June's hand, which he has not released all night. He winks at her, then hurries up the stairs toward the main lawn.

She sidles closer to where I'm perched on the arm of Ollie's chair. "What's he up to?"

My yearning to make fun of her unconvincing portrayal of *mild interest* is so strong I think my tongue is itching—but if I do it, she will get self-conscious and huffy. I glance repressively at Ollie, certain he will not be able to let the opportunity pass, but there's no teasing smirk forming on his mouth. For once in his misbegotten life, he is exercising restraint. "You'll see in a minute," I tell her.

When Terrance returns with what are quite clearly a violin case and a guitar case, a cheer goes up around the fire. Grinning, he raises them high over his head like trophies, then sets the guitar case against the free arm of Ollie's chair. It's unmistakable that he is throwing down a gauntlet.

Ollie laughs. "Oh man, I am so not up to the task."

"Come on. You used to jam with me all the time."

"That was before you were a professional musician," Ollie says.

"What about last summer?"

"Last summer I was drunk."

"So get yourself some liquid courage."

"Also, that guitar is so out of tune it sounds like a dying walrus."

"I tuned it before you got here," says Terrance. "Checkmate. Now come on."

"Just play, kid!" yells Howard, and the cry is quickly taken up: "Play, Ollie, play." I join in, patting his knees in rhythm to the chant. Even out of practice, Ollie is a fantastic guitar player. He's just also a perfectionist.

Finally, with a grimace of defeat, Ollie picks up the case and slides to the edge of his chair so he has room to play. I link arms with June and tug her into a better sight line.

Ollie fits the instrument into his arms and idly picks a few notes to warm up his hands. "Take pity on me," he says to Terrance.

"Something easy to start. 'Teach Your Children'?"

"Oh, sure. Three-part harmony, why not?"

"You forgetting we have a ringer?" Terrance says, taking out the tambourine he'd stuffed in the waistband of his jeans and handing it to his mother.

Michelle steps forward, smiling, and gives it a rattle.

"Got everything we need," says Terrance. "I'll take the steel guitar parts."

"That's Jerry Garcia on steel guitar!" bellows Howard, for no essential reason. He's been knocking back Ommegangs all night, and he is highly festive at this point.

As am I, in the interest of full disclosure.

"You remember the chords?" says Terrance.

Ollie rolls his eyes at Terrance, taps his foot to start the rhythm, then begins to play. With a smile, Terrance sets his bow to his violin, and then Ollie locks eyes with Michelle as they start to sing: him on melody, her on the harmony, their voices blending like they've been doing it all their lives. Because, of course, they have.

Here is a universal truth: When a hot guy picks up a guitar and skillfully plays it—and, even better, when he skillfully sings along—his baseline hotness becomes amplified by an exponential power impossible to quantify by any known means. I don't even really like this song or whatever band it comes from, but my ovaries are swooning like a pair of Victorian damsels. June, music fiend that she is, is doubtless enduring something similar watching Terrance play.

After a minute or so, Terrance turns, face lit with delighted surprise, to June. I was so absorbed in Ollie that I hadn't even noticed she was singing. She mumbles something I can't hear, but Terrance shakes his head and smiles at her, and damn, that guy's smile is so beautiful it's making *my* heart swell. She lets go of my arm and moves closer to them, and now I can hear her voice clearly, layering beneath Ollie's and Michelle's.

"Get in there, June!" yells Howard, and she smiles around her words.

It's amazing how everyone comes together in the space of three minutes. Terrance's playing was always confident, of course, but by the time he puts the final flourish on his last note, the singers, all of whom had started out a little tentatively, are smiling and singing loud without giving a damn about the little missed words or sour notes here and there. When they finish, the rest of us burst into enthusiastic applause. Howard sticks his fingers into his mouth to whistle.

"More!" he yells, and then there's a tumult of laughing and talking as everyone marvels that June can sing, discusses what the next song should be, and then starts it. Ollie's sitting in the middle of it, beaming like a goddamn headlight. This is about as in his element as he gets—high on music and on having all his favorite people around him at the same time. I feel a familiar twinge—the wish that I could share this with him and stand up there, singing. But my absence of pitch makes my voice sound even worse than any untuned guitar.

Ollie and Terrance play song after song after song. Some are more successful than others, but it doesn't even matter. This is the best Seneca July Fourth jam session I've ever seen.

Inevitably, things start to slow down after a little while, and a few people say their good nights. Ollie noodles on his guitar, notes and random bits of melody trickling from his fingers.

"June," Ollie says after a minute, "you wanna try 'Landslide'?"

I gasp with excitement. She loves that song so much. She's going to say she doesn't want to ruin it. I open my mouth to tell her who cares and go for it, but she speaks first.

"Can we take it up a step? I don't want to bottom out."

"Yeah, for sure. I'll play it in F."

"G might be better," says Terrance. "Stevie's voice is so low."

"So is June's," says Ollie. "She'll be good at F."

He reaches into his guitar case for a clamp and tightens it on the neck of his guitar. Holding his gaze steady on June's, he begins playing the notes. Finger picking is harder than strumming chords, but you'd never know it from the way Ollie's fingers flicker over those strings.

"I took my love, I took it down," June sings. "I climbed a mountain, and I turned around."

And I think I can safely speak for everyone around that bonfire when I say we all stop breathing. June Kang has been holding out on me for thirteen freaking years, because I had no idea she could sing like this. I knew she had a pretty voice, of course; but a gorgeous, soulful voice that's low and rich and throbbing with wistful yearning—that I did *not* know.

I edge over behind Ollie so I can get a clear look at Terrance's face. I think he thought he was going to tool around on that violin of his and add some spiffy accents to this song, but the bow is motionless in his hand and he's lifted his chin off the cushion so he can focus on June, and the hairs on the back of my neck stand up because good Lord, I am watching a man fall in love.

And then there comes a part where there's supposed to be a little electric guitar solo between the choruses, but Terrance is too busy gawking to play. June glances expectantly at Terrance, who abruptly returns to himself and fiddles out the solo with a wry smile on his face. She laughs, and the moment between them is even cuter than the adoring stare was. But June comes back in for her chorus right on cue, just like a boss, and finishes out the song with a swell of her haunting voice.

For the first breath after the last notes of Ollie's guitar absorb into the night, everything is still. And then Terrance sets his violin and bow on the chair behind him, catches June's face in his hands, and kisses her.

Oh. My. *Swoon*.

Howard, Rachel, and everyone else watching erupt into cheers, and I start jumping up and down and flapping my arms like some kind of demented jack-in-the-box. It takes me a second to notice that Ollie isn't cheering, so I smack him on the shoulder and point at June and Terrance, but he just glances at them briefly before he lowers his head again. His face pinches with discomfort as he massages a cramp in his hand. After a few seconds, June and Terrance break apart, grinning at each other with their foreheads pressed together, June blushing so deeply I can see it from here.

"Encore!" yells Howard, and the happy couple sheepishly laughs. But I shiver as I remember that moment with the four of us and the sparklers, and I swear I'm not just playing it up. . . . I think Terrance could be the guy for June. I'm not stupid enough to tell her so right now, of course, but I really, *really* think he might be the one.

14

June

BEFORE I FELL IN LOVE, I NEVER UNDERSTOOD WHEN PEOPLE would say, usually of somebody else's beloved, "I never meant for it to happen. I just couldn't help it." How ridiculous. Of *course* you could help it. There is an element of choice in everything we do.

And then Ollie happened. And it was like this quiet tap on my shoulder, a hand beside my face, pointing at him over there, across the room: *That one. That one for you.*

I fought it for a long time, because sometimes I lie to myself. But when I think about it now, I know exactly when it started.

Or at least, when it started for the second time.

After he moved away from New York, and finally gave up on trying to get in touch with me, I heard his name every now and then. As the years passed, I'd see him pop up in my social media feeds courtesy of the mutual friends we had (*Ollie Bierman liked Ruby Fairley's photo*). Every time, my shoulders hunched against the same sickening frisson of guilt-laced grief.

And then there I was one night, dressed as the flamenco lady emoji at my friend Rashmi's Halloween party, when I heard a voice behind me say my name.

It was just one word, but I knew who it was as soon as he said it. Not just because I recognized his voice, but because I heard the hesitation, the memory, the pain. I had no idea why or for how long or since when he was back, but he was. I took a slow, deep breath, and turned. And then the breath I was clutching exploded in a peal of laughter.

"No *fucking* way."

Ollie was dressed as the disco man emoji. Tight purple suit, hot pink shirt with popped collar, gleaming black wingtips. When he caught sight of my cascading wig and long, red halter dress, skirt hiked high on one thigh, he threw his hands up in celebration. "My dream girl," he said; and then he caught me into a tight, grateful hug. One hand curled around my head, holding me against his shoulder. We were laughing, and I was crying while I laughed, and then we weren't laughing at all. We just stood there, holding each other, an island of stillness as the party swirled around us.

I really couldn't tell you how long it was. I only know that when we pulled apart, something was different. He took my hand and said, "Let's get out of here," and I tugged my flamenco wig off, slipped into my black peacoat, and followed him out into the damp October night. It had quit raining by then, but the streets were wet, gleaming with headlight reflections and hissing softly as car tires rolled past. Chilly mist clung to my face as we walked, but my hand in his was warm.

"Where are we going?" I said, when the hem of my dress had soaked up enough moisture from the sidewalk to slap against my feet with every step.

"I don't know yet," he said, and shifted his fingers tighter between mine. But after a little while we spotted a quiet-looking wine bar and ducked inside, parking ourselves at a little table at the back. For a few moments we just studied each other, inventorying the changes.

In all the time I'd known him, I'd never been free to stare at him without reservation; so that night, I gorged on it. And it turned out that the added years really suited him. His light brown hair was razored into a much leaner cut than the floppy I-wear-jeans-to-work look I had last seen him sporting, and he'd acquired a trim beard that zapped the baby face right out of him. Leah would have bitched about it, and Leah, girl, you would have been wrong, wrong, wrong. A faint smile lifted my mouth at the thought of what colorful metaphors she would have employed to dissuade him from it; around Leah, that beard wouldn't have made it past its third day of life.

It had been five years and three months since Ollie and I had spoken; five years and two months since he'd fled the hemorrhaging wound of his life in New York and moved to L.A. Suddenly it was intolerable that I hadn't seen him in so long. And so we talked, all of those necessary stories spilling out as the level in the wine bottle slowly dropped. *How have things been? How is your family? What have you been doing? Where are you working these days? Are you back in the city for good?* That last one was from me, and the answer was yes, and then there was a restless bird inside me, beating its wings against my ribs.

"You know," Ollie said, staring into his wineglass as he twisted it from side to side, "I figured I'd run into you again now that I'm back in the city, and I knew we would end up talking about Leah. Part of me was dreading it because of that. But most of me was looking forward to seeing you. And now that I'm here with you, I'm finding that I don't want to talk about her at all." There was something defiant in his voice, and in his face when he lifted it and met my eyes.

"We don't have to," I said.

"Do *you* want to?"

Heart pounding, I slowly shook my head.

His shoulders dropped as he let his breath go. "Okay. Then we won't." He crossed his arms on the table and leaned forward. "So did you catch Tedeschi Trucks at the Beacon earlier this month? I almost emailed you to ask if you wanted to go, but I was afraid it would be weird. Well, I knew it would be weird. Do you want a glass of water, by the way?" he added, signaling for the server.

"Sure," I said, although I knew my hot flush wasn't just from the wine.

Once we had given ourselves permission to leave Leah outside the perimeter, our entire conversation exhaled. He told me about the wild stuff he experienced while he was trying to get up the ladder in the L.A. music industry, about the music publishing job he moved back to the city for, how excited he was to work with songwriters instead of just pop stars. When I said how glad I was, because it sounded like the perfect job for him, his smile made my brain go blank for several sequential seconds. "You were the one who gave me the idea in the first place," he said. "And you were right."

I told him about starting Elements; not just the CliffsNotes version I gave most people, but, because he was so genuinely interested, I gave him the meat of it: the exhilaration, the terror, the delight of being my own boss mixed with the craving for somebody else to tell me what decisions to make. I told him about how Pooja and I were thinking of adopting a dog, about how the rise of cellphone cameras had forced my dad to close his camera store but that he had found an unexpected new niche in children's portrait photography. "I don't know what it is. My dad's a shy guy, but little kids absolutely love him. I think he likes them because they're cute, but they don't expect anything of him except to make them laugh. And he's really got a gift of bringing out each kid's personality in the portraits. But of course having him around children all the time has got my mom in a lather for a grandkid."

Ollie laughed. "I bet. So, any prospects on the horizon, then?"

"'Prospects'?"

"I meant, are you dating anybody?"

"Oh." Warmth washed over me again. "No, I'm not." Normally

I would have launched into a story about my mother's or my aunt's color commentary on my debilitating singlehood, of which there was endless material ("Ji-Eunah, you don't want to let the boys think you are stale"; "Ji-Eunah, can't you find a way to look less tall?"), but with Ollie I didn't. I didn't want to. Instead, I took a sip of wine and, with my glass partially covering my face to assist in my casual demeanor, I said, "What about you?"

He shook his head.

"And does *your* mom give you a hard time about it?" I said, swiftly moving past his response.

"No. Caleb's baby gives me pretty good coverage for now," he said, smiling. But he held my eyes with his. He held them so long that something started heating up inside me, a lightbulb that had gone dark a long time ago, humming to glowing life inside my chest.

In the brief pause that fell, the soft acoustic guitar music that had been playing while we talked cut into silence, and I looked around to realize we were the only people left inside the bar.

"Sorry, guys, we gotta close up," said the waitress, walking briskly past with her hands full of the night's receipts.

Ollie and I shared a sheepish smile and began rustling about, gathering coats and scarves and bags. When he slipped his shoulders into his disco jacket, he grinned at me and gave the collar an Elvis-y little flick. Even that ridiculous getup couldn't make him look anything other than fine. I thought he might loop his fingers between mine again as we walked to the door, but he had his hands jammed in the pockets of his coat. All of a sudden he looked half a world away, and I felt embarrassed by that warm little spurt of hope that had leapt up inside me. Outside, the wind knifed through me and I shivered hard, wishing I hadn't decided to superglue the skirt of the flamenco dress into its signature frothy position.

"Well, I guess I'll head toward Seventh to try to get a cab," I mumbled, as I struggled with the skirt. "It was so great to catch up with you. Don't be a stranger. And if you ever do want to talk about her, you know—"

Ollie's voice cut through my babble. "June."

I glanced up to find him staring at me. "What?"

He shook his head, closed the distance between us in two quick steps, and fitted his hand to my jaw. "I am definitely not going to be a stranger," he said, low and intense. And then he kissed me. Hard. As if it was the only thing to do in that situation that made sense. As if it was the only thing in the *world* that made sense.

And god, it was like somebody'd plunged my cord into a socket. Electricity arced along every nerve ending from my heels to my head, making me gasp against his open lips. And then my fingers dove into his hair and we were moving, stumbling sideways into the recessed doorway of the nearest building, kissing ravenously as we clawed at each other's coats, desperate to reach unencumbered skin.

I was devouring him as if someone was coming to pluck him away, and he was doing the same to me. His hands raced over my body so fast and hot I was surprised my dress didn't scorch. But Ollie was the one who steadied us. After a minute, he pulled his mouth from mine and pressed one hand to me, palm on the top of my chest and his thumb and fingers in a V, resting against my clavicles. It summoned a pause, enough for the question to spread into the space between us.

"What are we doing?" I said it first, because it was important to me that he answer. I already knew what I was doing.

"I don't know," he said, still breathing fast. "But I promise you I know exactly who I'm kissing."

"Do you?" I said, as he moved his head to kiss me again.

He met my eyes and nodded. But there was something in his face that made me unsure. Something aching, something hurt, underneath the desire.

"I'm going home," I said, doing up my coat again. His hand, chased off my chest by my buttons, slid up to cup my neck. His thumb caressed my jawline. "You can get my number from Rashmi."

"If it's still the same, then I have it," he said.

"It's still the same," I said, digging my nails into my palms to keep from kissing him again. Yes, it was definitely still the same. I forced my feet to move away from him, one step after another, and only looked back over my shoulder once I was well clear. "Good night, Ollie."

He raised a palm in silent farewell. His smile was so tender, but so sad, that I wasn't sure I'd ever see him again.

I didn't hear from him for three days. When he called me, our conversation was both simple and confusing.

"I miss you. Meet me for dinner?"

"Yes," I said. And then I steeled myself to deliver the line I had spent the last three days pretending I believed. "But I think we should only be friends."

"Okay," he said. "Friends it is."

I felt a throb of hurt at his easy acquiescence—it wouldn't have killed him to feign a little disappointment—until I realized he had no intention of staying just my friend over the long term. He never directly came out and said it; I think he sensed a formal "I want to date you" conversation would have spooked me. It would have forced an examination of the how and why and what does this mean. And neither of us wanted that.

Instead, he insinuated himself completely into my life. It was effortless. In every way besides the obvious, it was as if the past five and a half years had not occurred. It was so goddamn good to have him around that I was stunned by how much I'd missed him;

shocked that I hadn't let myself feel it before. I hated how long he'd been gone. We spent so much time together, checking out concerts and trying new restaurants and playing board games while watching football in my living room, which he seemed to prefer to his own empty studio, that Pooja threatened to start charging him rent for his spot on the couch.

"Look, I know he used to date your best friend," she said one night in December, once Ollie had headed back to his place after a full NFL triple-header. "I also know I've never seen a guy make you light up like this. Liking him does not make you disloyal to Leah. You can't change what happened, and depriving yourself of something you clearly want is . . . it's like you're punishing yourself."

Of course I was punishing myself. Every time my skin brushed his and I flinched away, every time I forced myself to sit on the opposite side of the couch because I knew if I got close enough to kiss him I'd never make it back: It was punishment. Self-deprivation. Penance, long overdue.

I went on a few dates with Kurt, a guy I met online, and the first time he slept over, Ollie arrived at noon in time for the Sunday pregame show, bearing three bloated bagels and a cheerful smile. Kurt gave up just after kickoff and never called me again.

"That's a real shame," said Ollie when I told him.

I glared at him, even though it secretly delighted me.

"Listen, nobody who's worth your time is going to get scared off by some dude you've clearly friendzoned."

"Ollie."

"When you tell me that there's somebody you're legitimately into, I will back off. But until then, the cockblock stands. Although I consider it more of a blockade. 'Block' suggests something small."

"Oliver!" My attempt at sternness collapsed into laughter, and he stacked his hands behind his head and grinned at me. I tried to ignore the way it made his biceps pop above the sleeves of his Bills T-shirt. Friendzone, my ass.

Things finally came to a head toward the end of February a few weeks later, as I was sitting across a restaurant table from a guy I'd met on Tinder the week before. I was watching his mouth move as he talked, trying to summon the slightest interest in the conversation, when his voice straggled to a stop. "Is everything okay? You were frowning."

Because you're not Ollie. God, why the hell was I trying so hard to prove whatever I was trying to prove? And how many people's time was I going to waste along the way?

"I'm sorry," I said, getting to my feet. "I'm truly sorry to be so rude. But I don't think this is going to take off, and I don't want to take up any more of your time."

He gaped at me. "Are you serious? In the middle of a conversation?"

"I think my brain just took this extremely inopportune moment to let me admit that I'm in love with somebody."

He blinked, then raised his half-empty vodka soda. "Well," he said, voice sardonic, "cheers to the lucky guy."

I was texting Ollie before I even had my coat buttoned. *Sprung myself from Tinder date. Come meet me.* As soon as I wrote it, I realized I'd been waiting all day for the minute I could.

Ollie was waiting for me under the awning outside City Winery, watching the falling snow, and the minute he saw me coming, I knew he knew. He took off his glove and reached for my hand, his warm fingers tightening between mine the way they had that night we left the Halloween party together. It felt every bit as necessary, and as right.

"Listen," he said. "I've been sitting on this for a while because I didn't want to freak you out, but fuck it. I'm so in love with you. I want to be the first person you call for whatever you need to do or want to say or have to share. Hell, I want to be there to do it before you know you need it. And I want to hold your hand all the time, not just right now. I want to see you wake up on my pillow with your mascara smudged and your hair a mess, and I want to see you dressed up like this, this gorgeous, in these fancy shoes, for me."

I looked up at his beautiful, beloved face and I smiled, a little one-sided smile that belied the frenzied way my heart was banging against my ribs. "Ollie. You really think I'd put heels on for some Tinder guy?"

He glanced down at my shoes, the tiny flakes of snow glimmering on the black patent leather, then ran his eyes up my legs and raised his gaze to mine again.

Gulping in a deep breath of the rest of my life, I kissed him.

It's been the kind of relationship I would have cautioned anyone else about. Headlong, reckless, arguably suffocating—neither of us cares. That article I read about the neurology of addiction? It said the same brain changes that occur in addiction also occur when someone falls in love. And I believe it. What I'm less sure of is that there is even, sometimes, any distinction between the two at all.

15

Leah

OBVIOUSLY, OLLIE IS NOT POPPING THE QUESTION TONIGHT.
As the bonfire dies and the guests shuffle homeward, he joins me
in collecting cans and bottles from around the party area. Even
my unorthodox sensibility when it comes to romance can't see
post-party trash pickup and a marriage proposal happening
within the same evening. Now that I think about it, if he was going
to pick an occasion with family around, it's better suited to his
mom's birthday in three days. But after such a magical day, it feels
boring to just go inside and go to bed. Especially since the couple
of the hour has quietly vanished into the blackness to celebrate
their newly kindled love. I want to celebrate my love, too.

Abandoning my pile of empties, I sprint up to the house and
fling open the ground-floor door to the gear closet. This is a huge
closet, half the size of the average suburban garage, in which the
Biermans keep their lake-related stuff: life vests, inner tubes and
floats, skis. There are cobwebs in the upper corners. It smells like
plastic and mildew. The bug-strewn fluorescent light in the center
of the ceiling flickers as I scan the shelves for what I'm looking for;
and then I spot it and pounce.

"Leeb, what're you doing?" Ollie's mild voice comes from behind me, but I don't turn around. I am too focused on my task.

"Gnuh," I grunt, dragging the object forward from under the stack of rope that's obscuring it.

"For real, though. Why are you pulling out the tent?"

"Because we're camping."

"Right now?"

"Right now. I'm sick of tiptoeing to your room and not making any noise. We're reenacting our first date."

"We didn't sleep together on our first date," he says, amusement in his voice.

"Oh my god, you're so literal!" I say, then shriek as the tent abruptly comes free from under the rope, pitching me backward into Ollie. "I'm being spontaneous and romantic," I explain, shoving the tent against the shelves. I turn against him, and he smiles and settles his arms around my waist.

"Okay," he says. "I'm down for spontaneous romance. Why don't you go get the sleeping bags from the upstairs closet, and I'll set up the tent?"

By the time I have located the sleeping bags, brushed my teeth, and otherwise prepared myself for a night of spontaneous romance, Ollie has the tent up on the lawn. Stars sprawl overhead in a dazzling display, and fireflies hover about, blinking into the darkness to offer their own sweet, tiny lights—as close and comforting as the stars are remote. Below us, faint moonlight glimmers on the placid surface of the lake.

Once we have the sleeping bags unzipped and laid out across the floor of the tent, Ollie wraps his arms around me and pulls me close. He kisses me greedily, almost impatiently; the sex that follows has the same edge of hunger to it. By the time I collapse, wild-haired and exhausted, onto the innocent plaid flannel lining of the sleeping bag, I am grinning and extremely satisfied. Now that we've been together for so long, our sex has gotten a little bit . . . I wouldn't say *routine*, exactly, but I guess just *quieter* than it was the first couple of years. And also, if I'm being honest, a lot less frequent. But that, that was second-week-of-dating sex right there. That was movie sex. That was sweep-your-arm-across-the-desk-to-clear-it-'cause-shit-is-going-*down* sex.

"You know what? This was a great idea," Ollie says, pulling me onto his chest and nuzzling the top of my head.

"I know," I say. "I'm full of them."

"You are."

"And I'm full of spontaneous romance, too."

"Obviously."

"Damn right," I say. "And the fun's not over yet, so don't even think about going to sleep."

"Leah, have you never heard of the concept of a refractory period?"

I snort so loudly that I burst out laughing. "Not that, you ass. I just want to hang out some more. I miss those long talks we used to have, back when we first started dating and we didn't know anything about each other. Tell me something I don't know about you."

He's silent while he thinks. "Hmm . . . how about this: I don't do well responding to overly open-ended questions."

I turn my face and nip sharply at his bare shoulder.

"Ow, god damn it! What was that for?"

"I was serious."

"So was I!"

"You're never serious," I say, chastened. "But there's no pressure. It can be anything, it can be something small."

"Like you?"

I lie perfectly still and silent while he braces for reprisal. "This is me not retaliating," I say in a dignified voice.

"Satan's bedbug declines to bite," he says.

"'Satan's bedbug'?"

"I like this new 'grace and dignity' approach. Does this mean I can say whatever I want now?"

"Stop dodging my question."

"Okay, how's this: Every time I hang out with Terrance, it makes me wonder where I could be by now if I'd ever taken guitar seriously."

"Marginally employed?"

A burst of air blows through his throat in a short *kuh* noise: Agreement? Or something else? "Wow. Thanks, Leah."

Something else, then. *Shit.* I prop myself up on my elbow so I can see his face. "Well, it's true," I mutter. "It's not that you're not good; you know you are. It's just an insanely hard way to try to make a living. Which is why you never pursued it."

"Yeah . . . I know. But fear of failure is a shitty reason to hold back from trying something that might be important."

"A realistic assessment of your chances of success is not the same as fear of failure."

"Pretty sure that's different words for the same thing," he says.

"Come on, you know it's not. The fact that you started a real career instead of trying to make it as a musician in New York City does not make you a wimp. It makes you an adult."

A scowl drives a deep line between his eyebrows. "So Terrance is not an adult?"

"Gah!" I yell, and flop back down on my back. "That's not what I said. He's going to have two degrees in music performance, and you told me he's one of the best violinists in the country. The guy will never be hurting for good work. *That* is a career. Not . . ." My wheels spin in the mud as I try to think of what to say that won't antagonize him further. For as much of a smart-ass as he is, he is annoyingly easy to offend. "Not being in a band," I finish finally.

"It's not just being in a band, it would be writing my own music, and . . . You know what, forget it. It's too late now. I think going into the business side will be a better fit for me, anyway."

"The business side . . ."

"Of music," he says, impatience in his voice.

I flip onto my side again. "Wait. Are you for real with all of that?"

The mighty scowl returns. "Am I—why would you *not* think I was for real?"

Because every time he's brought it up, I thought he was just daydreaming out loud. "Well, because . . . you've been talking about it for so long, but you've never actually done anything about it. And I thought you liked your job."

"I like my coworkers. The work is . . . whatever," he says with a shrug. "Advertising's not what I want to do for the rest of my life. I want to work in the music industry. I know I need to make the move. I'm just freaked out about how hard it is to break into."

And for good reason, I think. I still can't believe he's serious about this. What, am I going to have to become some kind of rock 'n' roll wife? Hang out with him at concerts, gritting my teeth as I push my earplugs back in for the eleventh time? "Well . . . what aspect of the business are you thinking about?"

He runs his hand through his hair. "I don't know. Talent scouting is the obvious one; A and R. But that's what everybody wants to do, and those guys never get to have a life outside of work. I'd rather work on something long-term than always be chasing the next hot thing. So maybe talent management. Or June said to look at being a rep for songwriters, trying to get their work placed with artists or in commercials or whatever. Ugh, I'm getting overwhelmed just talking about it. I wouldn't even know where to start."

But in a blinding flash, I do. "Start with your dad."

He frowns. "The stuff he did was cool, but lighting and effects isn't really what I'm into. . . ."

"No, but he must know *everyone,*" I say, with the force of conviction. I'm positive I'm onto something here. "And if he doesn't know exactly the people you need to talk to, I'm sure the people he knows know them."

"Damn. You're right," he says wonderingly. "I never thought of it that way. His side of it was so specific . . . I didn't think about his contacts. Trying to get a job in music has always just felt like this mountain I was standing at the bottom of, with no idea how to get up."

"You start walking," I say. "One foot after another. Don't look at how far the top is, just walk. That's the only way to get up a mountain."

"You're amazing," Ollie says, and winds one of my curls around his index finger until he can pull me close enough to kiss.

A long time later, I glance at my phone: 5:16 A.M. "Well, we did it," I yawn.

Ollie catches the yawn from me. "Did what?"

"We talked all through the night. Just like on our first date. Which we were conceptually reenacting."

He peers at his own phone, half-lost under the pillow. "Damn. I guess we better call it."

"Wrong, Oliver. We're going to watch the sun come up."

He yawns again. "But I want to sleep."

"Come on, look at that," I say, pointing out the open tent flap toward the lake. The blackness of the night after moonset has separated into shapes—lawn, lake, tree line, sky—and I can see the beginning of a rosy glow appearing over the trees across the lake. "I want to do something to greet the day properly."

"Like what?"

"I would suggest skinny-dipping, but that water is freezing. How about the swing?"

"You'll get splinters in your ass," he yawns.

"I'm going to put my clothes back on. And so are you, because you're going to push me." I dig up his T-shirt and toss it onto his face. He groans, but he tugs it on.

By the time we've pulled ourselves together and straggled down to the old rope swing at the crest of the bluff overlooking the water, the sun is just about to peep above the horizon. Howard put this swing up when Ollie was a kid, and it's been one of his favorite places at the house ever since. Rachel keeps threatening to make him take it down, because who knows how strong that tree branch is, the swing reaches out over the drop-off to the water at its full extension, and so on and so on . . . but the swing remains.

I thump down on the bowed wooden seat—which squeals in protest and which, in fairness to Rachel, I do have to admit feels kind of precarious—then pedal backward to gain momentum for my launch. The grass is soft and damp with dew under my bare feet. I push back as far as I can get, then kick forward, legs extended.

Air rushes around me, cool and impossibly fresh. The grass vanishes, and with the dark water far beneath me, I'm sailing through the open air. Flight is a glorious thing. "I can fly higher than an eeeeeeea-gle," I sing, as I go soaring into the dawn. I'm no June Kang, but what I lack in finesse I make up for in enthusiasm. And in volume. "'Cause you are the wind beneath my wings."

I hear Ollie laugh, and when I swing back again he's ready behind me, pushing me right back into the air so I can fly again.

16

June

THE NIGHT OF THE JULY FOURTH PARTY, I GO TO BED EARLY, with the *pop-pop-pop* of fireworks ricocheting around the lake like gunshots. I skipped the bonfire; even had I not been extremely unsettled by the Caleb news, I was in no mood to watch Ollie and Terrance play, or to participate in the singing. I can't believe they're still doing it all this year. It's supposed to be carefree and fun; that is not the case tonight.

"Everyone was asking about you," Ollie says when he comes to bed, a little after eleven. "I missed hearing you sing."

"I sing for you all the time," I yawn, setting my tablet on the night table and switching off the lamp. "Did Caleb and your dad behave themselves?"

"Barely." He maneuvers across the bed toward me, avoiding Spencer, who has been curled at my feet in fear for his life from the fireworks. I fit my head into the crook of his shoulder.

"Are you going to talk to him tomorrow?"

"Yeah. It's going to be fine."

There were six distinct times today when I contemplated looking up the newspaper article about Caleb. I never went through with it, because it felt like the wrong thing to do. Sleazy, or underhanded somehow—even though it would just have been reading a newspaper story. It's entirely possible that reading it would have made me feel better; perhaps the allegation, whatever it is, is transparently bogus, and realizing that would set my mind at ease. But scavenging for information behind Ollie's back—any more than I already had—felt like a betrayal.

And then there was the last time, when I got as far as typing Caleb's name into my search bar, and the autofill suggested "Caleb Burwitz sexual assault" and my stomach almost ripped itself out of my body. Any situation where my brother-in-law's name pops up shackled to the phrase "sexual assault" on the Internet is not a situation that is going to be fine for a long, long time. But I wouldn't want to tell Ollie so, even if he'd known I'd heard the rumor. He gets tired of his role of peacekeeper between his father and brother, but I know he takes a certain beleaguered pride in it. Nobody else can manage them. Leslie always intends to help, but winds up getting aggressively defensive of Caleb; Rachel is too torn between them, and always too weakened by her guilt. I don't want to undercut Ollie's security on this front.

"Yeah, I'm sure it will be okay," I tell him. It's a harmless little lie, but as I sink toward sleep, unease vibrates inside me like the warning rattle of a snake's tail.

I am standing on the roof of the old apartment building, staring at the stars. As I stand there, face turned up to the sky, I'm wondering if maybe, when the earth eventually gets swallowed up by the ravenous, dying sun and everything goes supernova, she and I will find each other again. It's a thought she would have liked. "My carbon will bond onto your carbon," she would tell me, slipping her arm through mine to illustrate the link. I smile, and try to believe that it's enough.

And then I hear footsteps.

Footsteps that couldn't be anyone's but hers: quick and glad, launching her body toward me. A huge, perfect peony of joy blooms inside me, pushing so hard against my chest I can barely breathe, and I turn to her and she's there, she's really there, and I grab her into my arms and squeeze her against me until she starts to wriggle in that way she always did if you hugged her for too long, like a kitten or an impatient child.

"What is it?" she laughs, as the wind blows her long hair into her face, her skin pale against the inky sky.

"I thought you were gone," I say. How do I even begin to explain a thing like that?

She laughs again, and I drink the cool night air into my lungs, too dazed by relief to ask her where she's been or why she terrified me so. Because none of it matters now. She's here.

And then, with a ripping, grinding roar as if the earth itself had opened up, the piece of roof that she is standing on cracks and pitches downward. I notice too late how close her small bare feet are to the edge. I shout her name as I fling my hands out to grab her, but she's gone too far, too fast.

She does not scream. But I can see the terror in her face as she falls.

I crash out of the dream, hands clutching the blankets like they're a lifeline. I gulp air in and out, my eyes frantically searching the darkness to make sure I'm still right side up on solid ground, and Ollie sleepily stirs beside me.

"Sweetheart," he murmurs, lips against the back of my shoulder, "you okay?"

"Dream," I mumble, and he rubs his cheek against me.

"I'm sorry. Same one?"

I shake my head, trying to push the fear away. "No. It started off the same, but then it continued."

"Want me to get you some water?"

"Yes. Please."

By the time he comes back, I am lying on the floor, hugging Spencer, but I have mostly stopped trembling. I drink some of the water, then set the glass down on the table with a *thunk* and turn back to Ollie. "I'm scared to go back to sleep," I whisper, burrowing against him.

He hooks one arm and leg over me to pull me tight. "Do you want me to read to you?"

I shake my head.

"Do you want me to play for you?"

I shake my head again, and press my lips to his shoulder, then his throat. He kisses my eyebrow, my cheek, my lips. I welcome him, because I need him.

I lose myself in the heat of his mouth, the glide of his hands, the rasp of his beard against my face, the weight of his body on mine, the pressure of him inside me. With every touch and every gasp and every bitten lip, we promise that we are in love and compelled by each other. To each other. In these moments, all I need to keep me safe is Ollie's warmth, covering me, surrounding me. His breath mingling with mine: our very own blend of oxygen.

But when he drops back into sleep, hand curved over my hip while his chest rises and falls as steadily as breakers on a shore, I am alone again. The grief from the dream is still gnawing at me, hollowing me out, and I know that it won't let me sleep.

Faint gray light seeps into the room from the perimeter of the curtains, beckoning to me. I slip from the bed and tug on my clothes, throw a warm sweatshirt over top, and slide the screen door open.

Without the moon or stars, the darkness is almost impenetrable; only faint spots of brightness are dotted here and there along the lake . . . somebody's porch light left on, the row of street lamps at the park on the eastern shore. The murky glow from the towns beyond the horizon illuminates the sky just enough for me to make my way down to the water, past the lifeless remnants of the bonfire, through grass that clings cold and wet against my feet. This late, the lake is quiet: no fish, no birds, no waves, no motors. Just my footsteps on the dock, and the softest trickle of sound when a puff of wind nudges water to ripple against the pilings beneath me. I am completely alone.

I sit down at the end of the dock, draw my sweatshirt over my knees, and rest my chin on them. The silence of the lake gives me the strangest feeling that it's waiting for me to talk, and so I do.

"Leebee," I say, staring out over the black water, "I don't know what else to do but talk to you. I never did before because I knew you couldn't hear me, but being here I'm not so sure of that. I'm not so sure at all. And so, the first thing is that I love you, and I miss you so badly every single day that it still rips me up inside, and it feels like nobody understands that," I say through tears, wiping my cheeks with my thumbs. "It's just not right for you to be dead, it's *not right,* and I think the longer I live the less right it will feel, because the total of everything you're missing is just . . . my god, it's going to grow so high. It's huge already, it's a mountain made out of sunsets and jokes and trips and accomplishments and Sam, oh my god, everything Sam's been doing, just everything. It's a fucking mountain, Leeb, and I can't stand watching it get bigger and bigger and every day you're still not fucking *here.* How can you be twenty-five and gone forever? How?" I yell the last word into the sky, and it echoes like the cry of a wounded bird across the water.

"I just . . . I guess somehow I've been waiting for something to make it okay. Like, if I could make some kind of peace with it in my mind, then it wouldn't feel like this . . . obscene, gaping tear in the fabric of my universe. But there is *nothing* that will make it okay. Ever. Everything you're missing, it only makes it worse.

"And the thing I really cannot handle, Leeb, the thing that pulls at me the most, is Ollie. I love him so fucking much." I drop my face into my hands and sob, rocking back and forth on my hips. "I love him *so fucking much,* and the only reason I get to have him love me back is because you're dead. Because you died, he and I are together. You died, and so he didn't marry you, and then he ran away, and then we found each other again and we're in love and getting married and I can't imagine my life without him in it, I can't imagine loving somebody else like I love him . . . but I only have this because *you died.* How completely disgusting and messed up is that? How can I ever be completely happy, knowing what happened to give that to me?

"And I would give it all back in a second; I would give it up a thousand times in a thousand different lives if it meant we didn't lose you. I would do it with joy. But I *can't.* I can't make that choice, because it never was a choice. . . . I lost you, and then I gained what you lost. And now I have what you should have had, this future and this ring and this man who makes me laugh and lifts me up and has the kindest heart I've ever known and who makes me feel so known and loved and taken care of. I mean, god, the only reason I know how good he is to me is because you showed it to me. I was still dating losers while you were with someone who valued you, and I finally saw it.

"And I'm so *sorry.* I'm *so* sorry, because Ollie is the biggest piece of that mountain of everything you're missing. I know he'd be the biggest piece to you. The way he teases, the way he cares, the way he asks questions and listens to the answers, the way he adores his parents and can't wait to have kids, and hell, even the way he's a freaking miracle in bed. That was all yours. He was yours. And sometimes I wish I could enjoy it without always feeling this guilt at the back of my mind. But then I remember that I'm alive, so if that means I have to live with the guilt over stumbling onto what you lost, well, at least I'm *living* with it."

As soon as the last words fall out of my mouth, the silence takes them. The night absorbs them, and gives me nothing back. I get to my feet and stand, shivering, in the chilly air. Dark water is all around me, but I have a safe, dry path back to the shore. A gust of wind rushes down from the trees, brushing my hair against my cheek, and I clutch my sweatshirt tighter around my body. I'm still alone.

Of course I know that Leah cannot answer me. But finally spewing all that stuff out loud doesn't make me feel any more certain that she heard, or that she knows, or that she understands . . . or that she forgives.

17

Leah

I ALWAYS FEEL A LITTLE CHEATED WHEN IT RAINS WHILE WE'RE at Seneca. Like, c'mon, summer, you're supposed to do your shiny sunny thing every day so we can zoom around on the lake. That was the deal.

But instead, the day after the Fourth, we've been stuck inside since morning while a soft rain puddles on the flagstone terrace outside the family room. Terrance, too besotted to play hard to get, materialized after breakfast and has been stuck to June like green on grass. To my delight, Caleb muttered something about being tired of the fifth-wheel position and headed out to meet a friend, so the remaining four of us have been working our way through the Biermans' stash of board games, their faded cardboard cases battered from years of use. I was infuriated to discover that Terrance's easygoing veneer conceals a ruthless Monopoly shark.

"Why?" I demand, as he sweeps the board clean after yet another victory. "How?"

"Two older sisters," he says. "Give no mercy, for you shall receive none."

I pull the Scrabble box from the stack next to the recliner and slap it down on the coffee table. "You want no mercy? Prepare for annihilation."

"Now you've done it," Ollie says to Terrance. "Tiny Scrabble Assassin is out for blood."

"Is that so?"

"She's impossible to beat. She memorized all the two-letter words. Natural affinity for very small things," he adds, and I deliver a swift kick to his shin.

A snorting noise emerges from the direction of June's lowered face, but she's not bold enough to look up.

"By the way," says Ollie, "how *are* your sisters? I know Sonya's still in Florida, but I thought we would have seen Valerie this week."

"Ugh, drama. Val's not speaking to our parents right now."

"Yikes. Why not?"

"Oh, she let it slip that her new boyfriend, who she'd been praising to high heaven, couldn't come to the lake because he had to spend the weekend with his wife and children. My parents . . . did not dig it."

"Whoa," says June, slim fingers pausing mid-sort of her Scrabble tiles. "Did she know he was married when they got together?"

"Oh yeah. He's a partner in a different group at her law firm. But, you know, his wife doesn't understand him. The marriage is lifeless. He's just staying with her because of the kids. Valerie's the one he really loves. And on and on and bullshit on. All the tired crap you'd expect a cheating scumbag to say."

Uh-oh. This has swerved into dangerous territory, and Terrance clearly has no idea.

"Maybe he actually means it," Ollie says. "Maybe it's true."

Terrance gives a scoffing laugh. "Are you serious, man? That shit is *never* true. The dude is bored with his life, Valerie makes him feel relevant again, and so he tells her what she wants to hear. And my fool sister bought every word of it. So, she didn't like our folks telling her they raised her better than to be a home-wrecker."

I stab my finger at him. "Wait a second, why is *she* getting the blame?" I demand. "The boyfriend is responsible for his own actions."

"Of course he is. But Val should respect herself more than to be somebody's mistress. And she should respect the wife and kids enough not to intrude on their family."

"But what if it's really true?" says Ollie, leaning forward with his elbows on his knees. "What if the marriage is ending, and this guy means what he says about loving Val? Just because you have a kid with somebody doesn't mean you should stay chained to them forever. We all have friends whose parents stayed together 'for the kids,' and the kids sincerely wish they hadn't. Staying married to someone who makes you miserable isn't the way to be the best parent you can."

"I agree with that," June says. "My aunt and uncle can't stand each other, but divorce isn't really a thing you do in a nice Korean family. At least not in their generation. So instead they've been slowly poisoning each other for thirty years. It's kinda screwed my cousins up to say the least."

"Yeah. Can't argue with that," Terrance says, gently squeezing her knee. "But the cheating is a whole other issue."

"What are you going to say next, 'Once a cheater, always a cheater'?" snaps Ollie.

Terrance is staring at Ollie like his face is falling off. "Dude, is there something I don't know about you?"

Ollie sighs and takes a long sip of his beer before he answers. "My parents got together while my mom was married to Caleb's dad. The way people talk about cheating is always so black-and-white. The cheater is always the criminal; the other person's the villain. My parents aren't proud of how things happened, but the story's a lot more complex than the outline you'd judge if you didn't know them."

"What's the story?" says June quietly, after a pause.

"Caleb's dad is a piece of human garbage," Ollie says, with that hardness in his voice that only shows up when he talks about his mom's first husband. "She married him at twenty-two because she loved him and she figured that was as good as it got, and then she had Caleb a few years later. Seth was always controlling, but he got worse after Caleb was born. Nothing she did was ever good enough. He ran her whole life, made her quit her job at the library because he convinced her she wasn't doing a good enough job looking after Caleb. My dad was a fraternity brother of Seth's; he hadn't liked him too much when they were in college, but when my dad moved to Rochester for work he didn't really know many people, so he started hanging out with Seth. And then he met my mom and that was it."

"What happened?" says June.

"He fell in love with her. And the more he got to see how Seth treated her, the less guilty he felt about it. So, he stole her."

"Like Eric Clapton stole Pattie Boyd from George Harrison," June says, and Ollie shoots her a smile.

"That's what my dad says. Except my parents stayed married. They belong together."

Everyone is quiet for a minute. Then Terrance scratches his head and carefully speaks. "Listen, man, I'm not going to tell you what your parents did was wrong. We're all real glad you're sitting here talking to us. But I just think . . . I mean, what if the ex-husband hadn't been a bastard? What if he was a decent guy?"

"He isn't."

"I know, but—"

"My mom's broken wrist from when he pushed her to the floor says he isn't," says Ollie, voice pulled tight enough to crack.

"I *know* he isn't," Terrance persists, and my toes curl with discomfort until I remember that Ollie would only let someone he trusts push him this far. "Pretend it's somebody else. Pretend it's . . . pretend it's me, and my wife falls for some other guy. Still think all's fair in love and war?"

"Yeah," says Ollie flatly, crossing his arms over his chest. "I do. No, nobody should cheat, but I think we only get one real shot at true love. If the situation you're in is the wrong one, and then you find the right person somewhere else, and you *know* they're the right person—you have to go for it. You *have* to. Life will not wait."

There's a long, loaded silence. I count to four until I can't take it any longer.

"Soooo, yeah, he picked me up in the bathroom line at Off the Wagon," I say, and everyone laughs gratefully.

"And she was single at the time," adds June, to more laughter.

"I think some guy Leah might have been dating in another life just felt his balls retract," Terrance says.

"I get it, though," says June quietly. "Cheating isn't an honorable thing to do, but if that's your one right person and you know it, and if you wait then you might miss your chance . . ." She spreads her hands wide and shrugs.

Well, that's a new one. June occasionally gets exasperated with me because I see the world in terms that *she says* are too starkly black-and-white; but come on, cheating is a no-brainer. Under any circumstances. Yes, Rachel and Howard are wonderful people who were clearly destined to be together; and yes, Rachel's ex-husband is a bastard; *and also* it was shitty of Rachel to start boning Howard before she ended her marriage, *and* it was shitty of Howard to go after her before she had. All of those things are simultaneously true.

Ollie, now clearly wanting the topic to die its final death, just gives a little nod and takes a sip of his beer. It always takes me by surprise when he gets intense about something instead of being Mr. Mellow all the time, but I have to say, I'm psyched that this time it was about true love.

* * *

My impatience at being trapped inside finally boils over after dinner, when I forcibly move the party to the hot tub by changing into my bikini and marching in to wait until the rest of them join me. The deck upstairs shelters us from the rain, but the cool, damp night air makes a pleasant contrast with the bubbling heat of the water submerging me from the chest down. My excitement over June and Terrance is rising along with my alcohol content; they are sparking off each other like crazy. He's got an impishness to him that plays off her dry sense of humor perfectly. We're having so much fun that I don't even mind when Caleb reappears and sloshes into the hot tub next to Terrance.

I don't mind, that is, until I notice he's been drinking. His laugh booms loud, his face is flushed, and his smile has that blurriness to it that only alcohol can give.

"So, Caleb," I say, "leave any wounded people in a pile of smoking wreckage on your drive home?"

He doesn't get it. "What are you talking about?"

"You look like you're nice and loose. Did you drive home like that?"

The smile slides off his face. "I can handle myself."

"Can you? Or have you so far just gotten lucky?"

"'Lucky.'" The word is a whip-crack of humorless laughter. "Oh yeah, I'm *so* lucky. So lucky I got laid off from my job in software—the 'industry of the future'—while my buddy Bruce in finance just got a new gig that's paying him well over two hundred K."

Oh, no. Absolutely not. "You *are* lucky," I rage, but just as I'm opening my mouth to enumerate the ways—he can stand, he can climb stairs, he can effortlessly navigate every single structure on earth instead of just the micro percentage with a ramp and an elevator—June puts her hand on my forearm under the water.

"Don't pick a fight, Leeb," she murmurs behind my ear. "It's not

Caleb's fault that Sam got hurt. He's just a guy who's scared about being unemployed."

Her low, quiet voice cools me down like rain on a campfire. And she's right. Sometimes I get these random spikes of pain over the injustice of my brother's injury, but it isn't fair to take it out on other people. Belatedly, I notice Ollie gripping his forehead, jaw tensed.

"We're all lucky," I say, releasing my resentment with my breath. "We're in a hot tub on Seneca Lake, on vacation." I look for a smile from Ollie, but he won't meet my eyes.

"Amen," says Terrance, raising his beer can in a salute. He pulls June back for a kiss as she passes on her way inside to the bathroom. Goddamn, I miss that can't-keep-my-hands-off-you stage.

"And anyway, you'll find another job soon," Ollie tells his brother.

"Don't patronize me, Golden Child."

"I wasn't," Ollie says mildly. "Just stating the obvious. You will not be unemployed for long."

"I fuckin' better not. Bruce said I should consider going back for an MBA. Because now I'm getting career advice from one of the frosh I RA'd."

I can totally imagine Caleb as an RA in a freshman dorm. All the dudes must have loved him. Most of the girls must have loved him, too. I'm sure a few, with keen judgment and good taste, did not.

After a few minutes, June returns from inside with a fresh beer, wobbly after heavier-than-usual alcohol consumption. She mounts the steps to the tub, stretches one long leg over the lip of the tub like a stork, and lowers her foot onto the seat to step in, *oooh*ing at the heat. But as she lifts her back leg to clear the edge, she tips off balance and falls, crashing down with one leg in the water and the other one crumpled awkwardly along the edge of the tub.

"Ohhhh, that'll leave a mark," drawls Caleb, over her gasp of pain.

"Ow, ow, ow. Oh my god, ow. *Damn it.*" June's voice sounds like she's fighting tears.

"Are you okay?" says Ollie urgently, gripping the arm she braced against his shoulder as she tried to break her fall.

"I'm fine," she mumbles, then blinks and yanks her hand away. "It just really hurt. Yeeow. This'll definitely go down as my most exotic bruise. Pardon me while I go collect my faculties."

While she unwinds herself and straggles upright, Terrance leaps from the tub and grabs a waiting towel to fold around her. She shoots him a thin but grateful smile. He tucks his arm around her shoulders and leads her inside.

"Please don't say whatever it is you're about to," Ollie says to Caleb, whose smirk is threatening to burst right off his face. "Do not."

Eyebrow cocked, Caleb mimes locking his lips, followed by tossing away a key.

We sit in silence for a minute, then Ollie surges to his feet, sending a small wave undulating around the tub. "I'm just going to check on her."

"You sure you want to interrupt their game of doctor and patient?" Caleb calls to his retreating back, but Ollie ignores him.

Fantastic. I'm alone with Caleb again. I appreciate Ollie's chivalry, but he really could have left the comforting to Terrance. I stare out at the dark night while I drag my brain for some kind of small talk to make with Caleb. But then he beats me to it.

"All right, Leah. I want you to tell me something."

He leans forward like he did the day before, elbows on his thighs in an I'm-listening pose. There's a pause, during which I'm obviously supposed to volley back an encouraging "What's that?" Thing is, I'm not curious. So I don't ask.

"I have always wondered," he says, voice soft and playful, "how

my kid brother managed to bag a little hottie like you. He's so or-
dinary, and you're so . . . fiery. Feels like there's a piece of the picture I'm missing. But more likely there's something *you're* missing.
So, you know . . ."

I gape at him, dumbfounded. "No. I don't think I do know."

"When you're ready to make an upgrade," he says, leaning the
rest of the way across the tub and wrapping his hands around my
lower thighs, "my door is definitely open."

I freeze in panic that he's going to try to kiss me, but he pulls
back, fingers dragging along my legs. I shudder at the sensation of
his skin pressing against mine. And then he stretches his thick
arms along the back of the hot tub and regards me with a satisfied
smile.

What the actual fuck. Did that just happen? Did Ollie's brother
seriously just make a pass at me? My *boyfriend's brother*?

My stomach churns like the water in this hellhole of a hot tub.
Ollie is going to come back any minute now, and I don't even know
what to do. Or what to say. I don't want to make a big commotion;
I have to handle this without freaking out. Caleb is several light-
years out of line, but he is Ollie's *brother*.

Hoping he won't notice my shaking hand, I take a sip of beer,
my eyes meeting his over the upraised can. "There are so many
ways I could respond to that," I say.

"I can hardly wait to hear them," he says, grinning.

"So, your original question was how Ollie . . . 'bagged' me. I
think you want me to make some cheap joke about the size of his
penis or how good he is in bed. Because the implication is that
Ollie's deficient in some way. Which is, what?" I say, my tone evening out as I start to hit my stride. "He doesn't have huge muscles,
or drink a lot, or brag to impress people like you so obviously need
to, so that makes him, what . . . *lame*?"

Caleb's head kicks back in surprise. "Hey, it was just a joke."

"Ah yes, the universal excuse for shitty comments that don't land well. *Just a joke.*"

He makes a *tsk-tsk* noise against his teeth. "See, that's what I like about you. You're such a fireball. You keep me on my toes. It's good for me."

"I'm not anything *for* a human beer stain like you, except your *brother's girlfriend.* I am not a slot for you to try to stick your dick in; I am a person, and I could not possibly be less interested in any so-called *upgrade,*" I continue loudly, swooping huge air quotes as I say the last word.

"Okay," he snaps, throwing up one hand. "*Enough.* Like I told you, I was just kidding around. You don't need to insult me. Just drop it."

My jaw clenches at the sheer outrageousness of *him* getting offended with *me.* I tap my beer can loudly against the rim of the hot tub as another minute passes, and still none of the others returns. *For god's sake, Ollie.* June's bruised crotch does not require the attention of two additional people. I'm not sitting here with this lunatic any longer.

Without another word to Caleb, I stand up and step down to the chilly stone terrace.

"Where are you going?" says Caleb, and I'm satisfied to hear a note of alarm in his voice.

"Inside." I seize the nearest towel and whip it around my body, yanking it up to my armpits.

"Bring me back another PBR, would you?"

Before I can stop myself, I wheel back to face him and forcefully give him the finger. My other hand is jerked loose from the doorknob as it opens from the inside, and there's a beat while Ollie assesses the situation.

"I leave you two alone for five minutes and you're fighting again," he says. "What is it this time?"

I glance at Caleb's face and shiver. He's smiling tightly, but his eyes are narrowed in warning. My heart slams my blood through my veins while I waver. I don't want to let Caleb get away with this, but I have to figure out how to broach it with Ollie. The last thing I want to do is start a war inside their family. "Nothing," I say.

Every nerve in my body burns from the lie.

18

June

OLLIE HAS BEEN DOWN ON THE DOCK, TALKING WITH CALEB, for almost twenty minutes already: Ollie's smaller shape pacing against the backdrop of the sparkling water, Caleb's immovable as a boulder. From my spot on the deck, I can hear raised voices, but no actual words. I lower my gaze to the tablet in my lap, but I've forgotten my place again. I think I've reread the same sentence fifteen times.

I pinch my lip between my fingers as I raise my head to look at them again. Contrary to Ollie's hope, it doesn't seem like things are going to be fine.

"They'll get through it," says Rachel from the deck chair next to me, shading her eyes with one hand as she watches her sons. "They always do." But I watch her fingers drum the condensation on her glass of iced coffee, as restless as a pianist keying an arpeggio.

"I get the impression this is much bigger than a disagreement," I say.

She doesn't answer right away. "It's a misunderstanding," she finally says.

Ollie's mother gave him his gray-blue eyes, his love for books and obscure board games, and his sense of empathy. I can see so much of her in him: her gentleness, her peace-loving nature, and, specifically, a kind of dogged and stubborn love for Caleb that draws them together in the face of Howard's scorn. But what if it's misplaced? What if, despite all their defenses and excuses, Caleb doesn't really deserve it?

Just then, Ollie abruptly turns his back on Caleb and stalks toward the stairs up to the lawn. I'm on my feet before I even hear him shout my name.

"Tell me," I say as I reach Ollie in the middle of the lawn, but he grabs my hand and starts pulling me past the house, toward the front.

"Come on, we're leaving."

I scramble after him. "What? Right now? Slow down, Ollie. What the hell is happening?"

"Not leaving for New York," he says, voice pulsing with impatience. "Leaving here for the day."

"Where are we going?"

"I don't know. I don't care right now. Please just come with me." His jaw is rigid; his face has gone all angles and sharp lines again.

"Let me get my bag."

At the main road, Ollie turns us north. Anxiety scrapes at me like fingernails as we drive, growing stronger with each silent minute that passes. The car slows as we enter the outskirts of the town of Geneva, at the northern tip of the lake. Genteel nineteenth-century houses line the road on both sides, but their smug, placid beauty grates on me.

Once inside the town, Ollie turns onto the street that leads to Geneva's waterfront park and jerks the car into a spot. Without waiting for me, he slams the car door shut and strides down the grass toward the water. I hurry after him and find him on a park bench, elbows on his knees and his face in his hands.

"Okay, enough. You need to tell me what's happening, right

now," I say, and for the first time in twenty minutes, he looks at me as if he actually sees me.

"Caleb is in some serious trouble," he says. "He was at his friend Cooper's bachelor party in Rochester a few weeks back, and he got drunk and messy and hassled some girl."

"'Hassled'? Can you be more specific?"

"She filed charges against him for sexual assault. Said he grabbed her, pushed her against a wall, and groped her while he kissed her. He admits he fooled around with her, but he says it was consensual."

"Grabbing and pushing and groping doesn't sound consensual to me," I say.

He brushes his thumb briefly along my collarbone. "June, I literally did every one of those things to you that time I kissed you outside the bar at Halloween."

"I wanted you to."

"Well, he says this woman did, too."

"What exactly does he say went on?"

"He says they were flirting all night, and he had too much to drink—"

"Christ, I hate it when people blame their shitty behavior on being drunk," I spit. "Handle yourself like a fucking adult or accept the responsibility if you don't."

"I know," he says. "I said the same thing. But alcohol has a known effect. Cal says he was coming off a bad fight with Leslie and he got caught up in missing his party days, so things got too friendly with this girl, and they made out in the hallway for a minute. And then he came to his senses and stopped. And came clean and apologized to Leslie the next day. The end."

"No, clearly *not* the end," I say loudly. "Why the hell would she file criminal charges against him if she'd been into the make-out? Nobody puts themselves through that unless they were actually harmed."

"He thinks she's trying to get him to pay her off."

"Oh, give me a goddamned break. Every time a man's accused of something like this, he says the woman's looking for a payout. Either that or it's some elaborate revenge."

"Well . . . I think sometimes that's true."

I recoil like a whiplash, shock quivering through every nerve. "Ollie! Please tell me you did not just say that!"

He stretches his hand to me, palm up. "I said *sometimes*. Rarely. I know most of the time it's true. But at the same time, women are capable of dishonesty and manipulation. So, that could be happening here. Right?"

His voice is nakedly pleading. He wants so badly for me to agree. I swallow carefully, but I do not take his outstretched hand. "Okay, so how exactly do you think this woman ascertained the contents of Caleb's bank account?"

He lets his hand drop to his thigh. "I don't know. Expensive watch, fancy credit card getting a workout at the register? He brags. Especially when he's been drinking."

"This is Rochester, Ollie, not Vegas. Caleb wasn't using an Amex black card to pay for a night of bottles in the Tao VIP."

"Fuuuuuuuuck," he growls, dropping his head into his hands again. He drags his hands through his hair and jerks upright, then walks toward the lake as if he's trying to leave something behind.

I follow him and plant myself in his path, arms crossed over my chest.

"You're right," he says, crossing his own arms as he meets my eyes. In the sunlight, the hair dusted over his forearms looks golden against his tanned skin. "I just don't know what the hell to think. I know he can be an asshole sometimes, but he's better than he used to be. Except for this, he's been a good husband to Leslie . . . and he's a great dad to Eli. He's my *brother*, baby. I love him." His shoulders hunch upward apologetically.

Whatever Caleb has done, I hate that it's made Ollie feel like he has to apologize for loving him. I think Ollie has spent his whole life apologizing for loving Caleb . . . or apologizing for Caleb in general. I really wish he could have stopped by now.

"I know you do," I say. "And I know you don't want to believe he's capable of this."

"Of course I don't want to believe he's capable of this. I mean, how are you so ready to believe he *is*? You didn't seem surprised when I dropped a pretty big bomb in your lap a few minutes ago."

I flick my eyes to the patchy grass beneath my sandals, then make myself meet his gaze. "I asked Terrance yesterday."

"Oh god damn it, June!" Ollie yells.

"You wouldn't tell me!" I yell back. "I hated that you wouldn't tell me."

"So you couldn't trust my reasons, or value my family's privacy, or hold your patience for *one single day*—and you went running to your ex instead?"

"My '*ex*'? Give me a fucking break."

Hands on hips, we glare at each other. Ollie and I don't fight often, but when we do, it goes from zero to shouting if we let it get out of control. I close the space between us and curl my palm around his arm. He covers my hand with his own.

"So . . . Caleb," he says on a gusty sigh. "What the hell am I supposed to make of it?"

"Stop trying to make it make sense. What does your gut tell you?"

He's quiet for a long time. "My gut says it was a misunderstanding. Cal's a messy drunk, and I think he laid it on a little thick. I don't think he had any intention to force her into anything."

"Impact matters more than intent," I say, jerking my hand away. "Every single time. That's why drunk drivers go to jail."

He makes a small, strained noise.

"Look, I don't like this at all. Not one little bit. I'm not seeing how this is an innocent mistake. 'Misunderstanding' doesn't explain criminal charges. And money doesn't, either. Cal is not some high-profile celebrity; he's just a guy."

"He's not a rapist."

"She didn't say he was. She said he was somewhere in between harmless and rapist."

Ollie grinds his palms down his face. "Jesus, how are we even having a conversation about where my brother falls on the spectrum of sexual violence? He wouldn't do something like this. He doesn't have it in him to hurt anybody!"

"Are you *absolutely* sure about that? Think about his father," I say slowly, and Ollie's face blanches.

He blinks a few times, taking it in, then slowly blows out a breath.

I wrap my arms around him, and he pulls me tight and presses a kiss to my head.

"God, do you really think it's possible?"

I shiver as a bead of sweat rolls down the back of my neck. "How old was Caleb that time he got pissed at your mom and said, 'My dad is right, you're nothing but a lying whore'?"

"Fourteen," Ollie says.

"And Seth's the person who taught him how to be a man." I pull away a little until I can see his face. "Listen, I'm going to be really honest here, because I think it's called for. I know Caleb had a hard childhood in some ways, partly because your dad decided to punish him for being Seth's son. You feel guilty because of that, and because your dad so obviously prefers you. You've worked so hard to try to keep a good relationship with him, and you stick up for him when other people are down on him. I know you want to think the best of him. And I love you for all of that. So I've been trying for a year and a half to like Caleb for your sake . . . but I find it hard. Partly it's the way he likes to pick at you, but it's not just that. Something about him makes me uneasy. I don't know how to explain it. But it's always been there. Ever since the first time I met him, up here. I don't know how candid she ever was about it, but Leah couldn't stand him. And you know she was a damn good judge of character."

Ollie's face has gone from bad to worse. He looks like he feels physically ill. And I'm not far behind, because the memories are rushing in on me now, one after the other.

"Like, do you remember that comment he made about that girl he'd been dating, how basically she'd only been sleeping with him because he had money, and when he got laid off, she dumped him for a better target? Or the way he never even bothered to hide it when he stared at Leah's body? She didn't make a big deal about it because she didn't want to rock the boat with you and your family, but I know he made her really uncomfortable. And then there was that whole weird thing where he disappeared for two days . . . and when we finally saw him after everything happened, he had a massive shiner on one eye. I never did hear where that came from." I should stop, but I can't stop, because the horror on Ollie's face is not just from what I'm saying. There's something else here. Fear. Guilt. Why the fuck is there *guilt* on Ollie's face when I bring up Leah and Caleb?

"What?" I say. "What is it?"

He rubs his face with one hand, fingers digging into the skin. He doesn't answer me.

"Ollie, seriously, what's wrong? What did Caleb do? Did he do something to hurt Leah?" I clutch his arm and yank it so hard I scratch him with my nails. "Did he hurt her?" My voice is high and hysterical. "You have to tell me right now. You know I wasn't there when it happened. Is there something I never heard? Is Leah dead because of Caleb?"

"No!" he says, the word bursting out of him. "No. My god, June, no. Just . . . no. *No.* Caleb had nothing to do with it. You can't seriously think that."

Suddenly, it strikes me that I only ever heard the story once.

From Ollie, crazed with fear and panic. At the time, I'd barely even registered Caleb's presence. It never seemed relevant; the only thing that mattered was that Leah was gone.

"Why was he even there?" I demand.

"He was there because he was hanging out with us. There was nothing wrong about it. It was an accident. Jesus Christ, what do you think of me, that you could even ask me this?" Ollie's voice is as raw as a nerve exposed to the air.

"I love you," I say. "But you love your brother. For as long as I've known you, you've been cutting him slack, making excuses for him, smoothing over his problems. But something's not right with him."

He rests his hands on my shoulders and pinches as if he's trying to snuff out a match. "Stop it," he says. "Stop. Please, you've got to stop before this gets any further out of hand. I swear to you on the souls of our unborn children, Caleb did *not* hurt Leah. It was not his fault that she died. *It was an accident.*"

"I know it was an accident," I say. "But impact is greater than intent. You have to tell me this: Was there some kind of impact that he had?"

"No. I swear it to you. Caleb was in absolutely no way to blame."

I search his face, the most beloved face in my entire world. There's love, and fear, and grief, and need in his face—there's yearning for me to believe him. But instead of what I'm looking for, the pure and steady calm of truth, the thing I find is guilt.

19

Leah

"ALL RIGHT, LEEB. THE JIG IS UP. TELL ME WHAT YOU'RE UPSET about, right now, 'cause we're not leaving till you do."

Ollie, damn his coal-black heart, has chosen to make his stand in the middle of a footbridge spanning the gorge of Watkins Glen, near the southern tip of Seneca. It's largely a symbolic gesture, because the bridge is wide enough to allow me to walk around him and pass, or to retreat to solid ground—but he is banking on my being too proud to turn back. He is also banking on my being too nervous about the bridge to willingly walk its length without him ahead of me.

I try to peer unobtrusively around his shoulder, but the view— narrow stone bridge connecting to rocky cliff face, all of it damp with runoff from the surrounding forest and spray from the wa- terfall beneath—fails to fill my sails with wind, and so I stall. "This really isn't a good place to discuss it," I say, jerking my chin at the family that's passing to our left: dad in front, two young girls trail- ing behind him and mom bringing up the rear.

"You've had all day to discuss it, and you haven't," he says, arms crossed over his chest. "And as soon as we leave here, we'll be back at the house with the others, so as far as I'm concerned it's now or never. Cough it up. You know I don't play the 'What's wrong?'/'Nothing' game."

My cheeks heat at the injustice of this. "I'm not playing games; I just haven't figured out how to bring it up to you."

"Okay, fair. Progress. Let's get down to the main trail." He takes my hand and leads me the rest of the way across the bridge, then from there down some very wet stone steps to a pathway cut into the looming wall of striated dark stone. I wasn't exactly aflame with desire to come here today; hiking in the Glen had been June's idea. But after she changed the plan so she could spend the day hanging with Terrance and some of his friends on nearby Keuka Lake—thanks, June—Ollie decided he still wanted to come. So here I am, reeking of bug spray and failing deodorant, trying to fake excitement about trees and rocks and waterfalls, instead of practicing my slalom on the monoski or floating on a tube with a Southern Tier in my hand.

"So," says Ollie, gesturing at the alcove along the gorge trail that he's found for our stopping point, "hit me." He sits down on the stone wall with his back to the waterfall, and rests one ankle on his opposite knee. "What's going on in that head of yours?"

I sit down next to him and stare away from him, down the stream. The actual answer to his question is *Way too much*. My head started spinning at Caleb's bizarre come-on last night and hasn't stopped since. None of it makes sense. Not what Caleb did, not how I responded. Caleb—I guess—was behaving in character, if that character includes a much deeper capacity for inappropriateness than I'd ever suspected. But I don't know what the deal is with me.

If yesterday morning you'd given me the setup of what happened, and asked me what I would do, I would have told you: Slap the asshole in the face. Get away from him as fast as possible. Tell Ollie the whole thing, and let the family chips fall where they may. There is no ambiguity about what Caleb said and did to me. It was wrong, completely wrong. Completely out of line. He deserved nothing less than for me to do exactly what I just described.

But the thing is . . . I didn't. I mean, sure, I shut him down. Once I recovered from the initial shock. But I didn't call him out for touching me. I didn't get out of the tub right away. In fact, I stayed so long that when I finally got out, Caleb thought I was going on a freaking *beer run,* as opposed to trying to put space between myself and his repulsive notions. And then Ollie, when he met me at the door, gave me the perfect opening to tell what happened, but did I take it? No, I lied like a fucking chickenshit. Because in that moment, Caleb scared me.

"Caleb . . ." The gust of defiance that made me start talking abruptly peters out as I realize I still don't know what to say next.

"Caleb what, babe?" Ollie prompts.

Come on, Tessaro. This is Ollie. Ollie has got your back no matter what. "Okay. This is so awkward, but *I'm* not the one who made it awkward," I say, my voice heating up. "When you left us alone in the hot tub last night, Caleb hit on me."

Ollie looks like a cartoon character that just got clocked in the head with an anvil. "What do you mean?" he manages finally.

"Exactly what I said. While you were inside, Caleb made a pass at me."

"What did he say?"

"He asked me how you managed to 'bag a little hottie' like me, and he said when I was ready for an upgrade, his door was open."

Ollie groans and gathers the skin between his eyes into a pinch. "His sense of humor is disgusting. I'm sorry, Leeb."

I angle my head toward him. "Ol. He wasn't kidding."

"Of course he was kidding, babe. My brother wouldn't hit on my girlfriend, that's insanity."

"I agree with you that it's insanity, yet that is exactly what he did."

Ollie frowns and studies me in silence as he deliberates what to say. "Sweetheart. I'm really sorry that he offended you, but you know how he is. He likes seeing if he can get a rise out of people. And he knows you're an easy mark, because you always take his bait. But he obviously overstepped on this. I'll talk to him about it as soon as we get back and let him know he was out of line."

"I already told him that! I told him he was out of line!"

"Okay, well . . . good, then."

He's trying to be encouraging, but it isn't enough. "Saying he was out of line is the understatement of the freaking millennium," I snap. "I told him he was disgusting and to leave me the hell alone. I already said all of that. But I'm still really upset that it happened at all. I shouldn't *have* to tell him those things, because no decent person would have said it in the first place."

"Of course not. I'm sorry he grossed you out. I'll make sure he apologizes."

I knot my trembling hands in my lap, on the edge of telling him about Caleb grabbing my thighs. I want to do it so badly my mouth is watering. Ollie clearly isn't comprehending how bad what happened actually was. But if I tell him everything, he will punch his brother right in his smirking mouth. Which is no less than the asshole deserves. And yet if it happens here, at the lake house, with Rachel and Howard around, it would make the family implode. Howard would use it as an excuse to kick Caleb out and maybe even ban him from the house; and watching her husband and younger son feuding with her oldest would rip Rachel's heart in half. I just can't unleash that hell on Ollie.

"I really am sorry," Ollie says again, taking my hand and squeezing it. "I promise I will talk to him."

Abruptly, fury flares inside me like someone switched on a gas flame—I can almost hear the *whurh* noise of the ignition. "You'll *talk* to him? Great. I'm sure that will change everything. I'm sure he'll never say anything sexist or obnoxious ever again. He's been this way for thirty-two years without changing, but this talk from you will definitely do it."

Ollie's eyebrows skip upward. "Hey. I never said I could change him. You're right, he probably won't. But making sure he's polite to you, that I can do."

"Then why did you leave me alone with him last night?"

"I had no—"

"June's stupid sprained vagina was more important than keeping me comfortable around your dickbag of a brother, who you know perfectly well I can't stand?" I spring to my feet and face him, fists clenched.

"*Whoa.* Come on, be fair. I had no idea Caleb would do something like this. And yes, I am well aware you can't stand him, seeing as you find a reason to pick a fight with him every goddamn chance you get!"

"This is not my fault!" I shout. "Don't you dare make this my fault!"

Growling with frustration, he grips his head in both hands and then flings his arms at the air. "I'm sorry. I didn't say that to blame you. What he said was wrong—and no, it's not your fault. There's no question. But separate from that, the rest of the time, you *refuse* to just let him be. You can't ever let one single thing slide. Any chance you get, you're on his case about something. Like last night, the minute he walks in the door, minding his own business, you're accusing him of causing a car wreck on his way home from Geneva."

"You're mad at me for calling out a drunk driver?"

"Did you personally administer his breathalyzer, Leah?"

I blink, mouth open. "Well—obviously not, but—"

"He wasn't drunk. He would *never* drive drunk. His best friend from high school got hit by a drunk driver and has permanent nerve damage. He takes it seriously. But you always assume the worst of him."

"And I'm usually right!"

"Look," he says, after a long, angry minute, "I'm not saying he's not difficult. But I already spend half my time when I'm up here trying to keep him and my dad from ripping each other's heads off, and it's fucking exhausting. Can you please just . . . not add to that?"

I shake my head in disbelief. "How the hell can you sit there and tell me not to be upset?"

"I'm not! That's not what I said. Be as pissed as you want when he deserves it. And I'm not asking you to try to like him; if you don't, you don't, and that's fine. What I'm asking is for you to stop antagonizing him. And remember that anytime we're with him and my parents, you're going to see his worst side. I know you think it's weird that it doesn't piss me off when he rags on me for being the favorite child, but the reason I don't get mad is that he's right. He grew up with a stepdad who couldn't stand him, but who doted on me. For no real reason besides me being his own son. My dad's a necessary evil for Cal if he wants to see my mom, but if the shit ever really hits the fan with Dad, Cal will cut her off, too. That is the *one thing* I'm always trying to prevent."

I already know this. It's exactly why I'm not telling Ollie the entire story of what Caleb did. But even though he doesn't know, and he's not asking me not to tell, I hate that I'm covering for Caleb's appalling behavior. I hate that I'm making other people's feelings more important than truth, more important than justice. It's so wrong, so unfair, that it scalds me.

"Oh, bullshit," I snarl. "I'm sure Caleb gave your dad plenty of reasons not to like him. You always cut him too much slack, just like you are right now. When are you going to knock it off and grow the hell up?"

He shakes his head and looks away. "Leeb. I've apologized for him, and promised to talk to him, and promised that he will apologize to you. I don't know what more I can do. But you're just getting angrier. Is there something else? Something I said? Something I didn't say?"

"Marry me," my brain screams. *You haven't said, "Marry me." And last night June didn't say, "You seem awfully quiet, Leebee, is everything okay?" Instead she just brushed her teeth and washed her face and got into bed and passed out while I lay there silently crying. And she jetted out with freaking Terrance this morning before I could tell her, which means neither of the people who are supposed to look out for me even have the first clue what really happened.* But at least I've got one person left who won't let me down.

I look at Ollie, sitting there on the wall with his stupid shorts and his dorky hiking boots and his beautiful, earnest blue eyes, and I say the thing I know will hurt him: "No. You've clearly reached your limits. You're not going to make me feel better about this. I need to talk to Sam."

"What does Sam have to do with it?"

"Well, Ollie, Sam actually gives a shit." I turn abruptly and walk off down the trail. I crunch the pebbles under my sneakers as hard as I can.

I'm too far away to hear his weary sigh, but I know he does it just the same.

20

June

AFTER THAT NIGHT SEVEN YEARS AGO, THOSE FRANTIC HOURS of darkness when fear pressed so hard and high into my throat it made me gag, I never heard the story again. I read about it, in the articles in the Rochester and Syracuse papers that I devoured, late at night, in the white-knuckle grip of insomnia. Whenever I had to tell someone who hadn't heard about it before, I used a single brief sentence, polished hard and smooth by use. I never let my mind travel down the path of envisioning it, because I simply couldn't bear to.

A death that's an accident hurts in a uniquely awful way, I think. If someone gets sick, or their heart gives out, it feels inevitable; the failure was inside the body itself. Beyond the reach of others to predict or prevent.

A freak accident is unpredictable too, but it's the opposite of inevitable. It's a mixture of forces—physics, material failure, maybe bad judgment. Mass times velocity. Wrong place, wrong time. The unlikely confluence of those factors that destroys a human body—it could have just as easily blinked past without impact. When it doesn't, it's really nothing more than chance. Bad luck. Whatever you want to call it, it's horrifying.

But what's chained to this is that you can't stop thinking about the alternative. Of what could have so easily happened, if that spinning cosmic coin, arcing through the air for those brief moments while sunlight glanced off its edge, had landed on its other side.

Loving Ollie as I do, it was the last thing I ever would have asked of him: Please describe for me, without sparing a detail, the most traumatic event of your life. Tell me exactly how you watched the woman you loved die.

But now, something's changed inside me. It's wrong that I don't know. It feels like a betrayal of Leah—yet another betrayal of Leah—that I've never borne that pain. And, worst of all, it feels like there's something missing from the story I heard. Something to do with Ollie's brother, who's large and strong and outsized my best friend by thirteen inches and at least a hundred pounds. A man whom Leah disliked, distrusted, was with her when she died. I do not think he would have hurt her on purpose. But had he been in some way responsible for the accident, Ollie would have protected him. This much I'm certain of.

The lake is inscrutable, as usual. This afternoon, the air is pushy with the wind of an approaching thunderstorm, which suits my unsettled mood perfectly. A few warning drops have already splatted down on my skin, but I can't bring myself to join the others inside just yet.

"June, honey, would you mind helping me with the corn?" The rattle of the screen door scatters my thoughts and almost drowns out Rachel's voice as she emerges from the living room, nearly invisible behind two reusable grocery bags bulging with corn ears from the farmers' market.

"Of course," I say, extracting one of the bags from her grasp and setting it on the table beside me. I've barely spoken to her since Ollie peeled out for the drive to Geneva yesterday, so I'm sure she's been wanting to get me alone. I silently will her to heed the obvious message of my body language, and leave me be.

For a moment, the air is full of the squeaky noise of leaves and silk being stripped back from the golden spears of grain. The distinctive, earthy scent fills my nostrils; it smells like summer.

"I'm glad I got a minute to talk to you," Rachel says. "I've been a little worried about how you're holding up."

Never mind about my body language, then. "Oh. I'm fine, thank you," I say, because what else am I going to say? *I can't stop thinking about my best friend who died here, or why your sons, who witnessed it, have never told me exactly how the whole thing came about?*

"I've hardly seen anybody who seems less fine than you do," Rachel says. "You don't have to be polite about this. I'm asking you. You can be honest. It's an awful lot."

I raise my face to look at her. "I'm curious what exactly you're referring to by 'an awful lot.'"

Usually, the first time I let someone see the rapids upstream from my still-water river, they're so taken aback it makes me laugh. It's always the same. There's a little recoil, a little stutter, a pair of lifted eyebrows. But when I put her on the spot, Rachel Bierman's eyebrows don't move.

"Being back at the place where Leah died. Howard and Caleb, Caleb and Ollie. The accusations about Caleb. Trying to manage Ollie managing all of the above. That, my dear, certainly qualifies as an awful lot."

This time, it's my brows that lift. Bull and horns, meet Rachel. "Okay," I say. "I'm not fine. But I'm getting by."

She finishes stripping her corn ear in silence, then sets it down in the completed pile and turns to face me. "I just want you to know that you can talk to me. If you need someone. I recognize it might not always be the easiest thing to talk to Ollie. I love my son madly, but I know he can be . . . well, he doesn't like to deal with problems. He's always hated confrontation, ever since he was a little boy. He just wants everyone to get along and be happy, and when problems come up along the way he tries to hurry past them as fast as possible—but the problems are where you have to slow down."

I give a laugh that's more an acknowledgment of truth than it is an expression of humor. "Yeah. I have experienced that."

"Things weren't always so bad between Howard and Caleb. When Howard and I first got married, he tried. He really did. I have these pictures of the four of us from those years . . . we looked so happy. I can hardly believe it now." Her voice is as wistful as the last Sunday afternoon in August. "Then the year Caleb turned twelve, his father moved back to Rochester. His dad had always been distant emotionally, even since before our divorce, and I think Caleb internalized that and believed his father blamed him for our breakup. I tried to show him every way I could that it wasn't the case, but sometimes kids latch onto things. So, with his dad back in the picture and Caleb hungry for his approval, he soaked up everything he had to say. He never really turned on me, but his attitude to Howard completely changed." She rubs her forehead with one hand. "My ex is . . . well. I'm sure you've heard about my ex."

"I have."

"Ollie was too little to understand what was happening, so all he knew was that his dad and brother were fighting all the time and that it had something to do with me and with Caleb's dad. Things got pretty rocky by the time Caleb was in high school, so Ollie was nine, ten, eleven—that sort of age. He started out hiding when they'd get into it, and I'd find him in his room, practicing guitar. If you can believe it, his hands used to be so small that we had to start him on a kiddie one to learn on. A couple of times, he let them see that he was upset; but that just made Howard even more angry with Caleb." She pauses, lips tight, then continues.

"But as he got older, he figured out how to diffuse the tension. He'd change the subject or he'd tell a joke. Do whatever he had to do to let us pretend that everything was fine."

I'm torn between amused recognition of Ollie's personality and a stab of anger at the knowledge of when and why he developed this particular trait as a coping mechanism. "I wish he hadn't had to pretend," I say, yanking forcefully at the tight leaves on my piece of corn.

"Me too," she sighs. "We all spend so much effort trying to find the one we love; no one ever tells you that the one you love might disappoint you. Definitely no one tells you, when you've left a bad marriage behind, that the man of your dreams might disappoint you, too."

Carefully, I set my corn down and look at her. "What do you do when your child disappoints you?" I say quietly.

"You love them anyway," she says. "You tell them they must do better. You pray to God they will."

"What if it's something really bad?"

She shakes her head, so quickly it's as if she's trying to scare away a fly. "It doesn't matter. I couldn't stop loving my son, or love him less, any more than I could drain each drop of blood from my body. Parents are built that way. Once that love is forged, nothing can destroy it." Her voice rings with conviction, but she isn't looking at me. She is watching her own hands as they work.

"Rachel," I say, after a long pause, "did you ever hear anything weird about Caleb . . . related to Leah?"

Her gaze skids to me as her hands freeze on her corn. "Leah? No. Never. What makes you ask?"

I shrug. "Nothing in particular."

"It's a very particular question, June. Something must have prompted it."

I can't tell if she's afraid I've stumbled onto something she knows, or afraid I know something she doesn't. She stares at me while I swallow back the reckless words pounding on the roof of my mouth. Finally, I shake my head. "It's just on my mind. All of it. She wasn't the fondest of him, if you'll pardon my saying so."

Rachel's slim shoulders sag as she sighs again. "I can believe it. Caleb is . . . well, God knows I love him, but I won't pretend he hasn't been a trial at times. There's a lot of his father in him, for better and worse; and a lot of anger at me for leaving his father. I've probably put up with too much from him over the years, to try to make up for it. But I know he didn't do this thing he's been accused of."

I study her, wondering where her confidence comes from.

"But to what I said before—I can only imagine how much Leah must be on your mind right now, so if you need to talk to Ollie about her, don't be afraid to make him."

"Yeah. To be honest, we've never really talked about her at all," I say, and the minute I glance back at her face I know it was a mistake. "I mean, we have. Of course we have. But . . . we haven't belabored it, I guess."

"You said 'at all,'" she says. "I believed you the first time. And I think it's probably well past time you did talk about her."

I spent my teens and early twenties wishing I had a warm, cozy mother like Leah's, who wanted to talk to me about my feelings. At some point I hatched a hope that my mother-in-law might be that person for me. This is an object lesson in *careful what you wish for.* "We're fine. Honestly. Talking isn't going to change anything."

She cocks her head to one side and studies me with calm evaluation I don't like one bit. "Is that really true? Or are you worried that talking might change something? Because I promise you—"

"Let's change the subject, please." I use the ice-water tone that Ollie hates, and when I see his mother flinch at it I feel a warm burst of regret.

"I'm sorry," she says, rubbing a stray raindrop off her forearm.

"I know it's not my business. I'm just worried about you two, and I want to see you clear the air between you."

"I appreciate your concern," I say, then realize the words feel familiar in my ears. It's what Ollie said the other day, to Terrance's parents, when they told him they were worried about Rachel. Who is worried about me and both her boys. All these worried people.

"And there's the door slamming shut in my face," she says. "I suppose I deserve it. Just promise me you'll keep what I said in mind."

I stand to bring my bag of corn inside. "About which topic?"

Rachel's eyes don't falter from my face. "All of them."

21

Leah

OLLIE ONCE DESCRIBED ME AS A HUMAN BEACH BALL. Personality-wise, not shape-wise, although I will concede that a certain physical bounciness may have factored into his assessment. But he was thinking bright, and he was thinking cheerful, and—I know this because he demonstrated it for me, standing in the middle of the pool of the Fort Lauderdale Ramada where we stayed on our first weekend away together—he was thinking about how, when you press a beach ball down underwater, it pops right back up again the second you let it go. It cannot be sunk. It just wants to float with its belly up to the sun.

Although Sam's only response to my unanswered phone call was a quick text containing the words *sorry, busy* and an eggplant emoji, after a good night's sleep, my outlook on the world is substantially improved. Now that the memory of what happened has faded a little, I'm starting to accept what Caleb and Ollie both said: It was just a joke. A stupid, offensive, clumsy joke, but a joke nonetheless. Caleb couldn't have meant it seriously; I must have overreacted. Which, it pains me to admit, is not exactly unheard-of. Especially when it comes to Caleb.

Ollie himself has been reserved and penitent toward me ever since yesterday, when he silently walked five feet behind me all the way down the Watkins Glen trail. It was mean of me to tell him that Sam cares more about me than he himself does—I twisted a knife on Ollie exactly where he is vulnerable. Loyalty is everything to him. Normally I love him for that (like when it applies to me), but his insistence that Caleb isn't the asshole I find him to be is misplaced. He's said before that I'm too black-and-white in the way I judge people: Either they're good or they're bad. But I've never been wrong yet.

This morning is the enactment of the family tradition for Rachel's birthday. The ritual, which I have witnessed two times before, is that the rest of the family prepares her favorite breakfast—lemon ricotta pancakes with raspberries from her garden—and brings it to her bed on a tray and then gathers around to sing "Happy Birthday" to her while Ollie accompanies on guitar. I shamelessly love it, because the whole thing was Ollie's idea, back when he was seven years old, to make his mother's birthday special. And they've been doing it ever since.

The show gets under way around nine. I bet Rachel's been awake for a while, but is too good of a sport to get out of bed or display impatience. The tray is ready—complete with linen napkin, steel plate cover, iced coffee with striped paper straw, mimosa in a champagne flute—when, at the last second, Caleb says, "Wait, the hydrangea," and vanishes out the front door with a pair of kitchen shears. He returns a minute later with a frothy blue stem from the shrub outside, slips it into a bud vase, and sets it on the tray. The tray now looks like a still life encapsulating summer.

"Nice catch," says Howard, clapping Caleb on the back.

Caleb gives a shy twitch of his shoulders, then Howard lifts up the tray and the procession begins.

Caleb falls in after Howard, then Ollie with the guitar, then me and then June, grabbing my waist in an impromptu conga line maneuver. When we burst into the bedroom, Rachel takes off her reading glasses and sets her newspaper down, smiling. Her pajama top has blue blossoms on it that remind me of the hydrangea. She beams at us as we stagger through the song, then claps her hands when it ends.

Howard leans down to set the tray over her lap, and kisses her lingeringly on the lips. "Happy birthday, love of my life."

The boys hug her next, then she turns to me and June and waves us over. "Thank you, you sweeties," she says, as she hugs one of us in each arm. "This is the loveliest birthday treat anyone could ever have."

While Rachel eats, her family presents her with their gifts: a delicate gold necklace from Howard; a book of *New Yorker* cartoons from Caleb; the first season of *Downton Abbey* from Ollie. When she's finished, we all retreat to the deck table to attack the egg-and-sausage casserole that's been waiting in the oven.

"June dear, I keep forgetting to ask you," says Rachel. "How are you feeling after your fall; is everything all right?"

June slowly turns a dull red, while I eye-murder Ollie, who must not have mentioned the sensitive nature of June's fall to his mother and therefore did not think to tell her not to bring it up.

"Oh, I'm fine, thank you."

"I wonder if there's some sort of handrail we should put up, Howard. There are always handrails on the steps into pools."

"No, no, I was just clumsy," says poor June.

"Terrance took good care of her," says Caleb with a wink. "And Leah and I had some bonding time while everybody was checking on June. Right, little sis?"

"Oh yeah, she mentioned that," Ollie says mildly. "What was it you guys talked about, again?"

Caleb's jaw tightens, and he knocks back a big glug of coffee.

"Nothing important," I say.

"No, there was something funny he said. Something hilarious. You told me yesterday how absolutely hilarious it was."

"This sounds promising," says Howard, and I shudder. His tone is Hannibal Lecter musing about fava beans and chianti.

"No, it wasn't one of his better efforts," I say firmly, kicking Ollie under the table. "June, what did you and Terrance get up to yesterday?"

June, whose head has been pivoting like she's watching a tennis match, pulls up my rope without a missed beat. "Oh, it was really fun. His friend Dave who lives on Keuka has this awesome wakeboarding boat—"

"No way!" I squeal. "I've been wanting to try wakeboarding, but it doesn't work with the pontoon. Or so I am told."

"Terrance said he got you wakeboarding," Ollie says to June, with naked accusation. "You still don't want to give skiing a try?"

June shrugs. "Boarding was easy; there's one big board and you're strapped into boots."

"So you guys gonna spend the day over there again?"

"Maybe," says June. "I haven't talked to Terrance yet today. He's not my social director."

"You should," Ollie says. I wait for him to say more, because it's not clear if he means June should talk to Terrance or go to Keuka or both, but he just sits there with his arms crossed, scowling. June scowls back at him, and I shift uncomfortably in my seat. Ollie compensates for his usually sunny nature by turning into social toxin when he gets in one of his rare bad moods. And I'm pretty sure this one is my fault.

"No, you should not go to Keuka," I say. "We missed you yesterday."

June smiles and squeezes my top knot. "We'll see."

We'll see? Why is she being so evasive? I'm obviously stoked about her and Terrance, but it's annoying that she'd spend so much time away from me, when I'm supposedly the reason she is here at all.

As a grumpy lull falls in conversation, June, Rachel, and I stand up and start clearing the meal. Caleb grabs the large ceramic bowl that held the fruit salad, along with a couple of empty water glasses, but as he moves past Ollie to follow June inside, Ollie's leg sneaks out to trip him. Caleb, his two-hundred-plus pounds, and his breakable dishware all go crashing to the ground.

"What the fuck was that?" he roars, stumbling to his feet and looming over Ollie with his fists clenched.

"It was just a joke," says Ollie blandly, regarding his brother with cold blue eyes.

"Caleb?" Rachel calls from the sliding door. "What on earth happened, are you all right?"

"It's fine, Mom," Caleb calls back without looking at her.

"I'm surprised you didn't think my *joke* was funny," Ollie continues, quietly enough that Rachel can't hear. "You love to joke around so much."

Caleb's lips twist, one corner lifting in a sneer, but there's nothing he can say in front of Howard and Rachel.

"Leah, you didn't think Caleb's little joke the other day was funny, did you?"

"No," I say, "but this isn't what I had in mind when I asked you to discuss it with him."

"That's because he's a spoiled little punk," Caleb spits.

"You know, I really do feel like I need to hear more about this famous joke," says Howard.

"Caleb, Leah was about as amused by your joke as you were by mine. So I think you owe her an apology."

"It certainly does sound like it," says Howard. I can practically hear the scrape of metal as he sharpens his carving knife.

Caleb turns to me, and I recoil a step at the fury and humiliation in his face. "I'm sorry."

"For?" prompts Ollie, and I wheel on him.

"Knock it off. This is done. Let it go." I turn my back to him and kneel down to pick up the largest chunks of shattered glass and china.

"You going to let her pick up your mess?" Ollie says to Caleb, still in that same silky voice.

"You're the one that caused it," I mutter without turning around.

The deck shakes as Caleb stomps away; a minute later, there's the slam of a car door, followed by an engine starting and a fast, hard crunch of gravel as Caleb floors it up the drive.

"Howard?" Rachel's quiet voice is filled with disappointment. "On my birthday?"

"It was me, Mom," Ollie says, walking toward her. "We had a disagreement. I'll patch things over once he cools off."

Rachel's next words are so quiet I am certainly not meant to hear them: "I prefer it when you remind me of your father in ways that make me proud."

"Mom, he—"

"I don't care, Ollie," she says, sounding exhausted. "You're both grown men. No more of this."

Without another word, Ollie crouches next to me and picks a shard of glass between his fingers; then another one. He does not meet my eyes.

The thunderstorm blows in so fast you wouldn't believe. Ollie's told me stories, but I've never seen it happen before. One minute I'm floating in the lake, waiting for Ollie to start the motor for another ski run, and the next thing I know he's calling to me to come in.

"Why?" I holler back. "It's not that choppy. And it's not even close to dark!"

He yells back something I can't quite make out, pointing upward, and I belatedly notice that it *has* gone rather dark. A shelf of
heavy purplish clouds hangs in the sky to the north, steadily devouring the flat gray of an overcast afternoon as it moves toward
us. North is the direction of Lake Ontario, about forty miles away;
and I have heard that those Great Lakes can whip up some pretty
serious storms. And we are several miles from the Biermans' dock.

Ollie moves to the back of the boat and begins towing in my
line, dragging me steadily through the cool water.

"I can't believe I didn't notice before now," he mutters as he
gives me a hand to hoist me up out of the lake. "I don't like this at
all."

I shiver as the wind hits my wet skin, and plunk down on the
banquette with my already-damp towel wrapped around me.
June, whose company for the day was secured when Terrance
showed up after breakfast with a fresh-caught fish for lunch, is
huddled with her legs tented up under her sweatshirt while Terrance rubs her upper arms for warmth. Her hair blows in black
streamers across her face, but her lips are curved in a smile of
anticipation. June loves a good summer thunderstorm.

Ollie points us north and cranks the motor. The pontoon bobs
over the growing chop, but when we swing around the large point
of land that projects into Seneca halfway up the western shore,
Ollie utters a vicious curse. We are basically in the ocean.

Without the sheltering point to break its force, the wind is
gouging the lake surface into four-foot swells that roll relentlessly
toward us and crash against the front of the boat, drenching us
with spray even from a few feet back. The boat lurches and bucks
over the stormy water.

"This is one of the reasons Seneca isn't as popular," says Terrance. "It's almost three miles wide here, and there's fifteen miles
of open water till the northern edge. Things can get a little rowdy."

Now that Terrance mentions it, I realize I can't see the northern edge of the lake anymore. It's disappearing behind a wall of rain even as I watch.

"Do you think you could knock off the tour guide thing and help me?" shouts Ollie over his shoulder.

"Yeah, obviously—but we're not even close to your house yet."

June stands up, bracing herself with one hand on the seat back. "What do you need?"

"I need *Terrance* to check the tie lines to make sure they're all clear and ready. I need *you* to sit down. And put on a life vest."

"Ol, I don't exactly think we're getting swept out to sea," I say.

"Please just do what I ask."

As he says it, we jostle through another trough, and the tip of the wave blasts over the seats at the front of the pontoon, sending water skidding over our feet.

"Yeah, okay," I say, reaching into the cabinet where the vests are kept.

Silence settles while I distribute the life jackets and Terrance makes a round to ensure the lines we use to tie the boat to the dock are in position and ready to be deployed. I can't decide how alarmed I should actually be—Ollie's mouth is pressed in a rigid line, but I can't tell if it's from concentration, or worry, or both. And then, with a sudden rush of sound like a heavy sigh, rain drops out of the sky. It happens in the space of a single breath— the air I inhale is clear, and I exhale into water. The shelter of the double-decker platform overhead is meaningless; the wind drives the rain straight at us.

"Wow!" yells June, sticking her arms out and spinning in place like some kind of pagan storm worshipper.

"June, park it," snaps Ollie. "And stay parked."

"Yeah, take it easy, Storm Rider," says Terrance, pulling her hand to get her to sit.

"I'm not a fucking puppy," she snarls at Ollie.

"No, you're a girl recklessly moving around on a boat that is completely unsuited for water this rough. *Sit down.*"

"Everybody chill!" I say. "The crew needs to cooperate for the good ship *Pontoon* to dock safely at Bierman Harbor. Junie, Ollie's right, you should sit."

Rebellion flickers in her face, but she sits. Terrance leans close to her and murmurs something—probably how the most important thing is to keep her safe, *bluaaghhh*—but her fingers pick restlessly at the upholstery.

As it intensifies, the rain wipes the eastern shore of the lake from sight and most of the western side, too. All I can see is gray—opaque gray sky, churning deep gray water. The relentless pitching of the boat has turned even my usually sturdy stomach; I bury my head between my knees, shivering, while June strokes my back. Just as I'm contemplating whether I'm obligated to clean up my inevitable vomit while the storm is still going or if I can wait until the rain stops, I hear Ollie call out that we're almost there.

"What do we need to do?" says June.

"Getting it into the hoist is going to be hell with these waves. Terrance, can you take the front right? And June, back right. Mom and Dad will be waiting, so your job is to toss the lines to them so they can tie up. And try to hold it steady until we can get it up. But don't fall in."

"Thanks, I'll keep that in mind," June mutters as she hurries toward the back of the boat to get her line ready.

Ollie slows the boat as we approach the dock, and sure enough, there are Rachel and Howard watching us pull in, Rachel in an oversized yellow slicker like some kind of North Atlantic sea captain. The whip-crack sound of the big American flag on the dock snapping in the wind is audible even over everything else. It takes Ollie several tries to get the boat in at the right angle to fit into the hoist, but finally he does, and everything explodes into motion: June and Terrance toss the lines to Rachel and Howard, who tie them into place on the cleats while Ollie vaults onto the dock and starts the hoist motor to raise the boat up out of the water. Even on the tight leash of the two ties, the boat still rocks in the waves until it's lifted clear. As soon as it's steady, Terrance climbs to the dock and turns around to give June a hand, but she's already scrambling out at her end. Ollie glares at her like he wants to yell at her again, then shakes his head and reaches for me.

"Come on, Little Bean," he says, and it occurs to me that I haven't heard him use that nickname in a long time.

"Little Bean arriving," I say, and fearlessly grab his hand.

22

June

AS WE ALL LINE UP FOR RACHEL'S BIRTHDAY SERENADE, THE only thing I can focus on is Ollie's little nephew. Eli, with his apple cheeks and his riot of blond curls, is just pure sweetness. He leads the procession into Rachel's room, tooting randomly on a kazoo that Ollie gave him, and when his grandmother opens her arms to him, he flings himself onto the bed and crawls up to her to snuggle. Rachel wraps her arm around him and pulls him close. Watching them, I can't help wondering how much of all of this Eli will absorb: Caleb and Howard, Caleb and Seth. Will the man who branded his barely teenage son's mother a lying whore have any scruples about repeating it to his tiny grandson?

While they snuggle, Caleb gives Leslie a gentle nudge with his elbow, and she glances at him hesitantly. Smiling, he nods toward his mother.

"So, I guess now might be a good time," Leslie says, a blush creeping up her tan skin. "We wanted to tell you all that . . . well, I'm pregnant again."

"Little brudder!" shouts Eli, and Rachel gasps.

"Really, another boy?" she breathes, and Leslie nods, beaming.

"Another boy," Caleb says, voice full of satisfaction. "End of November."

Rachel blinks eyes bright with tears, and releases Eli to throw her arms wide to her daughter-in-law. "Oh, this is the best birthday gift in the world! Come here, you," she says to Caleb, who leans in next to Leslie and kisses his mother's cheek. "Oh my heavens, I love all my boys! But what do I have to do to get a girl?" Her eyes are like the beam of a searchlight, sweeping the room for Ollie, who throws up his hands in defense.

"Let me get married first, Mom," he says, to general laughter.

"That's wonderful news, Caleb," says Howard, thumping Caleb on the shoulder as he shakes his hand. "Congratulations to you both. Looking forward to another little sunbeam running around behind Eli."

"Well, I'm sorry, but I'm too excited to sit here and let you all watch me eat," says Rachel, setting aside her breakfast tray. "Let's eat out on the porch. Leslie, you sit next to me and tell me everything."

During all of the milling about, I covertly study Leslie. She has just announced her pregnancy with the child of a man who has admitted to cheating on her, quite recently, for no better reason than that he was drunk. A man who's been accused of far worse than simply cheating. But there she is, all sparkly eyes and gleaming teeth, gabbing with Rachel as if she hasn't a care in the world. Has she just filed the bachelor party incident under "boys will be boys" and buried it deep in her mental hard drive, only to be revisited as ammunition in a future argument? Maybe this isn't the first time. Maybe to her, Caleb's love for her and their kids is all that really matters. Maybe she doesn't recognize how much her husband's respect for her—or lack thereof—should matter, as well. I wonder how long it will take for her to realize . . . and what will happen when she does.

I catch eyes with Ollie, and from the subtle lift of his eyebrow, I know he's thinking the same thing.

* * *

After breakfast, we assemble on the boat for a family outing. Leslie has Eli so kitted out in rash guard, life jacket, and floppy-brimmed hat that he looks like a trussed goblin, scowling at her from behind a mask of thick white sunscreen. Caleb takes him to the front of the boat, settles him on his lap, and points out landmarks on the shore to him as they go flashing past. Howard stops the boat in a sheltered cove and dives in.

Ollie nudges my shoulder with his chin. "You all right if I go in?"

I turn to him, and there he is, right there; there are his deep gray-blue eyes under his strong brows, like upside down check marks, and his sharp nose with the seventeen freckles he hates because he thinks they make him look boyish. I brush a speck of sleepy sand from his golden brown eyelashes. "Yeah. I'm all right."

"I'll stay close."

"It's okay. I had no reason to freak out the other day."

He presses a slow kiss to my forehead, right between my eyes. "I don't blame you a bit." Then he stands, strips his shirt, and cannonballs into the water next to his father.

Caleb joins them, too, and begins coaxing Eli to give it a shot. Eli, unconvinced, stands on the back platform of the boat and deliberates with his index finger in his mouth.

"Come on, buddy," says Caleb. "Just lean forward and jump into my arms, I'll catch you."

"It feels cold," Eli says, looking down at where the lake water washing onto the platform covers his small pink toes.

"You'll like it once you're in," says Caleb. "I promise. It feels good."

Eli grins at his dad and, with a toddler's abandon, leap-topples into Caleb's waiting arms. As he squeals and giggles at the cold, Caleb clasps him close and smiles.

A memory flashes at me—being stopped near the shore like this on one of our first days at the lake, and being coerced into the water much like Eli just was. Until Terrance, at Ollie's urging, picked me up and threw me in.

I turn to where Ollie floats in the water, to ask him if he remembers, but the familiar hesitation stops me, that hand pulling back at my wrist that I will never not feel. Because that moment wasn't really about me and Ollie. It was him unknowingly flicking a tiny spark, like an ember from a cigarette, onto the waiting gasoline of everything I felt for him; and me bursting out yelling at him, not because he'd gotten me dunked, but because I was so exhausted from hating myself and already so regretful that I hadn't heeded my better judgment and skipped the trip to Seneca. And so angry and ashamed at how much I loved his laugh and the imperfect dent in his perfect chest and the way his eyes had lit up and he'd said "Yes!" when I described the sound of Mark Knopfler's Fender Strat as "buzzy." And it was Leah, floating in Ollie's arms, her head on his shoulder and peace on her face.

I have this silly little thing I do. Sometimes, when the pain gets too bad, I reconstruct the life she should have lived. Starting with the morning after, where—instead of screaming at the sight of her soccer duffel on her empty bed because it meant the night before was not a dream—I wake up to the sound of her scuffing around in the duffel for a bra, and she turns to me with her brown eyes dancing and says, "Come on, let's go, I smell bacon!" She returns to Manhattan with an excellent tan, and resumes her classes in the fall, and we finish out all the Groupon dates she never got to do, like sailing lessons on the Hudson and a ghost tour of the West Village. She earns her PhD with highest honors and has her pick of job offers.

I've been doing this for years, mentally rebuilding Leah's life. I started it while I sat under the blazing sunlight at her brother's graduation from MIT the year after she died, thinking about how proud she would be of him, so proud she'd barely be able to keep her butt in her goddamn chair. I sucked in the sight of Sam, shaking hands with his dean—sucked in every last photon of the image for all it was worth, and I beamed it out to her, wherever she might be. And the next thing I knew, my brain had summoned her, like some sort of hologram, and she was sitting next to me, smiling so hard I could see the shadow inside her dimple. She had a ring on her left hand that I had made, and Ollie's fingers twined between hers to her right.

For four and a half years, Ollie was part of the daydream. And then, right after he gave me that kiss on a Chelsea street corner that almost stopped my heart, he wasn't. Instead of him, Imaginary Leah marries some brilliant biochemist she meets in her degree program, who bears a passing resemblance to Idris Elba. Since I'm already pretending, there's no harm in telling myself that she would have outgrown her infatuation with Ollie, and found someone with whom she had more in common.

This is a lie, of course. Even in my imagination, I betray her.

23

Leah

WHEN I WAKE UP, I HAVE THAT GROGGY FEELING YOU GET after a nap, like you have to fight through melted marshmallows to move. The rain that lulled me to sleep is still falling, blowing cool, damp air through the open windows. Spencer snuffles in his sleep nearby, but otherwise the family room is deserted, lights turned low and all the drinks and games cleaned up. It seems like everybody went to bed, except a faint trail of music drifts down from upstairs, along with a low rumble that sounds like Ollie's laugh. Yawning, I get to my feet and shuffle toward the staircase.

The lights are mostly off up here, too; only the golden light from the kitchen doorway casts a beam of brightness across the dark floor beyond. Though quiet, the music coalesces into coherent sound: It's a spare, moody blues guitar, Ollie's favorite late-night music. I step toward the kitchen, but before I make it to the door my feet stop moving all by themselves.

Something is wrong in there. Nothing is wrong, and yet everything is wrong.

Ollie and June are in the kitchen alone. She is perched on the counter with her heels dangling against the cabinets below, palms wrapped around the edge of the counter. He is sitting at the kitchen table facing her, bare feet propped on the seat of another chair. They are four feet apart, not touching, not even close to touching. Literally no one else on earth would notice anything out of place. But because I know the two of them better than anyone else on earth, I see it. There is something going on between them.

I am a disciple of reason. I make my way by data and evidence, and the way those things translate to cold, hard fact. A gut feeling is rarely derived from pure intuition; there are countless subtle things that combine to give us the clues we receive. So, as I stand there in the shadows with anxiety ricocheting around my body, I break it down.

There's the music. When I said slow instrumental blues is Ollie's favorite late-night music, well, there's a lot of overlap between Ollie's late-night music and Ollie's hookup music. Next, there's June's body language: She may be nowhere close to him, but she's leaning toward him like a flower toward the sun. As I watch, she laughs with her head thrown back, then slowly rolls it forward, making her black hair spill against her graceful neck. Then there is *Ollie's* body language: open, relaxed, his left arm slung alongside his torso with his thumb hooked in his jeans pocket, and his right hand silently tapping out the guitar notes on the tabletop.

But even more than that, there's the look on his face. Enjoyment, interest, attention: more than I would expect just from talking to a friend. He looks like he's on a date with a girl he really digs. He looks like, if he were walking next to her while they talked, he'd be bumping her shoulder with his, tweaking the pompom on her beanie hat, pulling her to a stop just so he could kiss her for no good reason. *What the actual fuck.*

"Um, hi," I say loudly, pushing into the room. My voice ruptures the bubble of their chummy vibe with an almost audible pop, and they both turn to me with startled, faintly guilty expressions.

Ollie recovers first. "Hi, babe," he says, smiling, but he does not reach out an arm for my waist or a hand for my hand. "Did you have a good nap?"

"How long was I out?" I say, pinning June with my eyes.

She shrugs. "I don't know, maybe an hour and a half? It was a pretty good one on the Leah nap scale."

"Well, it's time to go to bed. Come on, Ol," I say, capturing his hand. "June, you're on your own in the girl room tonight. Unless you want to go fool around with Terrance. Come to think of it, why *didn't* you go fool around with Terrance tonight?" I tip my head to one side and wait for her response with narrowed eyes.

She opens her mouth, glances at Ollie then back at me. "Um, because I was having fun with you guys?"

"With me? *I* was asleep," I say, jerking a thumb at my chest.

She arches a single, pissy eyebrow. "Sorry . . . I didn't know I was supposed to be spending this trip trying to get laid."

"Well, I think it would be good for you. Good night." Ollie, courteously deciding to spare me the humiliation of having to physically drag him away from my best friend, gets to his feet and follows me from the room. I stomp the hall to his room and slam the door behind him.

"Leah!" he says in a loud whisper. "What the hell was that?"

"Are you cheating on me with June?"

"*What?*" The astonishment in his face is genuine, and it takes a little air out from under my soaring panic. "That's the craziest thing you've ever said to me in your life. No, I am not cheating on you with June. I am not cheating on you with anyone. I would never. Where in the hell is this coming from out of literal nowhere?"

"You guys . . ." I wave my hand vaguely as my voice trails away. What is there to say? *You looked enamored while having a conversation?* And yet, I know I sensed something. There's a concept in neuroscience called salience, which basically means the brain's ability to recognize when something is different or out of place. A black dot amongst a grid of white ones; a shout inside a quiet office. A charmed expression on your boyfriend's face, when he's looking at another girl.

Ollie catches my chin and turns my face back to him. "Us guys what? You're going to have to explain that."

I shrug, struggling to find the words to describe it. Whatever I think of to say sounds as ridiculous as he clearly thinks it is. "I don't know. I just felt something. You were alone in the kitchen talking to her with all the lights off and the sexy music on, while I was downstairs passed out by myself. When I walked in, it didn't seem like you wanted me there. I felt like I was interrupting something."

He drives a hand through his hair, then drops his arm to his side. "Leah. This is nuts. June and I are friends. We hang out without you sometimes, and you know that. You've never had a problem with it before. What changed?"

It's a simple question. I give it a simple answer. "The way you were looking at her."

He stares at me for a moment, blinks to scatter the intensity, then shakes his head. "Okay. Let me pause the insanity for a second to remind you that June is involved with Terrance. My friend Terrance. You were happy about this. I am happy about this."

"You're not," I say with sudden conviction. "You're so obviously not happy about it at all. Even Caleb is more into it than you are, and he doesn't give a crap about either of them."

"I'm done with this conversation," he says, turning away from me to take his watch off and set it on his night table.

"That's not fair."

"This *conversation* is not fair!" he yells, then flinches at the sound of his voice splitting the silence. "I don't even know what more there is to talk about. You accused me of cheating on you. I told you I'm not. I'm still in shock that we're even discussing this."

"What about all that stuff you said, about how cheating is totally okay if it's for the right person, and—"

"No. First of all, that's not even what I said, and second of all—"

"It *is* what you said!"

"No, it's not! But the important thing is it has nothing to do with us. I'm not cheating on you, and I have no desire to."

"You didn't want her to come." The words hit my tongue before I'm even aware of thinking them. "When I asked about her coming up here, you hesitated."

He sits down on the bed and drops his head into his hands, rubbing his face over and over. "You're giving me whiplash here. Which is it? I'm secretly sleeping with June or I secretly hate June?"

"Don't make fun of me," I say, despising the tremble of my voice.

"I'm not making fun of you," he says more gently. "I just don't understand what's going on. This is the second fight you've picked with me in two days. I don't understand the things you're saying or why you're saying them. I don't understand why you would throw such a huge accusation at me—and June—out of nowhere, for no better reason than us talking to each other while you were asleep. I've told you the truth, which is that I'm not cheating on you, and I never will."

"Have you ever? In other relationships, I mean? I never asked you, because it never occurred to me that you might have."

"I haven't," he sighs. "I'll swear on whatever you want me to. I've never cheated on anyone. Look, the stuff I was saying—I never meant to say that cheating wasn't wrong. You can't think I meant that. I guess I just meant that, under extremely specific circumstances, with a once-in-a-lifetime relationship . . . doing the wrong thing is worth it. My parents are the only people I know, the only situation I know of, where I could believe it *was* worth it. And obviously, I'm biased. But that has nothing to do with me, or with you."

I stay quiet, absorbing this.

"It's the truth, Leebee. I don't know what else you want me to say."

"How about 'I love you'?" My voice is flimsy, and God, I sound like such a sad sack. This isn't *me*.

"Ah, honey," he says, getting to his feet and taking me in his arms. "I do love you. I promise you there's nothing going on with me and June. There is *nothing going on*," he says again, pausing between each word.

Under the crook of his chin, where everything feels safe, I nod. Of course there's nothing going on. This is Ollie and June. They love me. Neither of them would ever do anything to hurt me. I let the yuckiness out on a long sigh. "I believe you," I say. "I don't know why I freaked out. I'm sorry."

"I'm sorry you were bummed that we left you down there. Usually you hate to be woken up when you want to nap."

"I know," I say, turning my face up for a kiss. "But the good news is, I'm feeling refreshed." I wrap my arms around his waist and wiggle my hips against him.

He smiles half-heartedly and eases away from me. "Mmm, I'm not really in the mood, Leeb. Arguing with you doesn't exactly turn me on."

"But we're done with the argument now!"

He shakes his head. "I just want to go to bed. Besides, you should talk to June before she falls asleep. You were pretty weird back there."

"Okay." I pull away, feeling small.

Ollie tugs me gently back to him and kisses me. "G'night, Little Bean."

* * *

When I get back downstairs to the bedroom, June is nowhere to be found. There's no note, no text, not even a crease on her impeccable bedspread to suggest she briefly sat on it. I pull the curtains aside and stare out at the dock through the murky night, but the rain is still falling steadily; no way would she be out communing with the lake in this.

By the time I've brushed my teeth and washed my face, there's still no sign of her and no response to my text. I make a brief round of the upstairs, but everything is dark and still. Ollie's door is closed, no light showing through the crack below. Maybe she took my suggestion and went to visit Terrance? But still, why not just text me that? Even if she was pissed at me for being so weird before—and, okay, I deserve it—she still should have told me where she'd gone. She knows I worry. Gritting my teeth against a frustrated sigh, I slip my feet into my flip-flops, toss on a jacket of Rachel's that I find in the upstairs closet, grab an umbrella, and head outside.

The night is wild with rain. It drums on the flimsy fabric of my umbrella, dripping from the edge in a diameter I belatedly realize is way too small to keep me dry. Within seconds, my feet are sliding in the flip-flops, which squish into the saturated grass with every step. I should have worn my Chucks; except then, they'd be damp and gross for the next week. God damn it, June.

Grumbling to myself, I plod toward the path to Terrance's house, but after the first few steps down, I realize I have made a significant tactical error. This path is *steep*. And it's dark, and it's pouring, and I can't see where I'm going for shit. I'm not even sure what I'm going to do once I get there; it's not like they're going to be kicking back on his porch with a bottle of wine. I take my eyes off my path so I can glance ahead at the shoreline, and my right foot slides in the mud, shoots forward, and I crash down on my butt in the grass. "God damn it, June!" I yell. I am going to kill her.

And I'm going to have such a fantastic time deciding *how* to kill her. Why the hell did she make me do this?

But once I'm down, I realize it's the best way to make progress. I put my feet in front of me, push off, and slide. With a shriek, I zoom the rest of the way down the hill. I lose one of the flip-flops halfway through, but I arrive at the bottom intact and still in possession of the umbrella. I lumber to my feet, collect my errant flip-flop, and trot barefoot the rest of the way down the path to Terrance's yard. I round the corner of the building until I'm standing on the pebbled beach, and stare back at the house.

As expected, there is no one in sight. Everything looks all settled in for the night. Except, now that I look closely, I think there's a light on in one of the bedrooms. It's a dim light, but it's a light, and it's in a room tucked up under the eaves—the kind of placement that suggests a kid's room rather than the master bedroom. Neither of Terrance's sisters is home now, so it has to be his room; and it's after midnight, on a rainy night when there's nothing to do but sleep. June has got to be what's keeping him up.

I check my phone again for good measure, but there's nothing. She ran over here for a booty call without even telling me, the little biatch. As I stand there, fuming, Terrance himself appears in the window, his dark shape silhouetted against the faint light behind him. I say his dark shape because all I can see is deep brown skin, because he is shirtless. He doesn't even seem to glance outside the window, just eases up the sash a few inches to open it. And then he turns his head and smiles at someone out of sight—without a doubt, a girl on his bed who happens to love summer thunderstorms, and just asked him to open up that window to the wind and the rain and the rich, watery smell of the air.

24

June

SAM TESSARO IS LIKE A SCAB I CAN'T STOP PICKING. I EVEN TOLD
him that one time over text, late one night when I was drunk and
defenseless. His response: *I wish I knew how to quit you.* That line
from *Brokeback Mountain*. I snorted through my tears and went
to sleep.

I started failing him the day his sister died. Some raw, unformed
impulse made me decide I ought to be the one to tell him—the
first of all of them. They were already in the car on their way up
here, a desperate drive through the middle of the night. It never
even occurred to me to wait until they arrived, or to call Leah's
mother, and let her handle how to tell her son; my brain went directly to Sam. And none of the Biermans were in a state to think
to tell me otherwise. So I called him. Me, incoherent with shock
and grief, barfing it all out to twenty-year-old Sam, making him
frantically stick my stumbling words together until he understood
that the person he loved most on earth was dead. The sound of
him screaming "No!," his voice cracking like a boy's, will echo in
my brain forever. God, somebody should have taken me out back
and shot me.

I was a mess. In the wake of it all, I was *such* a mess, at the
exact moment when Leah would have asked me to be strong, to

keep up her job of looking out for Sam. But I could barely get out of bed.

Instead it was Sam who found the strength to speak at her funeral, using words that placed her in the past—Leah *was,* Leah *loved.* I remember that, and I remember Ollie's face, red and wet with tears; and I remember the hurt that flickered across it when I flinched away from his hug. I couldn't stand to touch him; couldn't permit myself to take even momentary comfort from feeling him hold me. My guilt was eating me alive.

I avoided anything that reminded me of Leah, including Sam, for almost a year while I quietly drowned, until their mother called me, a few weeks before Sam's graduation.

"I think he'd be really glad to have you there," she said, in a voice almost unrecognizable as the bubbly woman I'd known for fourteen years. "He won't ask, so I am."

"Of course," I said, face hot with shame. "Of course I'll be there."

So I went, and there he was, Leah's beloved brother, still alive and thriving even though she was gone. And there was so much of her in him; I'd forgotten how much—his big brown eyes, his dimpled smile.

After that, I couldn't leave him alone. I pestered him for coffee dates, showered him with questions and unsolicited advice about his relationship (though Leah would have been the first to point out that dating was not my strong suit), and generally suffocated him while poorly concealing the fact that I needed him way more than he needed me. He tolerated my obsession with exasperated but affectionate patience. But every minute of uncertainty and awkwardness was worth it the time he called me at two o'clock in the morning, voice jagged as shattered glass, and said, "I don't know what the point is."

"The point of what?"

"Anything. Fucking anything. I miss her so bad I don't understand how it can be real."

"Me too," I said. And then we sat on the phone and talked about her for an hour and a half. That night I found out that the Tessaros were drifting toward divorce. Slowly, disinterestedly, relentlessly. And that Sam was also at sea, all by his lonesome. Neither Leah nor Sam had ever really been able to talk to their father, so not being able to talk to him *about* Leah was just standard operating procedure for Sam. He was, it seemed, just expected to move on. Meanwhile, any attempt to share his grief with his mother quickly devolved into him consoling *her* for what she considered a far greater loss: the dual blow of her daughter's death and his own disability.

"You're not a tragedy," I shouted into the phone.

"*I* know that," he said, humor in his voice. "But maybe you could mention it to my mother if you get a chance?"

I still remember the strange joy that surged inside me when he said it. It took me a while to recognize what it was, but I know it now: It was the sense of being needed. I'd never felt it before. Oh, I'd been loved—by my parents, my friends, a couple of misguided boyfriends—but never needed. No one relied on me for anything that I alone could give. Leah, as fiercely as I know she'd loved me, never really *needed* me. It was the other way around.

But here was Sam, with no one to talk to about his dead sister except for me. No one to listen for as long as he needed, without changing the subject or one-upping his pain. No one who knew her as well as he did, who loved her as much as he did. And feeling for the first time that I could be useful to someone—it gave me a sense of purpose. It pulled me, inch by inch, out of the morass of my own grief, because I had Sam to care about. And the fact that I could help somebody else showed me I was stronger than I'd ever realized before.

Ollie did his best to stay close to Sam, too, all the way from California. I knew it because Sam would always mention this never-ending text thread they had, that'd begun years before between the three of them. Ollie never stopped writing to it. When Leah's number eventually got reassigned, Sam figured out some way to send the texts to her email instead. Just so she could listen in if she wanted. God knows how many iOS updates later, that thread still lives.

Sam and I even had a whole conversation about Ollie, when he told Sam about his first girlfriend after Leah. That revelation arrived in a phone call, not over the thread.

"I know I should be happy for him," Sam said, staring down at the scuffed Formica of the coffee shop table where we were sitting. "But I'd really like to punch him in the balls."

"Sam . . ."

"And that girl, I hate her too. I think I hate her even more. I mean, for god's sake, they would have been *married* by now. How messed up is it to hate an innocent person just for being alive?"

I hate myself for it, I almost said. But I didn't. By then, I had learned that you don't relieve your own grief by piling onto someone else's.

By the time Ollie moved back to the city, Sam had moved to San Francisco, but we were excited to hang out with him as a group when he came home for Thanksgiving. He met us for dinner at an Ethiopian restaurant near his mom's place, but instead of enjoying our company, he stared at us like we carried a faint yet unpleasant odor that he couldn't quite place. Undaunted, we tried again after Christmas, but it was pretty much the same. Once we started dating, I volunteered to be the one to tell him.

"Wait," he said, voice dryly amused. "This is news?"

"Well, yeah. It is."

"Okay. I mean, I literally assumed this entire time that you were together."

"No, we—"

"It's okay. Whatever blows your skirt up."

I was silent for a while, rolling the hem of my sweater between my fingertips. "I obviously know it's complicated for you," I said finally, "but we hoped you might be happy about this. You mean a lot to both of us. And we hope that we mean something to you, too."

"You do. But 'happy' is a lot to ask for."

"Sam," I said softly. "It's been more than—"

"I know how long it's been, June. Believe me, I know. I didn't say you're doing anything wrong. I just said I can't get to 'happy' right now."

Shame rose hot up my neck. I should have known better than to think Sam could be *happy* for us. I told Ollie as much when I ended the call.

"He'll come around," he said.

So far, he hasn't. We have no idea if he'll make it to the wedding. I couldn't blame him if he passed. But still, I can't let go of my need to keep him in my life. And he's the only other person who knows the Biermans well enough to help me parse what all this weirdness means. Before the dinner for Rachel's birthday, I sneak away to the bench on the trail and call him. I pinch my lip while I wait for him to answer. *Please, Sam. I really need you.*

"How are you holding up?" he says, when he answers the phone, and the concern in his voice is like food thrown into my cage.

"Shitty. So, so very shitty. Everybody's being so weird, Sam. Ollie's brother is in serious trouble, but everybody's pretending like it isn't happening."

"What kind of trouble?"

"Sexual assault."

"Holy shit," Sam breathes. "That's insane. What happened?"

Briefly, I explain about the allegations against Caleb, and his inadequate defense. "And the worst thing is, Ollie doesn't seem to get it. He thinks it's just a misunderstanding."

"A 'misunderstanding'? It sounds like his brother seriously manhandled this woman. Pressing charges for assault is not a natural response to a *misunderstanding*. What the hell is wrong with him?"

"I mean, I get it," I say, even though I made that exact point to Ollie the other day. The instinct to defend him is just so automatic. "This isn't some guy in the newspaper; it's his brother."

"But you just said that Caleb literally is in the paper. He *is* that guy. Every bully and abuser has a family who doesn't believe he's capable."

I look out at the water and shudder. "Ugh. You're right. And we just found out this morning that his wife is pregnant again. With another son. I can't stop thinking about what he's going to teach those boys. Not even directly; by example is bad enough."

"Leah never liked him," says Sam. For him, as with me, Leah's assessments on character have been cast in bronze, immutable. It's one other little way we remember her: giving her the last word. "I think one time she called him meatloaf with legs," Sam adds.

A laugh pops out of me involuntarily. Dear lord, but I miss her. Which makes me all the more resolved to find out if there is something that needs to be brought to light. "Sam, did you ever . . . I don't know. It sounds so strange to say. But did you ever get the sense that she was . . . uneasy with him?"

"Yeah," says Sam. "She said he would eye-fuck her when Ollie's back was turned. Find little excuses to touch her. But nothing as serious as this. I would remember, because I'd probably be in jail right now if there had been."

"Right, that's what I remember too. But then with this assault thing . . . I can't stop thinking about it. Wondering if there was something more. Do you have any idea what he was doing with them that night?" I blurt.

"What do you mean? Caleb was *with* them?"

"You didn't know that?"

"No, I didn't know that!" Sam yells. "*You* told me what happened, and then Ollie, and neither of you mentioned that. She

couldn't stand that guy; I would never have forgotten it if I knew
he was there! Jesus Christ, June, what are you saying here?"

"Nothing!" I say, feeling a spike of panic at his response. "I don't
know. It's just . . . Ollie and I were talking about this thing with
Caleb the other day, and I started remembering how uncomfortable Leah was around him, and it made me think about that night,
and when I pushed Ollie about it, he . . ."

"He what?"

"He looked guilty. Like there was something more to it that I
never knew. Something to do with Caleb. And I don't know what
to do."

"You fucking ask him!"

I jump up from the bench and begin pacing back and forth, rak-
ing my free hand through my hair. "I did! I did. And he *swore* to
me that it was an accident, and Caleb wasn't to blame for it. And
I do believe it was an accident. But Caleb—"

"So you know what you do? You ask again. You demand to be
told. You stop giving a shit about feelings and decorum and you
rattle your stick along the fence of the whole goddamn family, and
you keep on banging until you shake something loose. And they
better pray it's you and not me, because if you don't get what you
want, I'm calling the Yates County police to demand they reopen
Leah's investigation."

25

Leah

THE MORNING AFTER THE STORM, THE LAKE IS PRETENDING IT never happened. Smooth, glittery water, deep blue skies . . . nothing to see here, move along. Likewise, June is pretending she didn't spend the night with Terrance. I wake up when I hear her moving around, and I sit up in bed, summon my best threatening look, and say, "Well?" in a tone of profound significance.

"I went to Terrance's," she says, not looking at me.

"I know," I say. "I went over there looking for you in the middle of a thunderstorm."

"I'm not sure why," says the maddening creature. "There was only one place I could have gone. And it was your suggestion in the first place, remember?"

Yes. I do remember. "Yeah. I'm glad you did. I, um . . . I was in kind of a weird mood last night."

She shrugs. "It happens."

"So . . . ?"

She doesn't respond to my extremely obvious prompt, so I give my throat an equally obvious clearing.

She turns to me then, frowning slightly. "You've got something . . ." she says lightly, pointing to her throat. And then she slips from the room before I can respond.

"June Kang, you come back here!" I bellow, but the witch is gone.

"You can't avoid me forever," I mutter to her an hour later as I plop down opposite her on the dock platform. Prime staring/observing position. Terrance is already next to her, hand curled over her knee, but I don't care. I'm his problem too, now.

She doesn't rise to the bait, but her lips twitch. *Gotcha.*

We attempt to play Scrabble, but it's so windy that I have my sweatshirt on over my bikini despite the sunshine, and the breeze keeps snatching our tiles away. Ollie is streaming Pandora on his phone, but none of the songs satisfy him; he flicks from station to station mid-verse until I slap my palm on the phone and tuck it under my thigh.

"Hey! Give that back!"

"You're annoying all of us," I say, and snap off a bite of baby carrot with my front teeth. "June, it's your turn."

June plays LABEL for eighteen points, then stands and stretches, yawning. I glance at the tummy revealed beneath her T-shirt hem and do a double take. "What did you do to yourself?" I demand, gently brushing the faint, nickel-sized bruise above her hip bone with my thumb. "That's a weird place for a bruise."

"Oh, I—"

As she twists to look at it, I see she has a matching one on the other side: same size, same position. "Wait, you have one on the other side. What on earth were you—"

And then I glance up at her face, which is bright pink and growing redder as I watch. She saucer-eyes me: *Shut up, Leah.* My mouth drops open and I glance at Terrance, who is gnawing on his nonexistent thumbnail, staring with intense concentration at the horizon across the lake.

I can't hold back a gasp of laughter, which Ollie hears. He turns to face me. "What?"

"Nothing," says June firmly, folding her arms low across her hips.

Half-smothered snorts of laughter are still jerking out of me, although admittedly I'm not trying *that* hard to stop. This is too good.

"*What?*" says Ollie.

"*Nothing,*" says June, settling back down next to Terrance. He gives her a small, private smile, and wraps his arm around her shoulders. His fingers trace a circular pattern on her skin. He doesn't look away from her again.

Ollie stares at them and frowns. "Seriously, what am I missing here?"

Something squirms uncomfortably in my belly. Why is he frowning at them? Aside from the fact that she ran off in the middle of the night without telling me, their obvious PDA is great news. This was the goal.

"You're not missing anything," June says quietly, not looking at him. "Play your turn."

"June's got screwin' bruises," I blurt, holding my hands above my lap like I'm gripping somebody's waist, wiggling my thumbs for extra clarity.

"*Leah.*" June's voice cuts like a lash across Terrance's low, quiet "Hey, now."

Ollie blinks fast a couple of times, swallows, then gives a mild lift of his eyebrows. "That's . . . definitely more information than anybody here wanted to be shared. Change of topic: Who wants to give up on Scrabble and hit the boat?"

"Think we'll head back up to the house for a minute," says Terrance, getting to his feet. June stands and busies herself with scooping up her iced coffee and phone. Embarrassment is prickling the back of my neck, and the urge to discharge it with an apologetic grimace is overpowering. I nudge her foot with my toe to get her attention, but she turns and heads for the staircase without looking at me.

When they're gone, Ollie abandons his chair and sits down next to me. "Leeb, what is going on with you?" he says, voice clipped with frustration.

"You know I have no filter," I say, but the tightening of his lips says that's not good enough. "I was just teasing her."

"But that was uncool. It's not your business to care about whether they slept together, let alone bring it up for group discussion."

I blow a stray Medusa curl out of my face. "Please, of course it's my business. She's my best friend. She spent the night at his place; you can't expect me not to pay attention to that."

"Fair enough. But you didn't have to announce it. And you *definitely* didn't have to give everybody the visual."

"Yeeeah, that might have been a bit much," I say, squinting one eye shut and scratching my ear.

"You embarrassed them."

"Okay! Jesus. I hate it when you scold me."

Ollie rubs at his eyebrow. "I just wish you would think about what you say sometimes before it flies out of your mouth."

"I try," I say.

He angles his head to the side assessingly. "Do you?"

"Yes! I don't always manage it, but I *am* trying to be better." Or at least, I am trying now. As of this very moment.

"Okay." He gives me a small smile.

"I'll smooth it over when she gets back," I promise.

"Terrance, too."

It is not a suggestion. And he's right. I don't know Terrance as well as Ollie's other friends, but I could tell my little joke went over like a lead balloon.

"Yeah. Terrance too."

Ollie kisses my forehead. "Thank you, babe. I think it's getting a little warmer; you want to float until they come back?"

As I bob belly-up on my favorite Rubber Ducky inner tube near the dock, replaying the awkward scene I created, I realize that June's Scrabble word reminds me of something. The summer that she and I moved into our new apartment after college, I went on a bit of an organization kick—the kind that every slob believes will forge them, through the flames of struggle, into a born-again tidy person. Every product in the home storage section at Bed Bath & Beyond sang to me as I cruised the aisles. June's position moved from enthusiastic participation to "Leeb, I'm not sure we really need that" to dead-eyed torpor as she trailed me around the store. But I persevered, and happily spent an entire Saturday night sorting hair elastics and laundry supplies into plastic bins of varying sizes. I assembled a two-tiered storage rack for the colony of shoes we kept just inside our front door. And then, drunk with achievement, I embarked on my final act: label making.

First I attacked the linen closet, assigning locations on the shelves for June's sheets, my sheets, towels of every size. Next was the kitchen: baking stuff, serving stuff, every type of glass. It didn't matter that our drinking glasses cost $2 each at IKEA or that our wineglasses had Santas on them. The important thing was that everything had a spot. I put one of those damn labels every place I could find, and after a week of activity, we couldn't open a single closet, drawer, or cabinet in our apartment without being confronted with a regiment of stickers imposing order on our cluttered space.

"Your room is still a shithole," June said, surveying the jumbled landscape from the safety of the doorway.

"Maintaining the storage areas will teach me discipline," I said, as I picked through the week-old mountain of clean laundry at the foot of my bed. "You'll see."

When I woke up the next morning, I felt something sticky on the skin of my forehead. Confused, I pulled it off and stared at it. Four letters, block caps: LEAH.

I yelled with alarm and looked around. My bedside lamp was also labeled. And then there was NIGHTSTAND, DRESSER, LIGHT SWITCH, DOORKNOB.

"Ha-ha," I barked, flinging open my bedroom door to find my roommate, the picture of innocence, quietly eating yogurt on the COUCH. There were several labels on the couch, no doubt due to its larger size. "Give it back," I said, but I was trying not to laugh.

"Give what?"

"You know what, you little asshole. Quit making fun of me."

She maintained her facade of confusion, but I figured the joke would lose its appeal once I stopped responding. Instead, the labels got more philosophical. GOT MILK? said the carton of almond milk in our refrigerator. The original label on my light switch was replaced with BRINGING LIGHT INTO THE DARK, and my favorite pair of jeans appeared emblazoned across the butt with a sticker that said LEAH'S ASS: MAKING GROWN MEN CRY SINCE FRESHMAN YEAR. I didn't remove the labels, because I was still trying not to acknowledge what was happening, but then Ollie came over for the first time since June's campaign had started, and burst out laughing at LIVIN' ON A PRAYER inscribed over the wooden rosary my grandma made me hang on the wall above our TV.

"Don't you start," I said menacingly, pointing a stubby finger at him, but it was with resignation and irrepressible giggles that I peeled two stickers reading THELMA and LOUISE off of my boobs the next morning.

"What? It wasn't me!" he said, fending off the half-hearted swats I was attempting through my laughter. "Look!" He flicked the covers back enough that I could see the single label precisely positioned on his naked body: SHERIFF JOHNSON.

Lying there on Rubber Ducky, I'm hit with a wave of homesickness. As beautiful as this week has mostly been, I want to go back home to that apartment, to that moment, where everything felt normal and perfect, and I didn't have this weird, amorphous anxiety that's making me pick fights with the people I love. Nearby, the breeze blows Ollie's tube gently against mine, and he reaches out and curls his hand around my foot. His smile is the prettiest thing I've ever seen. I close my eyes and listen to the wind whirring through the weeping willow as the sun bakes into my skin. Everything will be okay once we get back to the city. I'm sure of it.

I'm half-asleep when I hear voices, and footsteps drumming on the dock above me. I sit up to take stock, and my sunglasses, oily with sunscreen, slide off my face and drop into three feet of lake water. "Shit," I mutter. Squinting against the glare, I spot Terrance lowering the hoist on the Jet Ski while June waits nearby, watching a spindly limbed heron search for fish in the shallow water at the shore.

"Hey, if you guys want to go on the boat, we'll take you," I call, but only Terrance turns to face me.

"That's okay, Leah—June wanted to take the Jet Ski for a spin. Thanks, though."

"Well wait, we'll put the other one in the water, and then we can go with you." I straggle upward in my tube, trying to find a dignified position in which to have a conversation, but the damn thing is too small and too slippery and I pitch sideways into the water with a squeal. By the time I've retrieved the tube from floating away and stumbled around on the algae-covered rocks to recover my sunglasses, June is mounted on the Jet Ski with her back to me, arms around Terrance's waist.

"June, wait!" I yell, but the motor growls and then they're off.

"Damn it," I say, overhanding my poor sunglasses onto the dock. My eyes prick with sudden tears. I hate fighting with June, and she does, too; we almost never do it. But she is good and pissed at me right now. I know I was wrong to embarrass her, but how am I supposed to apologize if she won't even let me speak to her?

"I need a drink," I mutter to Ollie, as I trudge toward the dock ladder, Rubber Ducky trailing in my wake.

26

June

OLLIE IS WATCHING ME THE WAY YOU WATCH AN UNSTABLE
person playing with a knife.

Ever since my talk with Sam last night, I haven't been ready to
tackle my fiancé again on the topic of Leah and Caleb. The fear
and adrenaline that were pumping through me when I hung up
with Sam have congealed a bit with the morning. I'm waiting for
the right moment to appear; or maybe I'm just being a coward. As
much as I want to know the truth about Leah, I equally don't want
to know that Ollie's been keeping something from me, something
so important. I don't want to think about what happens next, after
I know.

Ollie knows something's on my mind. I'm quiet. I can't quite
meet his eyes. He wants to ask me what's wrong, but he's afraid to.
So instead of talking, we drive to the brewery, Climbing Bines, to
hang out with Terrance for the afternoon.

The brewery turns out to be just down the road from Ollie's
house, overlooking the lake. In the foreground, the eponymous
hops plants twine over their tall trellises, making lush green walls
in parallel lines. And in the distance, beyond a rolling cornfield,
the early afternoon sun gleams off the silver domes of a pair of

farm silos. The sky is so blue it almost echoes. Maybe one day, I'll be able to appreciate how beautiful this place is again.

We grab a couple of pints and sit down with Terrance at a picnic table in the sun. I let the conversation swirl around me, laughing where it's called for and occasionally chiming in. When Ollie gets up to grab another round of drinks, Terrance falls quiet and gives me a brief, wary glance as he decides what small talk to make. I watch a group of college-aged friends playing cornhole on the lawn while silence stretches out beyond companionable and into uncomfortable until I can't take it one more second.

"Okay, so this is probably awkward," I blurt out, "but I've been wanting to say that I'm sorry. For how I was. Before."

"'Before' when?"

"*Before* before. After everything happened." Which, of course, is only about 50 percent of what I owe Terrance an apology for; but there is no way I can share the rest.

He folds his arms on the table and leans toward me. "Hey, no. Don't worry about it. Are you kidding? Your life turned into living hell between one day and the next. Your best friend died. Obviously I understood that the stuff with us was the last thing on your mind."

"I know. But I should have talked to you; I should have called you back. Eventually. I mean, after our talk the night before, technically I was your girlfriend. For all of one whole day."

"Girlfriend for a day," he says, with a smile that's just a tiny bit sad. "There's the title of my debut singer-songwriter record, when I get sick of classical."

"Very catchy," I say.

"For real, though. I mean, yeah, I was bummed. But I figured it was because I didn't try hard enough to help you."

"What are you talking about? You were out with Ollie's family that whole night—you and your parents. You did everything you could think of."

He sighs. "I've never felt more useless in my life."

"No. Useless was me, frozen to the couch."

Terrance shakes his head. "You're too hard on yourself. You couldn't have done anything to save her, either. But what I meant about not trying hard enough—I meant after everything happened."

"You did try. I wouldn't answer your phone calls."

"Nah, I should have done more. I was worried about you. But I was so scared of saying the wrong thing or doing the wrong thing . . . making it worse instead of helping."

"I didn't want to be helped," I sigh. "I was in a black hole, and I thought I belonged there."

Terrance eases back on his bench and looks at me assessingly. "I was surprised Ollie couldn't reach you. You guys were good friends, and you'd just lost the same person. But you wouldn't talk to him, either."

"I couldn't," I mumble, staring at the table.

He makes a noise as if I have confirmed a suspicion. I jerk my gaze to him, but he's smiling. "You liked him, didn't you?" he says, nudging his chin in the direction of where Ollie is chatting with someone in line for the bar.

My face burns with embarrassment as I struggle for something to say, but Terrance gives a soft laugh.

"It's okay. I only guessed because I was paying such close attention to you that week. I knew nothing was actually going on. And while I will grant you that he's a good-looking son of a bitch, I was pretty sure I could get you past it."

I groan and rest my forehead on my palm. "I'm so sorry."

"Please, it's fine. June, seriously," he says, gently grasping my wrist and pulling it away from my face. "It's fine. I'm just teasing you. I have no problem with anything you did. There's nothing to feel bad about. Okay?"

Staring at my half-drunk beer, I shake my head. "Of course there is. You, and Leah."

"*Not* me. We've all gotten involved with someone while we were trying to get over somebody else. You never lied to me or acted in bad faith. Right?"

I meet his eyes. "No lies or bad faith. I really did like you."

"That's what I thought. So you didn't do anything wrong. And as for Leah . . ." His voice trails off and he shrugs a little. "You weren't trying to steal her boyfriend. Actually, I remember you trying to avoid him. That's part of what made me realize. But, God . . . I'm just so sorry about what happened. I never got the chance to know her well, but I thought she was fantastic."

"She was the best," I say, smearing away tears. "I'm sorry. I've been a mess all week."

"I don't blame you." He squeezes my shoulder and gives me an encouraging smile. "But you get to go home soon."

Home. Our sweet little apartment on our shady street in Brooklyn. Away from this haunted place, away from Caleb, away from this fear that's clanging inside me like brittle iron. If we can just get home, we can sort out the truth of everything.

"Man, I leave you alone with my fiancée and you reduce her to tears?" Ollie's tone is joking, but there's an undercurrent of real displeasure. He straddles the bench next to me and shoves Terrance's pint at him. "Now, which of his awful jokes did this to you?" he says, brushing my hair behind my ear.

"Ol, I'm so tired of being here." The words take both of us by surprise, but as soon as they're out, I realize how essential they are to say. "I wanted to be here for your mom, but it's been so much harder than I expected, and I'm exhausted. I want to go home. Can we leave tomorrow?"

For a second I think he's going to ask if I can make it through one more day, but then he slides his hand to cup my jaw. "Sure. Yeah, baby. Of course we can go home tomorrow."

"Thank you." We share a smile, and I can feel something in the vicinity of my shoulders relax. It will be so much easier to talk to him about Caleb and Leah once we're away from here.

"But if we're leaving tomorrow, then I think we need to kick up a little fuss tonight. Terrance, you in?"

"Always."

"All right, let me tell Mom we're going to stay out." He picks up his phone to write to Rachel, but he doesn't start texting; instead, a frown bends the skin between his brows as he reads.

"What is it?"

"Shit, June. We have to get back there."

My fingers bite into his thigh. Did Sam lose his cool and call the police before I had a chance to try again? "What's wrong? Is everybody okay?"

Ollie's head jerks up and his gaze collides with mine. He snaps his eyes to Terrance, then back to me. "Everybody's fine. But there was news about Caleb's case in the paper. Somebody else who was at that bachelor party is supporting the accuser's statements. He says it's true."

The newspaper looks so innocent, resting folded on the kitchen table like somebody brought it in with the day's mail. Which I guess somebody did—Rachel, sitting down with a glass of iced tea to sift through the Wegman's mailers and Allstate bills, then opening the *D&C* to thumb her way to the crossword, and instead she found her oldest son's name splashed across the very first page. NEW DEVELOPMENTS IN BURWITZ ASSAULT CASE, it says. *Rochester resident Paul Hutchins, 34, has shared exclusively with the* Democrat & Chronicle *his account of the evening of June 11th.*

The account of Paul Hutchins, it turns out, was enough to set my future mother-in-law to tears, her delicate shoulders jerking with sobs under Ollie's arm. Paul Hutchins, coordinator of a hospice care organization, member of the Edgewood Free Methodist Church, father of three young daughters, didn't like what he saw from his friend Caleb that night.

"That lying son of a bitch!" Caleb roars as he bursts into the house, slamming the front door behind him so hard it makes the wall shake.

"Control yourself!" Howard roars back, stepping toward him until Rachel's hand goes white restraining him.

Eli, just back from a visit to the playground, swivels his head with its floppy sun hat from his father to his grandfather and then bursts into tears. Leslie starts toward him, but Rachel says, "No. I need you to stay. Howard, take Eli down to the dock."

Howard looks mutinous for an instant, then relaxes his face and nods. "Come on, buddy," he says gently as he lifts Eli into his arms. "Let's go see if we can find some ducks."

For a long moment after they go—Howard shutting the door quietly as a counterpoint to Caleb's noisy entrance—silence sits heavy over us. Rachel draws in a shuddering breath and looks at her son.

"Mom," says Caleb, voice wavering. "Please don't tell me you believe I hurt that girl."

"What I believe," she says, "is that it could have happened exactly like this man says, and you still wouldn't see why it's wrong."

"I've never denied that I fooled around with her," Caleb says, glancing at his wife. "And I've already apologized to Leslie a million times for that. But I didn't *assault* her."

"He says he saw you in that hallway and you had her pressed up against the wall, kissing her. With one of your hands between her legs."

"Mom." Caleb's face burns red.

"He says he saw her struggling."

"I got a little carried away," Caleb says in a low voice. "I'd had too much to drink, and I had a serious lapse in judgment. None of this is new."

"It's new to me!" Rachel yells, slamming her palm on the table. "You told me it was mutual; you didn't tell me she was trying to push you away!"

"It *was* mutual! She was flirting with me all night. It didn't seem like she was trying to get away. . . . I . . . I thought she just wanted more air."

"She didn't want you to kiss her at all," Rachel wails. "It doesn't matter how much she was flirting with you; you don't trap a woman in a dark hallway and push her against the wall. Little thing like her, big guy like you . . . *were you out of your goddamned mind?*"

Caleb drags his hands through his hair so hard the skin on his face pulls tight for an instant. "This is crazy. I didn't *trap* her, I— I mean, Jesus, Ol, back me up here. Are you going to tell me you've never gotten too intense while you were kissing somebody?"

"There's only one time in my life I've ever manhandled somebody like that. But it was clear that it was mutual."

"See?" Caleb says, flinging his arm toward his brother. "Why is it fine when *he* does it, but I'm a criminal? Story of my fucking life!"

"It's fine because I can confirm that it was mutual," I say, voice shaking. "I was pulling him closer, not pushing him away. *That* is the difference between consent and assault charges."

"You know what I'm starting to wonder?" Ollie says, lethally quiet. "I'm starting to wonder how many women you've had this kind of *misunderstanding* with."

"Oh, give me a break," says Leslie, but Ollie ignores her.

He gets to his feet, unfolding like a panther who has spotted prey in the distance. "I never should have believed that shit when you said it to me the other day, because the thing is, I know better.

I know of at least one other person you never should have laid a single fucking finger on . . . but you did."

Ice water drenches down my spine. "Ollie," I whisper, mouth too parched to speak. "What are you talking about?"

Caleb pulls his eyes from Ollie's and stares at me, then looks back to Ollie.

"How is it possible she doesn't know?" he says.

27

Leah

THE GOOD NEWS IS, I FOUND THE TEQUILA. ALSO KNOWN AS Mexican party juice. The drink where the worm at the bottom of the bottle imbues me with magical powers of awesomeness.

The afternoon has passed in a haze of sunshine, margaritas, and waterskiing, and I am officially unbeatable as the queen of the lake. Currently we are floating on the boat, near the testing station in the middle of the lake. I wanted a closer look at it, because this thing has always weirdly fascinated me. I wish I knew what the navy engineers were doing with it.

"Okay," I say to Ollie, "I dare you to climb on top of that buoy over there."

"No way," Ollie says, settling me more securely on his lap. His damp shorts are cool against my skin. "I don't think the navy would like that very much."

"But it's just a buoy with some birds on it. And no one's even here."

"One time I rode my Jet Ski pretty close to one of those things," Terrance says, "and an alarm went off."

June and Terrance finally returned an hour ago from the world's longest Jet Ski expedition. Because, contrary to what Ollie seems to believe, I do actually know when to back off and let something go, I heroically swallowed the obvious question of whether they found some deserted cove in which to canoodle. If June only knew, she would be so impressed by my restraint. Tequila Leah is even less tactful than Regular Leah.

But June doesn't get to be impressed, because she still isn't speaking to me more than the absolute minimum required for conversation. The boys are doing this awkward dance around it. Terrance, made of more yielding stuff than his beloved, has clearly forgiven me for my faux pas, and is as friendly as always. Ollie has turned into an annoyingly hearty uncle, saying the words "you guys" to them every ninety seconds in an attempt to make up for his previous lack of interest. But June, rather than basking in the glow of new love, is sullen. Poor Terrance must be so confused.

"Well, I want an adventure," I say, smacking Ollie's thigh as I pry myself off his lap. "Feels like time to take a few spins on the waterslide. Terrance, you first."

"Why me?"

"Because you threw June in the other day. So she gets to watch you struggling to look dignified on your way down this slide."

He laughs and gets to his feet. "Sounds fair." He hands his sunglasses to June and heads for the ladder to the upper deck of the boat.

"Wait," I say, and grab a small empty bucket from the storage bin. I dunk it in the lake and hand it to him. "Maximum lubrication. For her pleasure."

There's a bizarre second where I freeze in horror with my hand over my mouth—*God damn it, Tequila Leah*—but then he snorts. He rolls his shoulders and shimmies his head like a fighter. "Oh, I don't need assistance. All-natural results, every time."

"Yeeow!" I yell, laughing, and he grins at me and starts climbing up. I glance at the other two: Ollie looks like he wants to barf; June looks like she wants to throw me off this boat and drive away.

What a party. "I'm putting out a want ad," I say. "Sense of humor badly needed. For the people in the front of the boat."

"Baby, do you want to come up here and push me?" Terrance calls from the platform. "Leah's right, fair is fair."

Hoooo my; "Baby," is it? Verrrrrry interesting.

"Nah, the view is better from down here," June calls back, and makes her way to the back near the slide so she has a better sightline.

I scramble up after Terrance, and the minute he splashes into the water a few yards away from the boat, I launch myself onto the slide feetfirst and howling like a banshee. The water embraces me, and then with a strong kick of my legs, I'm up.

Terrance is smiling at June, who is laughing at him, but I swim in front of him with my back to the boat and wave my hand in his face. "Hey, lovestruck. On a scale of one to ten, how pissed is she?"

His smile lingers at one corner of his mouth as he turns to me. "Hard to say. I have nothing to compare it to."

"One is me stealing the last of her almond milk without buying more. Eight is me telling her she ought to listen to my relationship advice because my record says I'm better at it than she is. I've never experienced ten."

He side-eyes me for level eight, and I deserve it. That wasn't one of my finer moments. "Hmm. I think you might be around a six."

"Shit," I mutter. "I really am sorry. I'm super-excited for you guys, and I have no filter, and it just kind of blurped out."

"Hey, it's no sweat to me. *Buuuut* I'm pretty sure she's not taking off her shirt because she doesn't want to risk any more comments."

I glance back at June. Who indeed is wearing her black T-shirt despite the heat of the late-afternoon sun. "As if I would—" I start, but Terrance arches an eyebrow at me. "Shit," I say again. "Well, since she won't speak to me, will you tell her I'm sorry? I've been trying to talk to her all day but she won't let me near her."

He shakes his head. "I love you, Leeb, but no way in hell am I getting myself any further into this. Don't forget I have two sisters. Trying to be the go-between for those two got me nothing but scorched."

"Fine," I say glumly.

"What I *will* do," he says, "is try to find a way to leave the two of you alone when we get back to the house. Now, will you please let me up out of this freezing-ass lake?"

Busted. As I trail behind Terrance on the way back to the boat, I mull over what he said. June is level-six pissed at me? Over a stupid *joke*? I mean yes, it was out of line and embarrassing, but I don't see how it deserves for her to get all that worked up. I didn't insult her, like Ollie did when he gave her grief for dating a tool like Rick the Dick. I was just celebrating the fact that she got laid. It's true that she doesn't like to talk much about her sex life, but she's never gotten upset with me for razzing her about it before. And meanwhile, it's our next-to-next-to-last day at the lake. I'm tired of being punished, and I'm tired of chasing her to make her talk to me. I want to have *fun.*

I stomp to the controls of the boat and flip the music from Ollie's phone to the local pop station, daring him with a scowl to say anything. Justin Timberlake pours out of the speakers and I nod, satisfied. Finally, something recorded within the last twenty years.

"Look alive, June," I say to her, handing her a Corona she didn't ask for. "Try to look like you're enjoying yourself."

"Actually, I don't need to drink beer to enjoy myself," she says, handing it back. As she does, I notice the three small bands of fainter color on the fingers of her right hand—she took her rings off before she got on the Jet Ski, so she wouldn't lose them at the bottom of Seneca Lake. I'll have a ring tan like that myself, if I ever actually get engaged to Ollie. Which, at this rate, will happen sometime after June and Terrance welcome their third child.

28

June

"I DON'T KNOW WHAT? OLLIE, WHAT DON'T I KNOW?"

He whips his head to me, eyes blazing. "When we were up here before, Caleb decided to make a pass at Leah. Said he didn't know what she saw in me, and his door was open whenever she was ready to . . . upgrade."

"You did *what*?" I yell.

"It was a stupid, misguided joke," says Caleb.

"You put your fucking hands on her!" Ollie shouts. "You put your hands on her bare legs, and you ran them up her thighs."

Rachel's horrified "Caleb!" almost drowns out my words.

"That's how it happened," I say, choking on my rage. "Isn't it? She was trying to get away from you. You animal. You reckless, careless—"

"Okay, all of you calm down and put away your pitchforks, or we're done here," snaps Leslie. "Eli doesn't need to grow up in the middle of this, and I won't hesitate to keep him away."

I haven't taken my eyes off Caleb's face for an instant. But instead of guilty, he just looks confused.

"What do you mean, 'That's how it happened'? How what happened?"

"Did you *grab her*? As part of your little *joke*?" I start toward him, but Ollie catches me by the shoulders and pivots me back to himself.

"We're not talking about the boat," he says, sounding exhausted. "It was a few days before. That night we were all hanging out in the hot tub. Right after you fell—I was inside checking on you. Because the last thing I thought would happen if I left my brother alone with my girlfriend was sexual harassment."

My brain is lagging way too far behind this conversation. "Wait, but—but she never told me about this. She would have told me something like that."

"She probably would have, if I hadn't done such a good job of convincing her it was no big deal," Ollie says bitterly. "Plus, you were pretty MIA those last couple of days."

Oh, Leah. I am so sorry. I didn't even know just how badly I let you down. I shut my eyes against the tide of shame and regret. "So what happened?"

"She told me to go screw myself, obviously," says Caleb. "As she should have."

"But it upset her," Ollie says. "A lot. She only told me about the comment at first, and I could see how much it bothered her, but for some reason it was more important to make excuses for you than to listen to what she was trying to tell me. Which is that you have a serious fucking problem with the way you treat women."

"Not me," says Leslie.

"Are you sure about that?" I say quietly. She gives a little shrug, as uncertain as it is defiant, and looks away.

Rachel gives a low groan. "God help me, what did I do that let this happen? What did I miss?" She surges to her feet and clasps Caleb's face in her hands. "You are my firstborn child. I love you more than I could ever express. How did I fail you so badly? How do you not understand how wrong this is?"

Caleb's face contorts as he fights tears. He scowls at the floor. "I never meant to hurt anybody, Mom."

"I believe you," she says. "But you have to do a lot better than this. If you're not trying to cause harm, but you're causing it anyway, then you *must* pay better attention. And give more respect to the people around you."

He nods and dips his head.

Rachel looks at Leslie over his shoulder. "Leslie, will you come and talk with Caleb and me?"

She nods, and they turn to leave the room.

"Wait," I say, my voice like glass breaking in the stillness.

They stop moving and look at me: three faces in a row.

I swipe my hair back from my face with sweaty fingers. "You still haven't told me about the boat."

Caleb frowns and shakes his head slightly. "'The boat'?"

"With Leah. The night she died. Why were you even with them? If you were creeping on her, you were the last person she would have wanted around."

He shrugs. "The three of us were hanging out together. I'd apologized to her and she accepted it."

"That doesn't make any sense," I say. "She wouldn't have been that mellow about something like that."

"Well, it's the truth."

"It can't be."

"June." Ollie's voice is low behind me.

I slice the air with my hands. "It can't be the truth. I don't believe you. You're going to tell me right now, what were you doing on that boat with them? *How exactly did it happen?*"

At last, understanding dawns in Caleb's face. Understanding, and satisfaction, and a little bit of pity. "You never heard the whole story, I guess. Well, you're going to have to ask the Golden Child for that."

As they trail out of the room, I slowly turn to Ollie. He's breathing fast but steady, as if that's the only thing keeping him from barfing out all of his intestines right here on this over-polished floor.

"Ollie?" I whisper.

He holds out his hand to me. His fingers are shaking. "Baby, give me your hand."

29

Leah

BECAUSE APPARENTLY I AM DOOMED TO NEVER ESCAPE THE doghouse, June and Terrance have disappeared again by the time I finish helping Ollie refill the gas tank on the boat. I call for her inside the house, but there's no response. And of course, no text, no note left anywhere in our empty room. So much for Terrance's promise to set her up to talk to me. The faithless wretch.

Just past the summer solstice, and as far north as we are, darkness is so long coming you almost think it won't come at all. But it does, slowly, all the bright colors of sunset fading to the deep purple-gray of dusk. The lake is quiet tonight; and with June and Terrance and Caleb gone, and Rachel and Howard out at dinner with friends, the silent house seems abandoned.

Ollie throws some white hots and corn ears on the grill, which we wash down with beers selected from the increasingly slim pickings in the garage fridge. It's so depressing when the fridge thins out—it means vacation is almost over. I'm out there, rooting around in search of one more Ommegang, when I hear a car drive up. I scoot back into the kitchen only to screech to a very obvious halt at the sight of Caleb, fending off an enthusiastic welcome from Spencer.

"Hey, Leah," he says, as if he is only back from a quick trip to the market. He sounds tired. Dark stubble shadows his cheeks, and his wavy brown hair is disordered.

"Hey." A spike of adrenaline makes me tense. Fight or flight time.

Caleb spots me eyeing the screen door, and jams his hands into his jeans pockets. "By the way, I really am sorry about the other night. I thought you were . . . kinda giving me vibes, I don't know. Obviously I was wrong."

My chest inflates with air as I prepare to let him have it, but then I remember. Future Leah is calmer and more measured, and considers her reactions before she lets them fly. Future Leah is serene. She does not needlessly antagonize her boyfriend's brother. And for what it's worth, Caleb does actually appear to be sincere. "Yeah. Thanks for apologizing."

He nods but doesn't speak further.

"So, we, um, we just cooked some dogs and stuff. Grill's still hot if you want some."

He throws me a faint but genuine smile. "No, thanks, I ate already. Where's Ol?"

"Deck," I say, bobbing my head in that direction. He heads to the sliding door. I linger uncertainly. "Come on," he sighs.

"Hey," says Ollie, sitting upright in his chair when he sees his brother.

Caleb screeches the screen door shut quickly behind us, flinching at the potpourri of bugs swirling around the porch light. "Hey."

"Listen," Ollie says, "I owe you an apology. I was out of line yesterday."

"Yeah," says Caleb, slumping into a nearby chair. He takes the beer that Ollie offers him and gives a few deep gulps and a satisfied sigh. "But I did worse to you when we were kids, I'm sure."

"You did," says Ollie. "But we're adults now."

"Are we?" Caleb throws a shadowy smile from behind his beer.

"Allegedly," says Ollie, tossing back the smile.

"Where are the lovebirds?" Caleb says.

"Unknown," Ollie says.

"Ah, young love and summer nights," says Caleb. "Good for them. So," he continues after a moment, "this is a dope old-married-person party you guys have going on here, but what say we take some drinks out to the boat and go night swimming?"

"I'm in," says Ollie, getting to his feet decisively.

I follow, far less decisively. I'm tired, and sad, and I had wanted to make it an early night. But after their argument, Ollie clearly wants to spend some time with Caleb, and I can understand that. I wish Caleb wouldn't make it so goddamned hard for his brother to have a good relationship with him.

We take the boat out, but don't even go out of sight of the house; we just stop the motor when we're about a hundred yards from shore, make sure our night lights are good, and float. There's no breeze to push us. This is when the lake is stillest: between sunset and sunrise. It rests in the dark, just like the rest of us.

Caleb, it turns out, spent the last two days on a spontaneous road trip to Toronto with his buddy Bruce. He keeps us laughing with stories about the hitchhiker they made friends with at some terrifying diner famous for something called a Garbage Plate, a middle-aged pothead named Francis who claims to officially be the world's biggest Buffalo Bills fan.

"The world, or just western New York?" I say, and the brothers treat me to identical glares of pained disappointment.

"I got his number," says Caleb. "We're going to meet up at a game this fall. This guy can put a hurtin' on a folding table like nobody's business."

"I'm so there," says Ollie passionately.

In the pause that follows, I see the light come on in my bedroom back at the house. June's home. I guess she decided not to spend the night with Terrance again; hopefully that means she's ready to forgive me. Warmth glows beyond the curtains covering

the screen door and throws a faint puddle of light onto the flagstone pavers of the terrace; it makes me yearn to be in there with
her, talking.

June's house when we were growing up was the perfect setting
for sleepovers. At my place, we had to combat Sam, who liked to
barge in on us the way annoying little brothers do, as well as my
mom, who was constantly checking in to see if we needed anything. My mom is a hoverer. But June had no siblings to interrupt
us or compete with us for resources like TV, ice cream, or pop-
corn, and her parents left us alone.

Our sleepovers were epic. Instead of staying in her bed while I
roughed it on the floor in a sleeping bag, she put her plain navy
bag on the floor next to mine. And then we lay side by side and
talked, hours and hours and hours of talking. I drew a graph once
that mapped the hours of the night against the topics of conversation: nine to midnight was school, friends, parents, boys. Midnight to one was advanced-level parents and boys: the things that
hurt us, drove us crazy, populated our dreams. And then one to
three was grab bag: frantic giggling, late-night punchiness, and
deepest, darkest confessions.

One time, somewhere around two-thirty, she asked me why I
loved her. I tried to dodge it because I didn't really know how to
answer, but in one of her rare bouts of obstinacy, she insisted. It
took me a while to get past "You're smart, you're interesting,
you're funny" and arrive at the meat of it: her kindness, her empathy, her sly humor, her pathological loyalty. But it was more than
that. I knew it, but I couldn't say it. It made me feel too naked,
even for two-thirty A.M. in the dark in a sleeping bag.

The truth is, I couldn't imagine my life without June in it. I still
can't. I have a big personality, and most of my other friends tend
to cede ground to me: plan making, decisions, minutes of conversation. June holds her own. She lets me be who I am, but she calls

me on my bullshit, and despite her supposedly "quieter" personality, she never lets me dominate our relationship.

I never really get it when girls talk about their weddings in terms of "marrying their best friend." Ollie is the love of my life, without a doubt, but he's my *boyfriend;* June is my best friend. She is my sounding board, my best source of advice and support and honesty, and she grounds me. She's the hand that holds my kite.

"All right, gentlemen," I say through a yawn. "You about ready to call it? June's home, and I want to talk to her before she goes to sleep."

"You sure she's by herself in there?" says Caleb, rolling his head back onto the banquette.

Ollie glances at the house. "Yeah, let's stay out here. I don't feel like going back."

I repress the urge to scream through gritted teeth. Why can't I seem to put a bullet in this wretched day once and for all? "Well, if I'm going to get outvoted, then I may as well make something of it. Who wants to go night swimming?"

No response.

"Caleb, come on, this was your idea!"

His long form, sliding downward on the banquette, does not move. "I know," he yawns. "But now I think I'd rather stay right here where it's warm and dry."

I wiggle Ollie's arm where it's wrapped around my waist. "Hey. Captain. Let's have an adventure."

He doesn't stir. "I might be all adventured out for the day, Leeb."

"No, c'mon," I say. "You're the one who doesn't want to go back to the house, and just sitting here talking is boring."

"Objectively, that water is very cold," he says without opening his eyes. "We discussed this the other night, and you were not in favor. I think you had it right the first time."

"Well, I've changed my mind." I shove his arm off, strip my shirt and shorts, and do a running dive off the back of the boat. I shriek as soon as I surface, because of course Ollie was right. It is *so cold* in here. The water has swallowed me whole, and it would take one of Howard's Viking bonfires to get me fully warm again.

"You little maniac," Ollie says, grinning at me from the boat.

"I just have to get used to it," I say, teeth chattering. "Come on, don't leave me out here by myself."

Shaking his head, he tugs off his shirt and dives in next to me. "Gaaaaaaaaaah, this is cold," he yells, frantically treading water to try to warm up. "Can we please say that we've done it and get out? I swear I'll never make fun of you for being short ever again. You're a giant. You're the tallest woman that ever lived. I will put it in writing, I'll get a tattoo, whatever part of me you want. Oh my god, I'm so fucking cold."

I'm laughing too hard to answer him. All my visions of sexy night-swimming kisses have popped like bubbles over my head, but it doesn't matter, because I'm with Ollie, and I should have learned by now that our reality—which usually involves us laughing like idiots—is always more romantic than the daydream, because it's *real*. "I'm holding you to that," I say, and swim quickly over to the ladder back to the boat.

Caleb is now on his back on the banquette, and as Ollie and I stand there dripping and shivering in our towels, I can hear snoring that sounds like it's coming from a congested bridge troll. *Yeah, what an "upgrade" that guy would be.*

"Let's go up on the top for a while," I say to Ollie, reaching into the bin for an armful of dry towels. Up on the platform, I arrange them into a cozy nest for us.

Ollie lies down on his back and pulls me against his side. "It's a beautiful night," he says, staring up at the sky.

You can always see the stars up here at the lake, as long as the sky is fairly clear; but sometimes there are nights like this, where it looks like there's nothing at all between you and all those lights, like you're staring into the raw black of open space. "Sure is," I say, stretching my left hand upward as if I could touch those tiny, distant diamonds.

My heart starts beating faster. After all the time I've spent this week both hoping and sulking, I know what I need to do, and this is the perfect moment for it. I just have to be brave.

"Hey, Ol?"

"Yeah?"

"I . . . well, I've been wanting to talk to you about something."

"Sure," he says, after a tiny pause. I know he's surprised. It isn't like me to preface conversations like this.

I take a deep breath and turn in the crook of his arm, so I'm facing him. "Well, I was thinking we should talk about when to get married. I'm ready to go for it. I've known you were it since the beginning. I don't want to wait around for years for no real reason."

He doesn't speak for a moment. And then, not for the moment after that.

"What do you think?" I say, pushing up on my elbow a little so I can see him.

He is frowning, staring up at the stars as if they hold the answer to the question I've asked him.

"Babe?"

"Uh," he says, the sound crackling dry and uncertain out of his throat. He clears it and tries again. "Um . . ."

A hairline crack of fear shudders through my confidence. "Ollie, why aren't you answering me?"

"I guess I wasn't really expecting to talk about this right now. I haven't thought about it that much."

The fracture splits like somebody drives a crowbar into it. "You 'haven't thought about it that much'? We've been together for four years, we're in our midtwenties, and you haven't thought about it?"

"I mean, I have. Of course I have."

"But not a lot. And not recently. Jesus Christ, Ollie, I thought you were going to *propose* to me this week."

He shakes his head slightly—confusion, not denial, but it amounts to the same thing. "Why? What did I—"

"It doesn't matter," I say, swiping at tears that arrive out of no-where. "Obviously I made the whole thing up in my head. So, okay. Maybe you haven't given it a ton of thought. But that's why I'm asking. We should talk about it. I mean, when—in a general sense—could you see this happening? Is there something specific you want to wait for?"

"No . . . I guess . . ."

That parched sound in his throat is back. He sounds like all he has in there is sandpaper.

"What do you guess?" I say, fists clenched from the effort of modulating my voice. I'm clinging onto my patience like it's the foot of the helicopter that's carrying me, legs dangling, away from an exploding building. "Just spit it out; we're in the circle of trust here."

He blinks several times, rapidly, and when he turns to face me, his eyes are hunted. "I don't know if . . ."

"You don't know *what*?!" Well, there goes the helicopter.

"I don't know if I want to get married." The words come out quietly, and so smoothly, after all of that croaking and hesitating, that it takes me a second to realize he has actually communicated. And then the crowbar smashes clean through me.

I sit up and stare at him. "You don't know if you want to get married at all? Or you don't know if you want to get married to me?"

He swallows, and suddenly I can't bear to hear him answer. I don't need to. "Oh my god," I whimper, pressing my hands to my face as if that will make them stop shaking. "You don't want to marry me."

"I think you are so fucking amazing," he croaks, but I yell "Stop!" before he can continue. This has never happened to me before, but I don't need experience to know what it is; I only have to look at his eyes. His eyes are full of pity.

"You're breaking up with me? Right now, right here, like this?"

"No," he says quickly, sitting up so we're at eye level. "I mean, I . . . no. I wasn't trying to. I just wasn't prepared to talk about this. But you asked me a really important question that deserves an answer, and I can't give you the one you're looking for right now. I love you, but I don't know if I see us getting married. And if that's what you want, then . . ."

"What do you mean, 'If that's what I want'?" I screech, my throat muscles straining. "Of course it's what I want! How can you even pretend like that might be a mystery? I thought you wanted it, too! We always talked about it; you said . . ." I suck in a deep, desperate breath as I try to remember exactly what Ollie said.

He shakes his head gently, and this time it *is* a denial. "I never talked about it, Leeb. I didn't shut it down when you'd bring it up, because I figured I just needed more time to feel sure. I really wanted to want that, so I kept waiting to feel like I saw it for my future. I was hoping it would click for me on this trip, with the two of us together, having fun . . . but it feels . . . out of reach."

"*'Out of reach'?* Marrying you is all I've wanted for the last four years! And you spent the whole time just trying to get interested in the idea? Good god, Ollie, have we even been in the same relationship?"

"I'm so sorry," he whispers. "I never meant to mislead you. I swear to God, I never realized that you were this serious about it. I thought it was just a 'someday' thing, you know? You've been putting so much effort into your PhD research; I assumed you were happy with the status quo. To be honest . . . marriage is the last thing I expected you to bring up just now. I thought . . ."

"Come on. Finish your sentences like a goddamn adult."

I feel a surge of satisfaction as his jaw tightens. "I thought you wanted to talk to me about the fact that we haven't been getting along so well this week."

"We haven't been getting along because all of a sudden you're finding fault with every single thing I do!" I yell.

"That's not true."

"Really? 'Cause it sure feels like it. No wonder you don't want to marry me, if you think I'm such a childish little fool."

"I don't think you're childish . . . or a fool. You're one of the most incredible people I've ever known."

"But not so incredible that you definitely want to spend your life with me. The way that I've felt about you since the beginning." When the words formed in my brain, I think I meant them as a question. But they get flattened on their way to my mouth, and exit dead and final, because there is no ambiguity left here. He should be arguing with me. Fighting for me. Telling me that he just needs time, that he might not be ready yet but he can't let me go.

Instead, all there is is silent lake air, silent darkness, silent stars, and Ollie's sad eyes.

Suddenly, I remember what I saw last night. It feels like weeks ago by now, but it was only last night—and I remember that light I saw in his face as he looked at my best friend.

"Does June have anything to do with this?" I say, my voice high and hysterical. I'm sure Caleb must be awake by now, but I don't even care.

"No. Listen to me," he says, gripping my forearms in his sweaty hands. I shake him off so hard I almost smack myself in the face. "Listen," he says again. "This is important. June has nothing to do with this."

"You swore to me there was nothing going on, but what does that even mean right now? How can I take you at your word when . . ." My voice limps to a stop. *When you're crushing the blood from my heart. When you've misled me about your feelings this whole time.*

"No. I swear to you. I need you to hear me on this, because I can't let you damage your friendship over paranoia. *Nothing* is going on. Absolutely nothing. Okay?"

I stare at his face, which up until ninety seconds ago I loved more than my own. His eyes are steady on mine, and in spite of the roof that's crashing down all around me, I believe him. If only because June would never do anything to hurt me—though it's obvious now that Ollie would. Ollie *has*. But never June. "She's going to hate you for this," I hiss. "And Sam will never speak to you again."

He nods and ducks his head. "I know. *I* hate me. Believe me. I'm so incredibly sorry. I wish so much that I could give you what you're looking for, Leeb."

"Don't fucking call me that! You don't get to call me by my nickname, or touch me, or have any tiny piece of me ever again. We are never going to be friends, so don't even bother saying it."

"I know," he says. In the dim light, I can see the gleam of tears in his eyes. How dare he look like *his* world is ending?

"God, I cannot fucking believe you!" I shriek, another swell of rage almost lifting me off my feet like a breaker rolling over a sandbar. "This whole week, while I've been hoping you would ask me to be your wife, you've been thinking what a loser I am?"

"No! It's not like that. I love you, I just—"

"Stop saying that! It doesn't mean a goddamned thing to me if it has a 'but' attached to the end of it. And if it's not enough love to sustain this relationship, then it's a pile of rotting garbage. Fuck your half-assed garbage love," I snarl. By this point, I am desperate to hurt him as much as I can. He thinks I need to filter what I say before I say it? He has no idea. "And my god, the shit I've put up with this week! The sniping, the arguments, the childish bullshit your father pulls—and your brother. Your brother creeping on me the entire time and you blowing it off like it's just a dumb joke. He *groped* me, Ollie!"

"*What?*"

"I didn't tell you because I didn't want to throw a Molotov cocktail into the middle of your awful family, because I had this foolish idea they were going to be *my* family—but you know what? Fuck all of you. Your brother is an entitled, inappropriate pig. When he made his little comment about how he would be available when I wanted an upgrade—as if I would upgrade to a douchebag like that—he slid his hands down my thighs, in the middle of the freaking hot tub."

"Caleb!" Ollie shouts, scrambling up, but I grab his shoulder and push him back down.

"No. You're not getting into it with him now. Just get this stupid shitty boat back to the dock. And then first thing in the morning, June and I are driving back to the city without you, and you will never see me again."

"Leah—"

"I just want to go home," I say, despising the broken and tear-logged sound of my voice. "Get me off this fucking boat, and get me home."

As I stand up, he says my name again and catches my wrist to stop me, and I pull back hard.

"Fuck you, Ollie! Get me home!" I fling myself away from him, toward the ladder down to the main level of the boat. I dive at it the wrong way—forward—like a fool, and my foot slips sideways in a patch of water near the opening for the ladder, and suddenly I'm in the air.

I can hear him screaming my name as I fall.

30

June

THEY SAY SOUND CARRIES OVER WATER.

I don't know why it does; probably Leah could have told me. But I never got to ask, because it was Leah's name that woke me that night, Ollie's voice screaming it over and over again, ragged and hysterical. I heard a door slam open somewhere upstairs, then a light popped on, then running footsteps, and then I was running too, careless of the dew-damp grass or the splinters that dug into my feet as I skidded down the steps to the dock.

I could see the pontoon, its night lights a small green constellation amid the blackness of the lake. Howard was already lowering the manual crank on the small fishing boat, the wheel spinning wildly.

"Howard?" Rachel yelled down from the deck, silhouetted against the floodlight behind her. The terror in her voice made me even more afraid.

"Call 911, Rachel." He seemed to notice me for the first time, then. "June, you should stay here. We don't know . . ."

I untied the cable lines while he finished running the crank down, tossed them into the boat as he started the motor, then jumped in after them. For an instant he stared at me, then as more splashing sounded from the direction of the pontoon, he threw the motor in reverse and backed us out.

"I knew it as soon as she fell," Ollie sobs, tears oozing from between the fingers pressed against his eyes. "I heard the sound her head—the sound her head made when it hit the railing at the bottom, and her body just flopped into the water. Just a few feet away from me, June. I dove in right where she fell in, as deep as I could, and I was flailing my arms around and . . . oh, Jesus. I kept thinking she had to be just a few feet away, but I couldn't see a thing, and I was reaching, and reaching, and screaming underwater until my lungs were burning and it was so dark I didn't even know which way was up."

His agony is so raw that I'm back there again, watching Ollie's slim white shape splashing in the dark water, hearing him hoarsely choke out the words "She fell. We were on the top of the boat and she was moving too fast near the ladder and she slipped and she fell. Dad, she hit her head." Caleb leaning over the railing of the pontoon, shining a useless flashlight over the water as he yelled for her. Howard, voice gentle but taut with fear, coaxing Ollie into the fishing boat. "It's going to be okay. Your mom already called for help. Come on, son. You're not going to help her in there. Come on back up and wait with me for her to find us." But the way he said it, something told me he didn't think she would.

He hung his arms over the edge of the boat to catch Ollie's and then leaned back, dragging his child, wet and shivering, into the middle of our little boat. Caleb tossed him a towel and he caught it, and as he wrapped it around Ollie's shaking shoulders, Ollie's eyes met mine, huge and dazed.

"She's a good swimmer, June," he mumbled. "She'll come up any second. We'll just sit right here and wait."

* * *

"I won't be able to stop reliving it until I die," Ollie says, staring out the living room window at the water, innocent and glowing with sunset light. "I barely slept for over a year. Not because I'd dream about it, but because I would close my eyes to try to sleep and I'd be back there. I remember it so clearly, reaching out to steady her, but she was just beyond my hand—and then she was gone. It happened so fucking fast. It happened . . . so fast."

I make a noise like a dying animal and fold my arms over my head in my lap. Huge, gulping sobs shake me from deep inside.

All these years I'd comforted myself with the notion that, if nothing else, at least Leah had been happy when she died. Snuggled up with Ollie until the moment she got that random urge to run down to the lower level of the boat. It was the way she inhabited the world—spells of happy indolence followed by sudden bursts of movement. But to know that she'd been running *from* him—running, and crying out in pain, because he'd just shattered her heart into smithereens?

"June." Ollie's voice is a broken whisper, his hand on my hair barely the pressure of a spiderweb.

"Don't touch me."

"*June.*"

"You *broke up* with her? Out of the clear fucking blue, in the middle of the lake, with Caleb eavesdropping on every word?"

"I didn't intend for it to happen," he says, voice dull. "That trip was supposed to be the magic cure for Leah and me. Things had been feeling off for the last few months, but I hadn't really accepted that the relationship might have run its course, so I told myself the vacation would fix us. And I *tried*. I swear to God I tried. She was so . . . vibrant, so fun, so addictive . . . I kept trying to feel swept up in her again, the way I always had. And sometimes I did . . . but it wasn't sticking. I'd get swept up, and then I would land again. And every time I landed, it got harder to get off the ground. So instead of getting us back on track, that week up here was when I finally started admitting to myself that maybe I didn't *want* to live in a whirlwind, and maybe I actually *liked* the feeling of gravity. And that maybe the girl I fell in love with when I was twenty-two wasn't the right girl for me at twenty-six. So I'm just beginning to process all of that, and figure out what I need to do, and all of a sudden she's asking me when I want to get married." He digs his fingers against his forehead, then drops them and stares at me with haunted eyes. "My options were to tell her the truth, or lie to her face about the most important thing in the world to her and then say, 'Just kidding'—what, a month later? Two months? When I was getting more and more sure that we didn't belong together at all? What else could I *possibly* have done?"

"You could've hedged it," I say, but he shakes his head.

"No way. She could sniff out bullshit from ten miles away. Anything less than 'I've been saving for a ring' and she would have understood the truth, no matter what I said. Because we both knew what she said was fair. We were together long enough for me to bite the bullet if I'd wanted to. If she'd been it, I would have been ready."

My heart threatens to explode with the injustice of it. My precious friend, burning with hurt—I know the one person she wanted in those minutes after everything disintegrated was me. And I never got to comfort her. I can just hear her, snatching back the pieces of her life from Ollie's grasp that she knew mattered to him: her own friendship, her brother . . . and me.

"I always knew," I say, throat raw, "that the only reason we got together is because she died. But I thought that was because you would have married her. Not because, if she'd lived, I never would have spoken to you again."

He grabs my freezing hands in his. "Don't say that. Please don't say that, baby. It isn't true."

"Of course it's true!"

"It isn't. June, it isn't true. Look, there are so many times I've wanted to tell you this, over the last year and a half . . . but I was afraid to, because it would have meant telling you what I said to her that night. But the truth is . . . last year, when I found you at that party? That wasn't the beginning of me loving you."

My breath rushes out of me all at once. "What do you mean?"

"I mean I started falling in love with you more than seven years ago. It happened so slowly that I don't know when it even started. Not the first year I was with Leah. But the second year, maybe a tiny bit. The third year, a tiny bit more. By the last few months, I was in serious trouble, and I just could not admit it. I kept telling myself that it was just a little crush, it would fade; I thought I just needed time for my feelings for Leah to stabilize again. I tried everything I could think of to squash it, but it kept on getting bigger. And I couldn't get away from you. I physically couldn't get away from you without getting away from her, and I didn't want to, because I loved her. I still loved her so much, and I wanted to make it work with her, and find a way back to how I used to feel.

"But it was like . . . my heart was a compass with only two directions on it. There was no point for 'away,' no point for 'somebody else.' Just you and Leah. The arrow started out pointing straight at her, but the farther it moved in the other direction, the more I knew that *was* the direction. So, that's the other thing I realized, that week before she died. Being around you so much, playing guitar for you to sing—I couldn't pretend anymore that it was just a crush. You were the one I wanted to be with. Just you. And that's never changed since. I moved all the way to L.A. to start over, but it didn't matter. Didn't matter what I told myself or who I dated. Nobody was you. And since we've been together, there's no question anymore. . . . My arrow will always point to you, no matter where I go. You're my north star."

With his thumb, he brushes away the tear that's trailing down my cheek. I never would have imagined that it could hurt so much to hear the man I love say things like these. It was bad enough when I thought my joy came at the expense of Leah's being extinguished. How could hearing that he'd been falling in love with me, while she was still in love with him, possibly make me *happy*?

"So you did lie to her, then."

"What?"

"On the boat. You said she asked you if it was about me, and you said no—but you weren't really telling the truth, were you?"

His thumb strokes over my cheek, again and again. "I was. It was true that nothing tangible was happening between us. The relationship wasn't ending because of how I felt about you; how I felt about you was a symptom of the relationship ending. The closer you and I got as friends, the more it showed me what was missing with her. Obviously, I would never have tried to lay a fingernail on you until I was in her rearview mirror. But I was crazy about you. And I wasn't sure what to make of things with Terrance, but that night when we were talking in the kitchen . . . I was pretty sure you liked me back."

He says this with a sweet, hopeful lift to his voice that shoots a dart straight into my heart. I remember that night so vividly. All week long, I had been fighting so hard against the craving to be near him, throwing myself into the fling with Terrance even though I knew my heart wasn't really in it. And then there we were: Leah asleep on the couch, and Terrance softly asking if I wanted to come back to his place; and I turned him down because I knew I could spend that time alone with Ollie. One innocent hour until Leah woke up, it was all I wanted. Just to have him to myself for one precious hour. It was all I thought I'd ever have.

"Of course I did," I say softly. "I was terrified you would guess, or she would. That's why I was spending so much time with Terrance that week. But—"

He kisses me, quick but insistent. "I knew it. I *knew* it. And I would have waited. Because she would have gotten over it. Over me, I mean. I wasn't the right guy for her, and she would have understood that after a while."

I make an involuntary noise of disbelief. "Oh my god, are you kidding me? Yes, she would have gotten over the heartbreak, but she never would have forgiven you for it. And she *definitely* never would have been cool with us dating. As if I would do that to her. 'So you know the guy you were in love with for four years, the one who ripped your heart out when he said he didn't want to marry you? Well, it turns out we really like each other, so . . . ' No. Come on. Never, Ollie. It would never, ever have happened."

"You don't know that," he says stubbornly. "By the time she found somebody better, I'd have been the leftovers at the back of the fridge. I would have waited. However long I had to."

"But you didn't," I say. "You moved away. I thought I'd never see you again."

"I moved away because you *wouldn't* see me. All those times I called you, I emailed you . . . I even went to the store where you worked one time, but you'd already left for the day, and I felt like such a lunatic I never tried again. You wouldn't even hug me at her funeral. It was such a basic thing, and I needed it so damn badly; I thought I could count on you for that. But I couldn't. I went to hug you and you flinched like I disgusted you."

I stare at a flimsy tuft of Spencer's fur as it drifts across the floor in the breeze from the ceiling fan. "I wanted to. But I felt so gross. I liked you so much; I'd hated myself over it for ages. And then that last night in the kitchen when we were talking, when Leah came up and it was obvious that she sensed something . . . I felt like the worst human being on earth. So I freaked out and ran over to Terrance's. I felt like utter dog shit because I knew I was using him for cover, I *knew* it, and then when she made that stupid joke about my bruises, I got so mad at her . . . and then she died before I could make it right—God, I was literally sick with guilt."

"*You* were sick with guilt? I fucking let her die! The whole reason I needed you so badly right then is that I'd just talked to her parents. Those people's daughter died on my watch. Because I didn't take her back to the house when she wanted to go back, and then I made her so upset that she fell and hit her head. And then I couldn't find her in the water. I failed her again and again and again. It was bad enough that it had happened, but to have to look everyone else in the face and know someone they loved was gone because of me? Jesus, *I* wanted to die!" He lets out a shaky sigh. "The point is, I could tell that you blamed me. And I understood, because I blamed myself. You were the only thing that would have kept me here—if we could have connected, just as friends. But you wouldn't speak to me."

"I didn't want to think about you. Didn't want to talk about it. And I couldn't have envisioned talking to you about anything else. The year after . . . was not a good year," I say.

"I know. It was the same for me."

"No, it wasn't."

"It's not a competition, June," he says bleakly. "We both loved her. We both wish we could have saved her. We both fell to pieces when she died. And we both rebuilt ourselves into different people. But we're here now, and we're together, and we love each other. That has to be enough."

"I don't know if it is."

He jerks in a breath. "What do you mean?"

"I don't know how we can recover from this," I whisper. "I can't look at you the same way again, knowing what that conversation was. Knowing that she was crying, and she needed me, because you had hurt her so badly . . . and that *that* is why she fell . . . how can I ever forget that?"

"No, no no no. No, baby, don't say that." He clasps my face between his hands and stares into my eyes. "You know I would take it all back if I could. Even if it meant losing you. I would do it in a heartbeat. But I can't. Nothing we can say or do can bring her back. There's nothing you have to prove to be allowed to be with me. There's no penance I have to do to be allowed to be with you. We can't go down that road. There's no further hurt that either of us can cause her, okay? We can only hurt ourselves. Or each other. And I am begging you right now to forgive me. Forgive me for hurting her and making her upset and clumsy. I know it might take you a while to get past it. But I love you. Please don't turn away from me."

A tear tracks down my cheek and catches on his hand. I close my eyes to shut out his beloved face. "Ollie, I have to."

31

June

MY GOD, HOW SHE WOULD HAVE HATED THE WAY SHE DIED. Vicious in its randomness. A hard but not forceful blow to the head, a teensy little concussion, just enough to knock her lights out for a moment. And yet, that moment was long enough for her to breathe in Seneca Lake instead of warm, sweetly scented summer air. Long enough for her to sink instead of pushing back toward the sky.

I hope—more than anything I've ever hoped for in my life, except the hope I'd had to find her safe—that she never woke. The thought of her mind returning to her while she was under and still falling, deep in the cold, black water, makes me want to tear off my own skin.

They found her just before dawn. I'd been on the couch with Rachel for hours, our shaking hands gripped together until we both went numb, listening to the relentless roar of the chopper making passes back and forth over the lake, scanning the water and the shoreline with its beams of light. Ollie, Howard, and Caleb were all out searching the shore. Terrance and his parents, too; they'd woken to Ollie's screams across the still water. He stayed with me for a while, until I couldn't take another minute of his silent anxiety and begged him to go and help the others look. But

I couldn't. I couldn't do it. Not when I knew there was a dive crew out there searching, too. I just sat and shivered with my face between my knees, and I prayed. And then the phone rang, and Rachel ran to it—there was a pause—then her low, keening moan. And then, I think, I started to scream.

This lake took her; and then it gave her back, lifeless. For that, I've hated it for seven years. Hated it in spite of knowing how beautiful it is, how enchanting; and how innocent. But as I drive away, the morning after the anniversary of Leah's death, I can't stop staring at it through the window. The water glimmers with light spilling from the sun, still low over the green ridge above the eastern shore. I watch it as I drive, all the way down to Watkins, and then I watch it in the rearview until it's gone.

"I'm home," says Ollie's tired voice, late that night. "I hate that you're not here. I spent the whole flight from Rochester convincing myself you'd changed your mind." He waits for me to say something, then when I don't, he continues. "Change your mind, baby. Get in the car and come back here. Come home. We can start figuring it out tomorrow."

From my old childhood bed at my parents' house, I imagine myself getting in the car, driving down the parkway with the night air blowing in the open window, stepping into Ollie's arms and feeling that peace slide down over me the way it does every time I hold him. But it doesn't feel right anymore. It feels like an illusion. It feels like we built our entire relationship out of jokes and music and sexual chemistry; and instead of a solid core, we were building it right over a sinkhole. We were so in love with being in love that we wouldn't even acknowledge the damn thing was there. But here it is, doing what sinkholes do.

"Maybe we made a mistake," I say quietly. "Thinking that we could ever be together with all this stuff between us."

"Fuck that," he says. "I know how I feel about you, and I know why I feel it. And I'm not letting you off the hook that easily. You don't get to tell me you had feelings for me seven years ago and then turn around and say it's a mistake for us to be together now."

"But it's bigger than us loving each other."

"It isn't, though. Not really. It's complicated, yeah. But you were always so much more to me than my girlfriend's best friend. You were my friend. That's the place that this love grew out of. You're not the person I met because of my dead girlfriend; you're the *right* person. That's how I know this isn't a mistake."

I stare up at my bedroom ceiling. In the orange glow from the streetlight, I can make out the shape of the light fixture; Leah always said it looked like a big glass boob with a chrome nipple. "I have never felt more disloyal to her than I do now. Knowing what I know about that night. And I've never felt more regretful that it happened when we were in the middle of a petty fight."

"You don't have to regret that," he says. "It was just one bad day in thirteen years of friendship, and she knew that. She wasn't upset with you."

The simple truth washes over me like clean water. "Thank you for telling me that. That helps."

He sighs. "I wish I'd known you were worried about it. I would have told you ages ago. Which reminds me. You know what *was* a mistake? Actually, two. The first one was not telling you the story about that night. The second was participating in this environment where we were never allowed to talk about her. Think about it: For two people who were extremely close to the same person, we've kept it all buried. All of it. The good stuff and the stuff that hurts. I miss her sometimes so much it kicks me in the gut. And before you say it, it doesn't matter that I was wanting to move on. If we were just broken up, I'd still miss her; missing her being alive is completely different. But I feel like I can't express stuff like that, because it's against the rules."

"'The rules'?" A shaft of hurt drives through me. "Ollie, that's so unfair. I've never put rules on this relationship."

"Not intentionally. But we don't talk about Leah. It's obvious that hearing me say I miss her is the last thing you'd want."

"Since when do you want to talk about her? The first time I saw you again, you specifically said you didn't."

"Because I wanted that conversation to just be about you and me. Which is what I want 99.9 percent of the time. But I never thought you'd take that to mean we'd avoid it forever."

"Well, can you blame me? If she hadn't been someone impor-tant in my life too, you'd never expect me to enjoy hearing about how much you miss the girl you loved before me. That's what your therapist is for."

"Right. So, there is a rule."

I kick the wall, hoping he can't hear me. "Okay, so there's a rule! Do you really think it's unfair?"

"I guess I just hoped we'd be able to share it. It's a big thing we have together. I mean, it's not like it's constantly on my mind. But every now and then—"

"Okay, fire away," I say. "Share."

"June . . ."

"I'm serious. Tell me."

"You might as well have just said, 'Come at me,' so, no. Not while you're already upset with me. I just think in the future, we have to be aware of it."

I fall silent, then, because right now I can't imagine a future that doesn't feel like this: raw and aching. Our relationship can never be what it was before. And I don't think it can be what I dreamed it would be, either.

The Tessaros' house is not the one I grew up visiting. They put the old one on the market a few months after Leah died, about a year before they split up for good. No, this small one-story ranch is the house where Leah's mother lives, the place Sam comes home to when he visits. He visits exactly three times a year: Thanksgiving, Christmas, and the anniversary. I used to come up to be with them on that date; since Ollie, I haven't.

I'm in the back, Sam texts me. I push the gate open and walk into the backyard. There's a pleasant terrace out here, under some sprawling old trees. When he sees me coming, Sam sets down his phone on the nearby table and smiles. *Oh god, Sam. You have your sister's eyes.*

"This is me not being obnoxiously needy," I say to him, as I lean down for a hug.

His shoulders shake slightly as he laughs. "Did I ever tell you I minded?"

"No, you just silently endured." I sit down opposite him and give him a once-over. He looks good: nice haircut, little bit of a tan, shoulders full as always under his T-shirt. He probably still pretends he doesn't like it when women objectify him for his muscles. *I know, I know,* Leah used to say, rolling her eyes; *you're more than just a hunk in a chair.*

"Everything satisfactory?"

"You'll do." I steal his Blue Moon and glug down a couple of thirsty sips, then tip my head back and stare at the canopy of leaves. "God, it's good to be away from that house."

"Ollie released you early?" he says, toying with the armrest on his chair.

"I released myself." His eyebrows prompt me to go on. I called him, that last night at Seneca, to let him know the truth—nobody was truly to blame for what happened to his sister, not even Caleb—but I knew I needed to digest the rest of it before I saw him. I'm silent for a long time, and he lets me be.

"She and Ollie broke up," I say finally. "Out of nowhere, on the top deck of the boat, after she asked him when he'd be ready to get married. He froze up, because it turns out that while she was day-dreaming about engagement rings, he was deciding that he was over the relationship. That's why she fell. She was crying, and try-ing to get away from him, and she lunged at that ladder the wrong way and she slipped."

Sam literally does not breathe for about a minute. I'm watching him so carefully that I start counting. Then he blows the words "That motherfucker" out on a long, shaky sigh.

"I guess it's good you didn't *immediately* say you were going to murder him," I say, my voice trembling with tears. I push up from my chair and slash my forearm across my eyes as I pace. "Ah, damn it, I'm so sick of *crying,* Sam! I'm so sick of this whole thing. I thought if anything, my biggest problem was going to be living with a brother-in-law who had somehow done something to make him responsible, but *Ollie*? Fuck!"

"See, the way this works," Sam says, after watching me gulp down a couple of big, angry sobs, "is that if you want a hug you have to come back here. I'm not going to roll over and clutch your thighs like a little kid."

I hiccup with laughter through my tears, and tug my chair next to him so he can get his arms around me.

"What are you going to do?" he says, chin poking my shoulder as he speaks.

"I don't know." I pull away and wipe my face, then grab the beer again for courage. "I'm so mad at him, and so heartsick, that I don't even know what to think. I hate that he hurt her. I hate that she died *because* he hurt her. I hate that I never even knew; all this time we've been together, I never knew."

"Does it really change anything?" he says, after a little while.

"Yes. It changes how I see him. He's not this pure good person anymore; he's a person who caused harm."

"None of us are pure good people. All of us cause harm."

"But not like this. I can't stop thinking about it," I say, gripping my forehead in my hands. "How devastated she must have been. How confused. I mean, she had *no* idea. She thought he wanted to propose to her that week. And then he goes and tells her, 'Sorry— just don't love you enough.'" I feel a lurch in my stomach at the reminder that who Ollie had really wanted was me—it both pleases me and sickens me at the same time. Partly, it sickens me *because* it pleases me.

"Yeah, I didn't say I *wouldn't* murder him," Sam sighs. "Didn't say I had to, 'cause he's mostly a solid dude, and he has good taste in women. But I didn't say I wouldn't, either."

With his face turned to the side, the line of his profile renders him a little boyish, a little more like his unguarded teenage self than I have seen in a long time.

"I miss when you just plain old loved him," I say.

He doesn't look at me, just raises his eyebrows as he picks at the label on his beer.

"Hell, I miss when *I* just plain old loved him."

Slowly, Sam nudges the beer across the table to me. The faint smile that lifts one side of his mouth is kind.

32

June

OLLIE CALLS ME EVERY MORNING FOR THE NEXT TWO WEEKS. He calls me every night. Mostly, we don't talk about why we're not together. He tells me that Caleb and his lawyer are planning to plead not guilty to the charges. There is talk of contacting the woman, to see if a written apology and a civil settlement will be sufficient redress for the wrong done. It is unclear to me whether Caleb truly understands that he harmed another person; it is unclear to me whether he ever will.

I want to ask Ollie why he didn't stand up for Leah better all those years ago. I want to say that maybe if he had, Caleb would have learned how to behave, and he wouldn't have assaulted that poor woman. But I guess it doesn't matter now. Ollie didn't, and Caleb did.

A couple of times, Rachel calls me. Each time, I send the call to voicemail.

The Friday night that falls two weeks after the disastrous conversation at Seneca, Ollie's voice has a different edge to it when I pick up the phone.

"The invitations came today."

"Oh yeah?" I say automatically. "How do they look?"

"'How do they *look*'? June, I don't even know right now if you'll still *marry* me." When I don't respond, he hurries on, voice skidding closer to panic. "Our wedding is in barely over two months. You have to come home. You have to talk to me."

"I'm talking to you."

"I mean *really* talk. Look, I'm . . . I'm starting to lose it here. I've been trying to be patient and give you space to work through this, but it feels like you're just drifting farther away. *Don't do that.* Yell at me, scream at me, fight with me, but *come home.* Please just come home."

"I'm not ready."

"Are you still going to Denver next week?"

The trip, to meet with the owner and staff of a new boutique that will be selling my line, has been on my calendar for months. "Of course."

"Please don't fly across the country for three days without even seeing me. Our relationship deserves better than that."

"I'm dreaming about her again," I say after a moment. "The rooftop dream. Except now you're there, too. She's running from you, and she trips, and you grab her but she slips out of your grasp."

Ollie's voice is low and tight. "I get that you need to punish me right now. But please don't do it like this."

"I'm not trying to punish you," I say, even though I know that's not really true. "You asked me to talk to you about what's really going on."

"Okay," he sighs. "I did. What else?"

"I keep thinking about Caleb, and how he hit on her. Did you ever even speak to him about it?"

"Of course I did. That's why he disappeared for two days. I didn't have a private conversation with him like an adult; I humiliated him, just like my dad always does."

The self-disgust in his voice gnaws at me. "What about the other stuff?" I say, in a softer tone. "The way he groped her?"

It takes him a while to answer. "We . . . at some point, that night, we were walking along the shore, looking for her . . . and I thought I saw something. I ran toward it but when I got closer I could see it was just some seaweed and a pale rock. I was so crushed and frustrated I slammed my hand onto it. And all of a sudden I wanted to break my hand. I wanted to smash every single bone. In my mind, I was trying to bribe God—my guitar hand for Leah's life. As if that was even a fucking fraction of a worthwhile trade. But I kept flinching at the last second, not connecting with enough force. Then Cal put his hand on my shoulder, and he said, 'Hit me.' I just stared at him, so he pulled me up by my arm and said, 'Hit me. I'm serious. I never should have touched her like that. Maybe if I hadn't, she wouldn't have gotten as upset and she wouldn't have slipped. Hit me instead of that stupid rock.'"

"He had that black eye," I breathe. "I thought it was from whatever he'd been up to while he was gone."

"No. He let me slug him, on some random person's beach at four o'clock in the morning, because we both knew only the divers were going to find her. I hit him in the stomach, and then I hit him in the face, and then I started bawling because my hand was on fire with pain and my girlfriend was dead and it was my fault, and Cal, he"—he pauses for a shivery breath—"Cal just hugged me. He walked up and hugged me for I don't even know how many minutes while I cried. So . . . I know you don't like him, but he's my brother, and—"

"No," I say quickly, the ache swelling in my throat. "You don't have to apologize for loving him. Or wanting to believe the best of him."

"Thank you," he says when he can speak.

"But does he get it at all, though? That this is a pattern? It's got to stop. He'll have two sons, Ollie. They deserve better."

"I know. I'm hoping this will be a turning point for him. Mom's been spending a lot of time with him and Leslie, it sounds like. They've been talking about his father, and Mom's marriage to him and why she left. I don't think she ever really talked about it with Cal, and probably that's overdue."

"She keeps calling me," I say, a faint smile in my voice.

"My mother?"

"Yep."

"Christ, how embarrassing. Jewish mother cliché usually isn't her thing. I'll tell her to leave you alone."

"No, I'm a big girl. I'll talk to her."

Silence pools between us before Ollie speaks again. "I miss you like crazy, sweetheart. I love you. And I want you with me, even if you're still upset. When are you coming home?"

The raw need in his voice matches the yearning in my heart. I miss him so much it's like half my body has been removed. But every time I start to go to him, guilt grabs me by the ankles. How can the person I love, the person I need, the person I want beside me for the rest of my life, be the same person who shattered my dearest friend's heart? Every time I look at him, I'll remember that the pain he caused her is what sent her falling through the dark.

Later that evening, I'm in the kitchen helping my mom prepare mandoo soup for dinner. NPR drones in the background; my parents started listening to it after they first moved here, to help improve their English. Diane Rehm was the soundtrack of my childhood.

"Ji-Eunah, pass me the scallions," my mom says to me in Korean. I smile a little, thinking how Ollie would twitch if he were here to hear it. He has this grand plan of learning enough of the language to understand the casual little asides my mom tosses out to me when we spend time with them. He got off to a great start the first time he met my parents and greeted them with a perfectly pronounced *"Annyeonghaseyo,"* but admittedly, he hasn't made much progress since.

My hands clench with how much I miss him.

My phone, which I'd left on the windowsill over the sink, lights up with a call. Rachel again. I huff a quick breath and ignore it.

"That's Ollie's mother?" my mom says, as I continue to ignore the glowing phone while I chop the last of the scallions. Three little words, heaping serving of judgment.

"Yes."

"You should answer it," she says.

With a sigh, I wipe my hands on a dish towel and tuck the phone against my ear, side-eyeing my mother as she sidles closer to me in hopes of overhearing Rachel's side of the call. "Hello, Rachel."

"The first thing you should know is that he didn't ask me to call you," she says, dispensing with pointless niceties like greetings and small talk. "In fact, he'd kill me if he knew."

"Rachel . . ." I say, gingerly closing the kitchen door behind me as I step onto our small deck. The humid summer evening swells around me, jittery with cicada song. "I really do appreciate that you care so much, but with respect and affection, I need to ask you to please stay out of it."

"Normally I would," she says. "But this is too important. He hasn't told me much about what's going on, but he did tell me he filled you in on the conversation with Leah, and how her fall happened."

"He did."

"I can completely understand you being upset about that. It's a very hard thing to hear. I'm sure it kills you to think of her being hurt like that, knowing those were the last moments of her life, knowing she slipped because she was so upset."

I wrap my free arm over my chest and brace my back against the deck railing. "To say the least."

"And that's because you're an empathetic person and a loving, loyal friend. But I want to ask you to give some of that compassion to Ollie. I don't think you fully understand what he went through as a result of it."

"He moved away," I say. "And I get it. I probably would have too, if I'd thought it would help."

"It didn't help him, June. He was in intensive therapy for PTSD for a good year and a half after she died."

"Oh, god," I whisper. *Ollie.*

"It wasn't just the constant flashbacks; it was the sense of responsibility. He felt like he'd made it happen, and then he'd failed to stop it. If he'd just grabbed her. If he'd just found her in the water. He blamed himself, and he couldn't let go of it. For a long time it was PTSD with depression, but eventually he made progress and things got better. But he was still vulnerable to it. He was never really the same—it was like someone had turned down his color saturation by 20 percent. Do you know when I started seeing my real son again?"

"No," I say softly. Although I have a feeling maybe I do know. I hope I do.

"When he found you. The color came back, all at once. I remember distinctly the first time I spoke to him after you two connected. He didn't specifically tell me he felt better—he certainly didn't tell me why—but he did mention he'd run into you, and that's all I needed to know. I'd always kind of wondered . . . well. Perhaps I shouldn't say that. I'll just say it didn't surprise me, is all."

I clutch my hand to my forehead, dizzy. "I had no idea. About any of this."

"I know. He never would have told you, so that's why I'm butting in. He had a hard enough time admitting to us how much he was suffering while it was going on, and you're the person he most wants to look strong to."

Ollie wants to look strong to me? I've always wanted to look strong to Ollie—hell, that's the whole reason I made myself go back to the lake in the first place. The thought of him hiding his pain out of insecurity pierces me with tenderness. And with sorrow for the missed opportunity to let it bring us together. "He never told me any of it. I guess because he didn't want to tell me about their breakup. But god . . . I can't believe I never thought to look deeper. He's so even-keeled; I took for granted that that carried him through. I guess I just kind of figured he managed to cope without completely falling apart like I did. I—I don't know how I could have thought that."

"Because that's what he wanted you to believe. And please understand, when I told you how you were what finally brought him back—I didn't tell you that to make you shoulder the responsibility for his mental health. That's not fair and that's not your burden. But it is a testament to how very much he loves you."

"I know," I say in a tiny voice.

"And because he loves you that much, I'm just asking you to try, if you can, to forgive him for Leah. Nobody could hate him or blame him more than he's hated and blamed himself. But you know the truth is that it *wasn't* his fault. It was a horrifying, random accident. I know you're hurting, but I also know you love him. So . . . please, honey, don't make him bear the weight of blame."

"I'll talk to him," I say, desperate to get her off the phone so I can call Ollie. "I'll call him right now. Thank you so much for this. I love you."

"Love you too," she says. "You two belong together. That's worth me being a meddlesome pain in the ass."

I hurry back into the kitchen and stop inside the door. "*Umma*, I'm sorry; I need to go home to Brooklyn."

My mother doesn't raise her head from the cutting board she is washing—in the sink that, I belatedly notice, is right next to the open window overlooking the deck. Her long, girlish black ponytail snakes down her back.

"Go home, Ji-Eunah," she says.

33

June

I DON'T EVEN CALL; I JUST DRIVE. I HIT A SNARL OF TRAFFIC ON the Bronx River Parkway that makes me pound the wheel in a homicidal rage, and then the closest street parking I can find to our place is four goddamned blocks away. Because unlike in the movies, New York City doesn't really give a shit *how* bad you need to see your person right now. But then, finally, I'm standing on the sidewalk outside our building, staring up at the light in our living room window. That light is for me, and it means welcome home. How could I have ever thought I could walk away from that?

I throw the front door open so hard it bounces back. Ollie barely has time to toss his book on the floor before I'm in the Eames chair with him, twined around him, squishing him; but from how tight his arms are wrapped around me, he doesn't seem to mind. "I'm so sorry," I mumble into his neck. "I'm so sorry, I'm so sorry."

"Hey, hey," he says wonderingly, "what are you sorry for?"

"Because I never asked you. All this time, I was so obsessed with the fact that Leah was gone, and what it meant to me, and how much *I* hurt; I was so sure that I was your second choice that I never talked to you about it. I couldn't handle seeing what I thought I knew. So I never asked you to share it with me. Even though anyone with any empathy would have known you went through hell after what happened. I never tried. . . . I never tried to help you with what you were dealing with. Even the other day . . . after you told me about it . . . you told me you didn't sleep for a year, and I still didn't get it. I'm so sorry I failed you," I say, holding his face in my palm.

He cups my head and kisses me. "You didn't fail me. That street goes both ways. I could have tried harder to talk to you about it. But I didn't, because I was scared."

"And then I reacted exactly the way you were afraid of."

"There was no way you wouldn't. I knew that. One of the reasons I love you is how much you love her. *Love,* present tense. Because it's so alive in you," he says, brow wrinkling as he fights back tears. "She's been gone seven years but you still *love* her, so much. It's right here." He taps gently over my heart. "*She's* right here, and she always will be. You wouldn't be who you are if that wasn't true."

"But I should have done better for *you.* It's true what you said a few weeks ago, that neither of us can cause her any more pain. But you . . . it must have hurt you so much when I told you about my dream. I'm so sorry for that."

He brushes my hair back behind my ear. "You didn't know."

"Well, tell me. Please. So I do know. It's part of you, so I need to know it."

I can feel his shoulders rise as he steels himself. "Okay. My therapist that I mentioned . . . I was seeing her because I was having flashbacks and anxiety attacks that turned out to be PTSD. It sounds so ridiculous to say that; I mean, this is something combat veterans have. People who've witnessed horrors."

"You witnessed something horrible, too."

"That's what she said. So . . . I told you I barely slept . . . that was from flashbacks every night, every time I saw a flat body of water.

I didn't tell you I woke up every day for a year and a half and thought, *Did that really happen, did I really kill someone?* Followed by *Whose life am I going to ruin today?* I didn't tell you I started drinking way too much. I didn't tell you I walked out along the Santa Monica pier more than once and seriously considered how long it would take me to drown."

I whisper his name and burrow closer to him, aching.

"It did get better after a while. I had to stop trying to avoid it and learn how to actually cope with it."

"Like you were trying to tell me that night we went for the sunset cruise."

"Essentially, yeah. And other things. I had spent such a long time obsessing about 'If only,' and I had to force myself to let go of that. Because it was just another way to torture myself."

"I'm so sorry, baby," I whisper, stroking his chest. "I wish I had known. I wish I'd known then. I went through some pretty bad stuff too, but I didn't think to reach out to you. I wish we'd helped each other instead of silently going through hell on opposite sides of the country."

"I wish we had, too," he says. "I missed you so much."

"I know. I missed you, too. But I had to avoid you, because I hated myself so much for being in love with you."

He tips my face up to him with the backs of his fingers. "You loved me?" His voice is soft with wonder.

Heart in my eyes, I nod. There's no point in concealing it anymore; it's always been the truth, whether I liked it or not. And he deserves to know it. "I did. I had for a long time. But it was like you said, I couldn't get away from you without getting away from Leah. I was trapped. So I lived off crumbs and kept telling myself I would outgrow it eventually. I almost begged off the Seneca trip, but I was weak, and I wanted to be near you more than I really wanted to be away."

He stares at me for a moment, and then our lips connect and

everything drops away except the two of us. Clinging tight, wrapped around each other, we stumble to our bed and make the most devastating, searing love of my entire life. For the very first time, my love is oozing out of every pore, blowing out on every breath, set free and opened up and wholly given: every last shimmering minute of it that I have ever felt, even the ones I was ashamed of for so long. Ollie owns each and every one of them, and he finally knows it. It terrifies me. But I will never withhold anything from his precious heart again.

We lie together in the aftermath, the ceiling fan softly blowing air over our cooling skin. I nudge closer to him and tug the sheet over our waists.

"Okay, so after *that*," he says after a while, stroking my naked back with open fingers, "you can't tell me you still think we only got together because she died."

He wants me to agree with him, but I don't know if I can. Instead of answering, I raise my head and give him a long kiss.

But Ollie is no fool. "June, baby, you've got to let go of that. I can't stand the thought of you carrying this around forever. That taints us so much."

"You know I don't think we did anything wrong."

He winds his hand into my hair and massages the base of my head. "Yeah, but you think our marriage is going to be a by-product of tragedy. Our marriage, that we're going to be sharing for the rest of our lives, and building a family on: the result of a tragedy. That makes me feel gross. And I don't want there to be anything gross about the fact that I love you."

"It's not gross. . . . It's just the truth."

"It's not. I loved you and you loved me. That means this was always going to be our big love, so we would have found a way to make it. If things hadn't happened the way they did, I would have waited for a while and then I would have told you how I felt about you."

"Which would have forced me to choose between the two of you," I say, frowning. "She never would have stayed friends with me if I was dating you."

"Yeah, she would have been really upset with you for a while. But she would have forgiven you eventually. I've always believed that, and I do even more now that we've talked about it all. I want you to believe it, too. And it's not about self-absolution. It might be hard for you to see from your perspective, but from mine, I am absolutely sure. She just loved you too goddamned much to cut you out of her life for good. *Even* over me," he says when I open my mouth to argue. "I know how much she loved me, I don't want to make light of that. But you had been like a sister to her since she was twelve years old. You were always the person who was meant to be in her life for her whole life. I was the boyfriend she had in her early twenties. Don't you see the difference?"

As a thought exercise, I consider it. I think back to the guilty, ashamed, but utterly insistent love I felt for Ollie seven years ago. The way it burned through me like wildfire as soon as I finally gave myself permission to feel it. What if he's right? What if, once Leah had recovered from their breakup, I had told her how I felt about Ollie? She would have been hurt, of course, but would she have cut me off forever? She would have known I'd never break that rule for anything less than, well—less than true love.

"Maybe you're right," I say, rubbing my cheek against his chest. "But we'll never know. And we can't pretend like things didn't happen the way they did just because we don't want to live in the shadow of it."

"We can't wish it away, but we don't have to live in the shadow. We can't. We are alive. We love each other. We don't have to apologize for either of those things. Not to Sam, not to anyone. Not even to Leah."

"I know you're right. I do. I just . . ."

He rolls onto his elbows and looks at me intently. "Okay, here's another way to think about it. Maybe it's true that we wouldn't be together if Leah hadn't died. I don't accept that, but I know I won't convince you right now. But no matter what, we can be grateful to her. Because we never would have met if she hadn't lived."

I close my eyes then, and I see her: bending over Winfield on that dark, snowy road; holding my hand as we waited for the vet to return. Playing wheelchair basketball with Sam at the local park, her eyes glinting with the thrill of the challenge. Spearing a monster stack of ravioli at her family's Easter luncheon, laughing as red sauce splashed onto the front of the stiff yellow dress her grandmother had made her wear to church. Snuggled next to me in her purple sleeping bag on the floor of my bedroom, her head almost touching mine because she insisted best friends should share one pillow for encouraging deeper conversations.

"She really did live, didn't she?" I say softly.

Ollie threads his fingers between mine and smiles. "Jesus Christ, she lived. Do you remember how she always had to order a drink flight any time she saw one on a menu? Didn't matter what kind of alcohol, she just wanted to try as many flavors as she could."

I laugh, because it used to drive him nuts to see her leave the stuff she didn't like undrunk. "*Yes*, and the chronic over-ordering of appetizers. Same compulsion."

"And the gifts. The effort she put into them, the behind-the-back investigations to try to get the perfect thing."

That reminds me of something. "She was saving up for a Les Paul for you," I say, toying with the divot at the base of his throat.

"You're kidding me," he says, affection mingled with sadness in his voice.

"You don't remember me asking you about your dream model? And then pushing you to tell me what would be your dream model that didn't cost three thousand dollars?"

"*That's* what that was about? I thought you were just interested in guitars."

"That's why she recruited me to find out what you wanted. She knew you'd be onto her in two seconds if she asked you herself."

"Oh, man. Classic Leebee," he says softly.

"She used to buy my tampons for me and smuggle them to me at school until I could drive myself to the store because I was too embarrassed to ask my parents."

"No way," Ollie says, delighted. "I never heard this one."

"Yeah, and she never teased me about it, either. Actually, it was her idea. I was dying of embarrassment at the prospect of having to tell my mom I didn't want the pads she used to get me, which were the size of a phone book, so Leah biked over to my house after school with a package of tampons stashed in her backpack. Which made me even more embarrassed to be so helpless—but she just rolled her eyes and said, 'I solved your problem, didn't I? Next item.'"

He laughs appreciatively. "She was the most relentlessly practical person I've ever met."

"Yes!" I say. "That's exactly the right way to put it. Relentlessly practical. God, it could get annoying, couldn't it?"

"So annoying. I was always trying to catch her pulling some kind of dumb-ass move, but she never did . . . but she would catch me trying to catch her."

I put my face against his shoulder and laugh, because I can so exactly see it. "She put up with so much shit from us, too. Do you remember the label maker?"

"Of course."

"I saved the ones from when she finally started retaliating.

Hang on a second." I pull on my underwear and T-shirt, open the door to our closet, and take down a brown cardboard box from the top shelf.

"Why is something of Leah's in a box with your tax returns?" he says. "Come to think of it, why are your tax returns in our bedroom closet at all?"

"Oh, this is all Leah," I say, kneeling on the floor as I root through the box. "No tax returns. I had nightmares of coming home from work to find you weeping over this box if I wrote what it was."

"*June.*"

"I know. But anyway, here they are." I sit cross-legged next to him and place the labels, their backs still faintly tacky all these years later, on the sheet between us.

He picks one up, throws his head back, and laughs. "What did she stick this one on?"

I peer at his hand and read upside down. JUNE'S JOKES. "Oh, that was a pair of wrinkled potatoes tied together with kitchen twine."

"And this . . . was this the dog shit one?"

He's holding JUNE'S SENSE OF HUMOR. "Yep. She scooped a stranger's dog poop off the street so she could bring it home to insult me."

"You deserved it," he says, eyes crinkled with humor.

"Please. She enjoyed every minute of it."

Still smiling, he leans backward, opens the drawer to his night table, and tosses a narrow strip of paper at me. I snatch it, trembling.

I had thought all of Leah's things had been known already. In my house, Sam's, their parents': counted and cherished, the things that had survived the occasional, hesitant purges—I thought we collectively had known what and where they were. I hadn't really wanted to consider that Ollie might have some of his own. But any new Leah relic that finds its way to me feels like getting a microscopic piece of her back, against the odds. Learning something new about her that I'd never known before. This is something she touched, something she made. Even though that must be a sweet, personal love note he's saved, I still want to see it, because she wrote it. And it says—

OLLIE BIERMAN MASTURBATES TO FURRY PORN. "Where did she put this?" I say, through my laughter.

"Oh, on the keypad of my closed laptop. So I didn't notice it. Until I went in to work the next day and opened up my laptop in my morning meeting."

And when a pause in our laughter falls and we just sit there, smiling at each other, it's like a fist that has been clenched inside me for almost two years is finally, finally relaxing. Ollie and I are talking about Leah. Not briefly, not guiltily, not hesitantly. I am not afraid to remind him of what he lost; he is not afraid to let me see how much she meant to him. We are just talking about her, like two people who deeply loved the same person who is gone.

And good lord, we cannot get enough. Neither of us can stop. Neither of us can sleep. We just talk: Leah, Leah, Leah, one o'clock, two o'clock, three o'clock, four. I make us coffee and bring it to him in bed and climb back into my spot, tucked up against him with my head against his chest.

Finally, I notice a rim of light around the edge of the draperies in our room. I shove them aside and open one of the French doors to the coming morning. The air rushes in, damp and cool and sweet.

"That's perfect," says Ollie softly. "We did it."

"We did."

"Do you think she knows?"

"I don't know." I smile. "But I hope so."

"Don't know how anybody out there could miss having their ears burn like that . . . no matter how far they'd gone. Hey," he says, after a peaceful pause, "c'mere."

His arms are open like a V, and I crawl between them and lie down. With dawn on its way, I finally feel ready to sleep.

"You know something? I have never felt closer to you than I do right now," Ollie says.

I think about that fist inside me, and how I kept it clenched so tight that I never saw what it was holding. But now the fist is open; I can see the riches that lie nestled there. Honesty, courage, vulnerability, truth, trust. A pile of tiny diamonds.

"Me too," I tell him. "Me too."

Leah

I THINK EVERYBODY MUST HAVE ONE FAVORITE DAY. ONE DAY that you especially remember, when time slowed down just a little bit, because even the universe was in thrall to how gorgeously *right* everything was.

Mine is my twenty-third birthday. Not because I did anything fancy or exciting, or because anyone threw me a big party—it was a small party, with exactly the right people. Ollie, June, and I had taken the train up from the city the night before, and we'd all had dinner with my parents and Sam. Ollie and June slept over, and after an obese breakfast, the four of us parked ourselves in the backyard next to the pool and played games all afternoon. We played hearts, which June usually won; and then Scrabble, where I smoked everyone, because it's what I do.

I jumped into the pool for a victory dip, and Ollie jumped in after me.

"Excuse me, I'm trying to swim here," I said, pretending to be outraged when he waylaid me, when in reality I was heating up being cuddled against his smooth wet skin.

"I want to snuggle with greatness," he said, and gave me a kiss that went a little deeper than mixed company prefers.

"Gross!" yelled Sam from the deck, but then he burst out laughing as June nailed him on the chest with a Scrabble tile. "Hey! What the hell was that?"

"You're just mad that you got beat by a girl," she said, and fired another one at him.

"Bullshit," he said, catching the tile against his shoulder and throwing it back at her.

"*Two* girls, in fact," she said. She was grinning demonically, most of her face hidden behind her huge black sunglasses. The chic effect was ruined, however, by the filthy baseball cap she had borrowed from Sam to shield her face, and the orange-and-pink paper party hat she had perched on top of it. Sam was wearing one, too.

"Two girls who were probably cheating," Sam said, which earned him a rapid-fire pelting. "Go ahead, keep throwing them. It's not gonna be my ass who picks them up."

She paused, considering, then shrugged and launched one that caught him right on the top of his forehead.

"All right, you're done," said Sam, grabbing a handful of tiles and throwing them at her.

Ollie's belly moved against me as he laughed, and as we turned and grinned at each other, I fell for him all over again. The lashes over his beautiful eyes were spiked with water, and he was smiling at me, and the sun was warm on our faces and the water lapped at our skin, and the breeze rustled in the branches of the trees and I could hear my brother and my sister laughing and yelling nearby, and at that moment, I almost exploded from love.

I was the luckiest girl in the world.

ACKNOWLEDGMENTS

My first and biggest thank-yous go as always to the best, most patient, and most supportive agent in the world, Meredith Kaffel Simonoff; and my editor, Kara Cesare, who is truly the stuff that authors' dreams are made of.

I am tremendously grateful to Dave Pichichero and his father, the indomitable Dr. P., for introducing me to the unique (and slightly terrifying) beauty of Seneca Lake and hosting me there for many days of boating and diaper floating and gluttony. My only regret is that I didn't get to spend any time defying your expectations for human food consumption while I actually *was* pregnant.

Thank you to Allie Larkin for your thoughtful read, thereby saving me from myself in countless ways; to Yumi Kim for helping me make sure June was as accurately sketched as a white girl from rural Virginia could manage; to Dan Waldron and Cory Barber for educating me about the unique lifestyle that is Bills fandom; to my family and friends for your love, encouragement, and early reads; to the general Lake Dick crew for being so stoked and supportive about this book; and to my husband, Allen, for being the most patient and loving human on the planet.

Thank you also to my entire team at Random House, who worked so hard on this: copy editing, formatting, art (oh my god, this cover), rights, marketing, publicity, and editorial support—

You are the wind beneath my wings. Mucho love to my entire writing tribe, for lifting me up and keeping me sane.

And finally, I couldn't do this without my readers, so enormous thanks to all of you from the bottom of my heart; and special thank-yous to all the amazing bloggers and 'grammers whose passion for books translates to such incredible support for authors. Love and gratitude always.

ABOUT THE AUTHOR

A native of Virginia's Blue Ridge foothills, BETHANY CHASE is the author of *The One That Got Away* and *Results May Vary*. She lives with her husband and son in New Jersey.

Facebook.com/bethanychaseauthor
Twitter: @MBethanyChase
Instagram: @bethanychaseauthor